Troglodytes

Uncorrected Galley Proof
Advanced Reading Copy

For Limited Distribution
Not For Sale

Reviewers are reminded that changes may be made in the proof copy before books are printed. If any material from the book is to be quoted in the review, the quotation should be checked against the final bound book.

Other Books by Ed Lynskey

The Dirt Brown Derby

Pelham Fell Here

TROGLODYTES

ED LYNSKEY

Mundania Press

Troglodytes Copyright © 2009 by Ed Lynskey

All rights reserved under the International and Pan-American Copyright Conventions. No part of this book may be reproduced or transmitted in any form or by any means, electronic or mechanical including photocopying, recording, or by any information storage and retrieval system, without permission in writing from the publisher.

The scanning, uploading and distribution of this book via the Internet or via any other means without the permission of the publisher is illegal, and punishable by law. Please purchase only authorized electronic editions, and do not participate in or encourage the electronic piracy of copyrighted materials. Your support of the author's rights is appreciated.

Warning: The unauthorized reproduction or distribution of this copyrighted work is illegal. Criminal copyright infringement, including infringement without monetary gain, is investigated by the FBI and is punishable by up to 5 years in federal prison and a fine of $250,000.

This is a work of fiction. Names, characters, places and incidents either are the product of the author's imagination or are used fictitiously, and any resemblance to any actual persons, living or dead, events, or locales is entirely coincidental.

A Mundania Press Production
Mundania Press LLC
6470A Glenway Avenue, #109
Cincinnati, Ohio 45211-5222

To order additional copies of this book, contact:
books@mundania.com
www.mundania.com

Cover Art © 2009 by Skyla Dawn Cameron
Book Design by Daniel J. Reitz, Sr.
Edited By: Judy Doyle

Trade Paperback ISBN: 978-1-59426-721-5
eBook ISBN: 978-1-59426-720-8

First Edition • June 2009

Production by Mundania Press LLC
Printed in the United States of America
10 9 8 7 6 5 4 3 2 1

Dedication

For Heather, With Love Always

Acknowledgement

The opening chapters are derived from a short story contracted to appear in Blue Murder Magazine (David Firks, editor) and later published by Judas Ezine (Anthony Daeur, editor).

Author's Note

This P.I. novel is a pure fiction. The setting and atmosphere are drawn from my two stays in Ankara, Turkey, including my trip to tour Cappadocia's underground cities constructed by the troglodytes. The Otel Pamuk is invented as are the Shannon and Harrington Hotels. The car bomb blast of the U.S. Embassy is a total fabrication. In sum, I found Turkey nothing short of charming, its people gracious, and its landscape vivid.

CHAPTER 1

"Watch this."

I tipped the ink pen upside down. The squat, balding Turkish Customs official at the Ankara International Esenboga Airport fixed his olive dark eyes on the ink pen's upper half. The blonde in a candy red bikini did a striptease. She wore no G-string or pasties, just a love-me smile and dimples. He grinned at me.

"Here, you keep it."

I gave him the ink pen (an old gag gift). Still grinning, he nodded. My diversion was a big hit. He stamped my passport in smeary, red ink, forgetting to quiz me on my business in Ankara. With no handy lie, I'd used the striptease ruse. He waved me on in the line, barking, "Next!"

After pacing over to the conveyor belt, I wrested off both my bags. Doubts racked me. Why was I here some 7,200 miles from home in Pelham? Right: The Job. I shouldered through the airport doors and schlepped into the rain, splashing up a recent memory. My latest client, the socialite Lois Mercedes, had phoned me three days earlier. She'd fed me a wild-ass tale. Her husband Sylvester had flown to Ankara on a business trip two Sundays before and dropped off the radar screen.

"Sylvester can be clandestine at times."

I had to wonder what she was hiding behind a word like "clandestine" spoken in an autocratic, nasally cadence. At the same time, I tried to envision a missing persons search in Ankara. Put up flyers?

"A week out of touch is no big cause for alarm. Maybe his work has him snowed under."

"Quit condescending to me. He's missing. I'm worried sick and want him found. Are you interested or not?"

I wasn't. Not really. Even before 9/11 I'd hated flying. I was out of luck. No causeway linked Virginia to Ankara, and I was stone-cold broke. All summer I'd busted my hump at an heir finder agency in Charlottesville and stunk at it. Much of the job was computer-driven, checking databases and stuff. I did better at burning shoe leather. Few heirs traced meant I'd earned few commissions.

"Have you contacted the U.S. Consulate?" I asked her.

"Why bother? They won't lift a finger."

"Has your husband angered any recent enemies?"

"No."

"Has he gotten any death threats?"

"No. Why?"

Missing persons cases sometimes ended in foul play, but I didn't raise that point. Yet. "I'll fax you my standard contract," I told her. "It gives my per diem plus my expenses. I'll ask for a larger than usual advance since I'm headed overseas. Give me a good fax number."

She had.

Now I was soaked to the bone. My bags plopped in a puddle. Things looked up when a yellow car, the word mounted on its top and a "T" prefix on its license tag, rode up. I flipped out the rear door and leaned in.

"Otel Pamuk?"

The short cabbie tossed me a wiry smile. "No sweat. Get your bags. We'll be off."

"Man, you're heaven sent."

He mistook my idiom. "No, I'm Mr. Ahmet."

"Frank Johnson," I said to round out our self-introductions.

Mr. Ahmet threaded his blocky Trabant, a Russian import, through a snarl of beat up sedans and, seeing me shiver in the rearview mirror, he switched on the heat. I nodded my thanks. Ankara lay twenty-one miles to our south. I'd dry off before we broke the city limits.

Once out on the blue-top two-laner, we ran at a snappy seventy. The airport microbus leaving every half-hour, though a little cheaper, took longer. Mrs. Mercedes had deep pockets, so why scrimp? Bad attitude, I thought. I'd account for every penny of hers I spent.

Wiping my nose on a Kleenex, I surveyed the scrubby landscape flying by us. Turkey here in 2005 hadn't fallen into ruins. My last stint here had been in 1991 on Uncle Sam's dime. I was an Army MP buck sergeant. We'd just kicked butt in the first oil war over the border. Bush II waged a new oil war in Iraq, but in the interim I'd traded in my three stripes for a PI ticket.

"Tourist?" Mr. Ahmet's eyes flitted to the rearview mirror.

"You bet. Which sights are worth seeing?"

"Only one if you see no others." He used a thoughtful tone. "Go south on Konya Road to Cappadocia. It means 'land of beautiful horses' in Hittite. The troglodytes lived there. We're proud of it."

"Thanks for the recommendation." At a glance down, I saw the road map at my feet was spread open to Cappadocia. "Do you go there much?"

"From time to time, yes. I was born there."

Troglodytes? I shut my eyes. Checking out how people grubbed below ground like moles did nothing for me. I replayed on my last talk with my employer, Robert Gatlin from Middleburg in the fiefdom of Virginia's horse squires. Pursuing his business ventures -- a few even legitimate -- Gatlin the burly lawyer always in the brown corduroy suits had amassed a fortune.

These days he was big into defending the poor, huddled masses, what he referred to as "sticking it to the Man". If his mugging for the cameras ended up in the tabloids or on CNN, it made his day a real gas. How had we remained a team or, if I was crazy enough to think it, friends?

"Yes, Frank, I did steer Lois Mercedes your way," Gatlin in his baritone had told me over the phone. "You said you need the work. She's loaded."

"I'm in hock to the Feds, sure. But me flying off to Ankara? I don't know about that."

"Why not? You excel at bird-dogging missing persons. Your passport is valid. Your previous stay there will be invaluable."

"Fourteen years ago, I did. Different world now, Counselor."

"Is it? With a war next door, it'll be like old times."

The CNN reporter talking in the background (I had cable now out at the doublewide) said another GI had died in Iraq. I frowned. That made one more Gold Star mom. Before the war ended, we'd see a galaxy of them.

"This damn war really chaps my ass."

"Everybody feels that way, Frank."

"How do I get past Customs with the IRS hounding me?"

"Your job takes your overseas. If the IRS expects payment, they better let you do your job."

"Fine, I'll be off then. I'm that cash-strapped."

I knew Gatlin beamed from ear to ear. He'd notched another victory. "Excellent. Relax, eh? You'll do splendid."

"What's the skinny on her old man?"

"Mercedes told Lois this was a business trip."

Warding off a head cold, I sniffed and bumbled right into Gatlin's trap. "What sort of business?"

"No, that's our question for you. We agree his excuse was a smoke screen."

"Hey, wait. Is he a spook? I'm not sticking my nose in that damn mess."

"Lois says he's a businessman."

"What else do you know on him?"

"Admittedly not too much. I'll send his dossier. Work on that head cold, too. You sound like Donald Duck."

"Include any recent photos. Kodachrome, not that digital shit. His known associates in Turkey is useful. Keep on your cell phone. I'll be in touch."

"Thanks, Frank."

I hung up. I'd paid my damn taxes, just not enough by the IRS's quirky calculations. I needed to get a good CPA in my corner. Gatlin knew a sharp lady on Chain Bridge Road in Fairfax. Until then, look out Turkey, here I come again.

※

It took Mr. Ahmet twenty-three minutes to ferry me to downtown Ankara. It was still a busy but not frenzied city. We exchanged few words. He edged to the curb. I paid him, liberal tip. Shambling my bags through the revolving glass door, I recalled there wasn't a drop of Kentucky bourbon in Ankara.

On this trip that fit my AA purgatory to a tee. There also wasn't a fiddle lick of bluegrass music. That sucked. Stopping, I sized up the Otel Pamuk's lobby. Fresh carpeting and stuccoed walls, both muted red, made it livable.

"Frank Johnson, welcome to Ankara." Omar was still the lean but more bald proprietor. It was good to see a face I knew. "Glad to have you back. It's been -- what? -- fourteen years? More, even."

"Hello, Omar. A long time, yeah. Put me in the back." We shook hands as the jet lag melted my brain into play doh. My body clock felt out of sync.

"Room 348 is made to order."

"No, get me a room on the first floor."

Call me a wimp with my aversion to streetside bomb blasts. More thieves broke into the ground units, but I'd love to catch pawing my duffel.

Omar humored me. "Room 148 is better. After you've settled in, we'll chew the bone out at the bar."

"Chew the fat," I corrected him. "Dogs chew bones." A few Yankee idioms threw him. Otherwise I rated his English as good as mine.

"Then we'll chew the fat."

After hefting up my bags, I scurried off to find Room 148. It was the same dive as in 1991, but I found no roaches in the sink. There was a desk and chair to do my reports. After chucking my bags on the swayback bed and bureau top, I ran a check in the closet, under the bed, and behind the shower curtain. No bogeymen lurked there to shiv me in the back. After I flipped on the nightstand lamp, I blew my nose and left the room.

CHAPTER 2

The Otel Pamuk's corridor was as shadowy as my doublewide any month I didn't pay the light bill. Craving an Efes, the native Turkish brew, I invaded the lobby and parked at the bar off to the side. I scotched the Efes idea. My AA was an international deal.

Omar mixed a Tom Collins for an American, a linebacker-gone-to-seed type with a Jersey accent and a chip on his shoulder. His flinty eyes dared me, but I'd better things to do on my Happy Hour. Omar moving by the beer taps nudged a passkey on a cocktail napkin at my cuff.

"Mr. Mercedes' stuff is in Room 213. He always stays there. Go up and look, if you like."

Nodding, I palmed the passkey. "That's where I'll start."

"I'm worried. That's why I called his wife after he never returned."

"Give me a rundown on two Sundays ago. After he left his room, what happened?"

Omar swabbed a beer ring off the bartop. The American rattled his ice cubes for a refill. "What's there to tell? Mercedes rode down in the cage elevator. He wore a beige suit. A white gardenia was in his left lapel button."

"Cufflinks, white handkerchief, hat?"

"I saw none of those."

"Did he take any bags or a cell phone?"

"I don't think so, no."

"Did he get his coffee here?"

"No, he cut straight for the door."

"Then which way? To the cabstand?"

"Nobody saw him after he left the lobby."

"He carries a fat wad, his wife says."

Omar shrugged. "He paid in your dollars. He probably squandered the rest. Both hotels on the hill run crooked casinos. Laws ban the Turks, but for you Americans, the sky is the limit."

"No, Mercedes' wife tells me he's a big roller. He jets off to Vegas or Monte Carlo for his gambling."

Winking, Omar trashed an empty Efes bottle. "But the ladies in the Vegas and Monte Carlo aren't nearly as sweet as our Turkish Delights."

Shoving off from the bar, I waved. "I'll take your word for that."

I sardined into the cage elevator and rode up its shaft. I remembered why I'd liked Omar on my last stay here. He took good care of his guests. The cage elevator braked, the front grill retracted, and I got off. The patchy corridor reeked of ammonia, helping to unclog my nose. Undoing Room 213's lock the passkey made a prim snick.

The doorknob rotated, and I curled in to see the same furnishings as down in my crib. I fell to it. Shakedowns can take a few minutes, but I wanted to take a closer look. I found no wallet or keys. The hotel note pad next to the phone hadn't been scribbled on. The wastebaskets in the room and john were empty. While I was tossing his duffel, a lacy, red bra trickled out of his shaving kit. I picked up the bra and placed it on the nightstand.

"Mercedes is in an interesting business."

Then a discrepancy bugged me. His tailor-cut wardrobe and alligator loafers with the silver buckles didn't belong in here. If he could afford nice stuff, why not roost at the tony Harrington or Shannon, not slum at the Otel Pamuk? Could be he liked to stay incognito. How then did his lady friend slink past the front desk without detection? I parted the monk's cloth drapes and peered out the window. It was unlocked. I saw a waist-high wrought iron balcony. An athletic lady could drop from it to the alleyway below.

I'd left the door cracked, and the shadow must've sidled in behind me. My peripheral vision saw a bogey coming at warp speed. Dumb, was my first thought as his sap walloped me over the head. Seeing a pink starburst, I lurched a step. My eyes went all fuzzy. My hand up, I sensed the next sortie. That one to my temple knocked out my headlights.

I did a gravity check. Kissed the bottom dark as an eelpot. Swam up to the light of consciousness. Finding I was prostrate on the floor, I dragged up and collapsed on the bed. Dazed. Nauseated. Touching both swelling knots, I winced. From bad experience, I knew concussions weren't anything to shrug off.

Groaning, I stood up, steadied my legs, and moved forward. My ass braced at the doorjamb. Patting my pockets, I groaned again. The mugger had lifted my wallet fat with the twenties from Mrs. Mercedes' check. Mercedes' photo was gone. I glanced at the nightstand. The mugger had also swiped the lacy, red bra.

Something wasn't kosher. This had gone too rough for a theft. Despite the pair of new bruises, I was thrilled to feel a pulse. It jetted my hot, angry blood. I left Room 213, caromed off the corridor walls, and bumbled into the cage elevator. My shaky thumb jabbed the Lobby button. This trip down went easier than my last one in Mercedes' room.

Chapter 3

The office behind the lobby's front desk smelled musty even with my head cold. I sat, a plastic bag of ice cubes numbing my aches. I saw no family photos on Omar's desktop. Whistling, he returned. He brought two Styrofoam cups, one for me. Steam swirled off it into my face. My ice cube bag flopped on the dehumidifier. I scalded my tongue on the black Turkish coffee he'd laced with saccharine. I set aside the Styrofoam cup.

"Your head is lumpy." The corners to his lips twitched, his amusement at my expense.

"I better carry a goon stick."

He sat behind his desk and lost the humor. "One of my hotel guests is a thief and mugger."

"Maybe. I found the balcony window ajar."

"We keep the windows secured. He broke in through the balcony."

"The attack felt as if he slipped through the door."

After a slurp, he put down his Styrofoam cup and tugged out his desk's side drawer. My eyes flicked down. It was crammed with the junk -- screwdrivers, twine, and airplane glue -- a pack rat innkeeper kept around. The drawer also had a false bottom that lifted out after he removed the junk.

"Here, this might keep you alive better than a goon stick." He put the jet beauty of a Luger on his desktop. I'd fired a few on the outdoor range at my late cousin Cody Chapman's gun shop. "Take it. Go ahead. I own a harem. My grandfather bought them for a song after the big war."

"I did get tattooed." I sized up the Luger. "Did the Yank go off after I went upstairs?"

"Beats me. I had to work in the kitchen. Nobody is back there this afternoon."

I looked at Omar for several moments. He blinked first. "Did anybody use the cage elevator?" I asked.

"Maybe, maybe not. Didn't you see your attacker?"

"Just a glimpse of his war club. After my eyeballs quit twirling in their sockets, we'll go over your guest roster."

"It can keep. Do you need a doctor?"

"I'll let you know if I do. Did Mercedes use his room phone?"

"I checked his phone records. Nothing. He used a cell phone or maybe a phone box. Several are near us on this street."

"Makes sense. That way he kept things hush-hush." I tried to make it sound offhand. "Did he get any visitors?"

"None that I ever saw."

My bruises throbbed. I regarded the Luger. A Browning 9 mil had been my favorite piece. Older and wiser, I preferred no firepower. But this deal had turned nasty. Omar stood up a cartridge on his desktop. The bullet was a 124-grain load. From my days at Cody's gun shop, I knew the Browning and Luger used the same ammo. With new respect, I fisted the Luger's angular grip and actioned its toggle lock.

"It packs eight rounds but don't use hollow points, just the round-nosed loads."

"Where's the damn safety? I forget."

He showed me how to let it off. "The empty brass flies back at you. Be ready for it."

"Appreciate the warning. My eyes have quit twirling. Let's have a look at your guest roster."

He set out the heavy, black book on his desktop. "We use a computer system, but I also write down our guests. Computers crash. Blackouts strike Ankara."

"I remember them."

I scanned the handwritten entries and saw the other Yank had registered as "Joel Nashwinter, Washington, D.C.". I got up from my chair and ducked out the office door. My sightline to the bar showed Nashwinter wasn't on his barstool. I told Omar.

He grabbed at his desk phone's headset. "Should I ring him?"

"No, he's probably gone up to sleep it off."

"Was anything of value stolen?"

"My wallet held three C-notes." I decided to stay mum on the lacy, red bra. Terse PIs collect, not divulge information.

"Let's keep the cops out of this."

"Same thought here." I turned to leave. "Just so you know, I'll be in and out knocking around the city."

"Take our subway."

"I better stick with s. The tried-and-true works best for me."

~~~

Later in my crib, I took a bottled water, four ibuprofens, and a new paperback I'd bought off a book stall at Dulles Airport to bed. A lady between my sheets was better. I ripped the paperback in half and lobbed the top shank into the wastebasket.

The water flushed down the ibuprofens. After ten pages, my nerves quit singing on the razor's edge. Bored by reading the downsized plot left me drowsy, and I tipped headlong into a black chasm. This third trip down, however, was by my own volition.

Chapter 4

Early Monday I started the day with a headache royale. The aftershocks from the mugging still reverberated in me. In no particular rush, I decided to take things a little slower. Had I racked up a concussion?

Doubtful, it was just the head cold. I removed the earplugs to shut out the around-the-clock street din. A few old MP tricks still worked while on travel. I teetered sitting on the edge of my bed, but I didn't black out. So far, so good. I made it to standing upright and gimped into the john. The "Watch Your Step!" sign posted in the shower stall was there for good reason.

I aced a navy shower and toweled off. Once dressed, I used the book and phoned around to Auto Europe, Orbitz, and three other car rental joints. Most reps spoke serviceable English, but none had rented Mercedes a compact. Scratch that idea.

I jotted a note on what I'd learned to stick in my detailed final report and logged in my latest expenses. I unstashed the Luger I'd from under my mattress. The Luger fit in my pocket. Only a fool bucking for a Jake Barnes Special stuck a handgun in his waistband front. I rapped my knuckles on the door. Solid-core wood was good stuff to keep out the local goons. The corridor was dim like inside every morgue I'd visited.

But the bakery bread smells filled the well-lit lobby. I hurried back to the restaurant annex where Omar had put out a buffet breakfast. While not extravagant, it rivaled the spread at Gatlin's last New Year's bash in Middleburg. The fruit -- cantaloupe, figs, plums, dates, and honeydew melons -- grew on the nearby farms. Turkey unlike many nations could feed its own.

For now I skipped the fruit. The pound cake was tasty. On my way to the bar, I wolfed down a third wedge. My haunches crowned the barstool nearest to Joel Nashwinter where he'd sat yesterday. A cup of Turkish coffee was my order. As Omar poured it, Nashwinter's stubbly face hatched a toothy grin.

"Fags belly up to the bar and order coffee."

"Have we met?" I wiped my runny nose on a cocktail napkin. "As a rule, I don't take shit off strangers until after I've had my first cup of coffee."

"Frank, easy. Mr. Nashwinter is only jerking your leg."

"The right idiom is 'pulling my leg'," I told Omar. "Just the same, you got the 'jerk' part right."

Nashwinter stiffened. "Are you dissing me?"

"You said it, not me, friend."

"How about a third knot to go with your other two?" Nashwinter's hands balled up into chunky fists.

"Did you slug me from behind yesterday?"

Nashwinter grunted. "Rabbit punches ain't my style. Now, go fuck off."

Omar parked the cup of coffee on the bartop.

I nudged the cup of coffee over to Nashwinter. "This is for our friend. He's sobering up to answer a few questions."

Nashwinter snorted. "Questions. Go piss on ice -- "

The Luger I put at Nashwinter's temple switched off his mouth. "Bottoms up, friend."

"What do you want to know?" Nashwinter eyeballed the coffee. I read his impulse to flip it over and scald my lap. But the hot round chambered in my Luger ten centimeters from blasting out his brains cooled the idea.

"Frank, maybe you should put up the Luger." Omar

sounded jittery.

"Name?" I asked Nashwinter. "Your reason to be here."

"Joel Nashwinter." He gave a croaky gulp. "I'm a beer salesman from D.C."

"Do you know Sylvester Mercedes the other Yank camped here?"

"Maybe I've spotted him cruising through the lobby. Mercedes isn't a big talker. But I haven't laid eyes on him lately."

Omar smiled. "I believe him, Frank."

"Maybe but Nashwinter, you oughtn't booze it up. It makes you an asshole. Assholes don't sell beer."

Nashwinter, taut-lipped and livid with a big lug's anger, gained his wobbly legs to straddle the barstool. He looked at Omar. "Stick this on my tab. I'll be up in my room."

"Better go easy on the sauce," I said to his bulk lumbering over the carpet to catch the cage elevator. He hoisted up his meaty hand, his middle finger extended.

Omar looked at me. "What does he mean?"

"It means he understands me," I replied. "Can we talk in private?"

Nodding, Omar signaled me to follow him. We left the bar. He unlocked the same office door behind the front desk. Once in the cramped area, I toed the door shut. We sat in the same chairs.

"Here." I shoved the Luger at him. "Take this damn thing back."

Bewilderment wrinkled his forehead. "Sure, but why?"

"Because my waving it around is stupid. If word leaks back to your cops, I'm jailed for a firearms possession beef."

"You use it as a last resort. I thought you knew that."

"Getting cold cocked scrambled my brains. Take it. I've got enough on my plate."

"If you say so." He relieved me of the Luger. "If you need it, it's in this same drawer."

"I'll know who to see. Thanks, too."

"Mr. Nashwinter has nothing to do with Mr. Mercedes' departure." Omar hid the Luger under the drawer's fake bottom. "You see, Mr. Nashwinter just wanders in and out of the different bars and restaurants peddling his company's beer."

"How good is his beer?"

Omar screwed up a face. "It's truly goat piss."

I ranged up and pulled open his office door. "Can you get away for a few minutes? Somebody needs to watch out while I'm casing Mercedes' room."

"Use the cage elevator. Wait by the door. I'll be up soon to join you. I need his room to rent."

"I'll look around, and we can truck his stuff down to my crib."

"Capital idea. See you up there."

※

Twenty minutes later Omar clanged up in the cage elevator, and a speedy tread brought him down the corridor. Smiling, he apologized. There was a stampede on breakfast where he was still short-handed, and he'd pinch hit. I smiled back. We small businessmen wore many hats.

Omar flipped on a second lamp. My next toss checked Mercedes' desk drawers for a bus ticket stub or a *taksi* voucher. Nothing. I hit the redial button on his phone. The operator came on. I hung up before I unhooked Mercedes' suits in the closet, dumped them on the bed, and gathered up the bundle. Lugging the Samsonites, one in each fist, Omar trailed me down the one flight of stairs to my room. I put down the bundle and let open the door.

"He packs a lot of stuff," said Omar.

"Not me. I travel light," I said.

"What's that smell?"

"Maduro tobacco. Mercedes must be a heavy smoker."

"He should switch cigar brands."

We heaved our cargo in a pile beside my nightstand. I heard a mouse squeak. Omar squinted at the pager clipped to his belt and then called the kitchen on my phone. Listening, he frowned. I also heard a snooty voice blaring out. A German lady who'd almost strangled on a fig pit threatened to sue him. His swarthy cheeks flushed red as he replaced my phone receiver.

"Did she think that Turkish figs are seedless?"

"Sounds like she's out to score a fast buck. Go calm her down. I've got this."

His Turkish oaths faded as he beat a path from my room down the corridor. I nudged my door shut and tackled the pile of Mercedes' clothes and luggage. Twisting the pockets inside out, I scraped up a handful of lint and thirty-seven cents in loose change. The maduro tobacco scent, rich and heavy, permeated the fabric. Mercedes liked his cigars, but I didn't find them or a vintage Dunhill lighter sophisticated men preferred. My fingertip traced the dress jacket's seams, but I felt no suspicious lumps. Frisking the rest of his duffel turned out no booby prizes.

That lacy, red bra bugged me. The last sawbuck in my pocket said Mrs. Mercedes hadn't worn it. Was Mercedes a rich, globetrotting playboy? I didn't give a rat's ass, but then I wasn't paid to like or judge my clients. They tossed me their hot potatoes, and I handled them. It paid the bills.

So, Mercedes in a suit with a white gardenia boutonniere had sauntered out of the Otel Pamuk's lobby two Sunday mornings ago cool as you please. A lacy, red bra lay hidden in his room. I bet he'd entertained a working lady, and using the balcony she'd sneaked out the back way. My phone shrilled (European rings sounded tinny), and Robert Gatlin expected a progress report since I was seven hours ahead of him.

"Two black-and-blue knots."

"Huh?"

"Why didn't Mrs. Mercedes call me? Do I report to her or you?"

Gatlin cleared his throat, a lawyer's stalling tactic. "Uh, she's asked me to oversee the general operations."

The uncharacteristic strain I heard in his reply set me on edge. "I bet she did.

What's this lady got on you, Counselor?"

"Nothing," he said, too fast in denying it. "Why do you ask?"

"I tossed Mercedes' crib where a goon mauled me, but not before I fished a bra out of his shaving kit. I doubt if he's a transvestite. So, he gets a little nookie while he stays in Turkey, and I get the idea this ain't your typical missing guy case."

"The Mercedes allow each other discrete trysts."

"Uh-huh. His dossier doesn't mention their open marriage. In fact, I got little more than the basics."

"He's a clandestine fellow." I didn't like hearing that word again as Gatlin rattled on. "I gave you all we know. What do I tell Lois?"

"Tell her more than her husband is gone. His cash vanished, too. He either blew it at the casinos, or the same goon made off with it."

"Any clues on who assaulted you?"

"Only that he swings a mean sap."

"Well, be more careful. Stay in touch."

The black phone's dial tone buzzed in my ear. *Be more careful?* I had a yen to go back and swap the black phone for Omar's black Luger. But I didn't just yet.

Chapter 5

My next gambit was logical enough. I'd amble up and roll the PI's dice at the two hotel casinos. If Mercedes had played at either, the odds he lost his stake there looked good. His photo in Gatlin's dossier had showed a paunchy, middle-aged man, how my own mug shot might look in a few short years.

With his slanty eyes too close together and a yam for a nose, Mercedes' face didn't stick out in your mind unless you got paid to remember it like I was. An addendum in Gatlin's precise handwriting said Mercedes was a "big sightseer". That detail was useful on where to focus my search in Ankara.

My emergency traveler's cheques (from Mrs. Mercedes' sizable advance) rolled up inside a fake shaving cream can fell out. My lucky Kennedy half-dollar and an olive wood rosary also skittered out. Believe it or not, I said one before each case I took on. I also removed my PI photo ID in an old wallet. Scurrying down the shadowy corridor to the lobby, I sneezed.

At the front desk I plucked several Kleenexes from a box. This head cold, I hoped, was on the downswing. A wasp-waisted, busty young lady smiling her capped, immaculate white teeth cashed my cheques for a wad of Turkish Lira (minus the Otel Pamuk's 6% commission) big enough to choke a camel. I stuffed the TLs on a money clip and pocketed it.

She smiled again as I stuttered "*tesekkür ederim*". Less

confident of my only Turkish supposed to mean "thank you", I cut out the revolving glass door. Feeling the sun's warmth on my knotty shoulders was a balm as I slipped into my tourist guise.

Grade schoolers in their blue-and-white uniforms swarmed by me. Smelling the wood smoke left me to pine for the fall mornings coming up back in Virginia. How long would this damn missing persons case drag out? Was it a needle in the haystack? Would I miss my Indian summer? More than halfway up the hill I noticed the shops were all closed.

"Watch, the casinos will be shut, too."

Both mid-rise hotels etched a bold relief against the hard blue sky. Seeing all this four-star luxury left me nervous. Gatlin did his best to teach me how to enjoy a rajah's lifestyle, but I'd never get it right. My orneriness stemmed from my dirt Irish forebears. The Johnsons had fled the big potato famine blighting The Emerald Isle. A few renegades settled down to raise burley tobacco and a little Cane in Southwest Virginia where I still had relatives. I saw them at family reunions every decade or so.

I approached the first hotel, going from a flat-footed shuffle to prowling on the balls of my feet. The hair on the nape of my neck bristled as I shouldered through the Harrington's door. The tacky lobby fit what I'd expected with plenty of tinted glass, native pink marble, and copper bric-a-brac. The cathedral ceiling and flush of light created an airy space. I crossed the spongy carpet. The sign over an exit read "Casino Below", so I used the stairs. Every flat surface on the corridor below dripped with gold leaf finish like at the gold shops, and the casino was perking. Its batwing doors admitted me.

"Halt." A brawny Turkish man a cut under my height pointed his asp baton at me. "Passport, sir."

I'd enough sense to bring it. He eyed the cheap photo, then me.

"Next time wear a necktie. I'll let it slide for this

time."

He lowered his asp baton and hand-motioned me on, but he kept my passport until I was ready to leave. That worked okay for me. The room I entered was green-lit and smoky. The atmosphere felt too clubby like everybody belonged here but me.

An obese Greek, his face a nodding resemblance to Anthony Quinn, wheezed at playing video poker. I thought of flashing him Mercedes' photo but put it off. A croupier spun the clacking roulette wheel. It stopped, and a chorus of moans went up. I saw the middle-aged ladies in yellow gowns and fanny packs glued to the black jack and baccarat tables. Their chinchilla and sable stoles trailed on the carpet by their Aigner pumps. Their glares showed they'd also hit a skid.

All the time the brawny guard kept a sharp eye on me. I didn't play their games until a slot machine beckoned me. After checking for any coins left in the slots, I plunked in mine. I glanced right. The brawny guard hadn't lost interest in me. My busted up head added to my menacing look. After I fed the slot machine, I circled the floor again when he cut me off.

"Mr. Johnson, you're aren't playing much."

"I don't real feel lucky. Do many Americans come to gamble?"

"They do and stay upstairs. But you don't. I checked."

"I'm at a hotel downtown. Sylvester Mercedes comes to this casino, and I'm looking for him. Have you seen him?"

"Your questions harass our guests." The brawny guard used his asp baton to prod me. "You just better move it."

Angry, I made a stand at the casino exit. "What's with the strong-arming?"

The brawny guard undid a pair of steel handcuffs off his belt. He dangled them several inches from my nose. "We can do this without making a scene. Or not. Your choice, sir."

Before I could react, he pinned my arms behind my back and hitched the handcuffs to my wrists. The steel jaws bit into my skin. His shoulder slap stung me. The sweaty Greek and unlucky ladies smirked over at me, diverted from blowing more of their money. The brawny guard shoved me through the batwing doors.

"I'll escort you upstairs," he said. "Outside the Harrington I'll free you. Then you'd be smart not to return."

We retraced my earlier route, the brawny guard's rough hands shepherding me along.

"I need my passport." I stepped before him into the service elevator. Its scarred doors clacked shut. Jerky chains lifted us in the cab. My pulse revved up to knock in my chest.

His hammy palm slapped the Emergency button. The elevator sighed and stalled between the floors. My heart was a claw hammer. The brawny guard shifted around to me. If a beatdown was on tap, I vowed he'd lick a few of his own wounds. I flexed the arches of my feet, ready to bust him in the balls.

"Relax, sir." His keys jingled, and his cuffs popped off my wrists. "It was an act. Sorry if they pinched, but our guests don't like browsers."

I kneaded my stiff, sore wrists. "Who are you?"

"Mustafa. You see, Mercedes is my friend. He's been gone, and I've been worried. I've asked around with no luck. Then you show up with your questions. What's going on?"

Maybe it was a chump's play, but I decided to trust Mustafa with part of my story. "Mercedes' wife Lois in the U.S. hired me and I flew over. A private detective now, I was once an MP in Ankara. Mrs. Mercedes hopes I can help her pick up his trail and find him."

"You're a police detective."

"No, I'm private. Big difference. See?"

Smiling, Mustafa nodded. "I lived in the States. That's

how I came to work here. Americans are big spenders, but few can speak a word of Turkish."

"Is that how you know Mercedes?"

"He flies in from time to time, and his gambling fever drives him to the casinos. We talked and had a few beers."

"Did he tell you what he does in Ankara?"

"Business, he says. That's all I know. Where are you staying, Mr. Johnson?"

"It's Frank. I'm at the Otel Pamuk, the same place as Mercedes."

"No doubt you've heard Omar's fairy tale. How Mercedes left the hotel lobby and never returned."

"You don't buy it?"

"Let's just say I don't trust Omar. I better get back. My pit boss growls if I leave for too long." Mustafa cuffed a black button, and a jolt cranked us going up again.

When my passport changed pockets, I was relieved. "Guard this. Swiped passports are hot commodities on the black market. I get off at noon. Meet me in the Otel Pamuk's lobby. We can grab a bite and talk some more. Okay?"

I nodded. "One last thing. Did Mercedes come by here on the Sunday he was last seen?"

"The casinos are closed on Sunday. But the night before he took a bath at the black jack table."

"Does he lose big often?"

"Every time he comes to the casino."

"Does he come alone?"

"Yes."

The service elevator released me by the kitchen. Pots and pans clanged together. Mustafa gave me the directions to the lobby before going down. Back in the sunlight, I saw a kid maybe six or seven. He thumped an orange tennis ball off the hotel's glass façade and shagged its rebound. He was a future Andruw Jones. I left the Harrington, strolling down the hill.

I'd done PI work in a few cosmopolitan cities, but

Ankara on the central Anatolia steppe rated as one of the most picturesque. New York and Detroit had me darting wary glances over my shoulder, but Turkey's capital city just awed me. I felt more relaxed and at home, in fact.

By now the streets teemed with people. The alleyway beside the Otel Pamuk I took still opened to a honeycomb of kiosks. Gold jewelry draped on necklace busts and heart-shaped gift boxes gleamed under the hot lights behind the glass fronts.

The last karat of gold I'd bought, a wedding band with an inscription to my ex, sat on a river bottom. All the grief the gold band had brought me curbed my buying impulse. Marty, my ex, had stood cute and compact, a sandy blonde with an open smile.

The trouble came when her smile grew a little too open. One afternoon home early I'd pulled up at the doublewide, and her lover boy hightailed it out back. I was too shell-shocked at catching her red-handed to blow my stack much less get even.

Marty slapped together her bags and took off in a taxi. But payback, as the proverb goes, was hell. I asked around and hired a hit man named Limpet. We concocted a dandy plan. Lucky for me I had a friend like Gerald Peyton. Maybe bloodier than I liked, but things worked out. Gerald had a knack for pulling my fat out of the fire. Funny but that hadn't impressed me before this moment.

I watched the young lovers murmuring, pointing their fingers at the gold, and their breaths fogging up the plate glass. They ogled the rings, necklaces, and bracelets. Beady-eyed merchants hovered nearby. This tough crowd, though, wasn't swayed to buy much.

"Help you, sir?" A keg-chested merchant had buttonholed me.

"Thanks but I'm just looking."

"I sell just what you need." A sleeve tug coaxed me into his shop. He was a pushy, little fucker. "Make your girl look like a million bucks. Cleopatra wore one of these." An opal pendant on a herringbone gold chain glittered cool as ice in his fingers.

"Sorry, no gold for me." I took out Mercedes' photo. "Have you seen this man? He stays at the Otel Pamuk."

The merchant ignored my question and Mercedes' photo. "You can make her a queen." He stroked a smaller, heavier gold necklace without the fancy pendant. "She's worth it."

"What does an ounce go for now?" The merchants sold their gold wares by weight.

His wrist flick downplayed my curiosity. "We can iron that out. But you have to take the first step and decide which is the right one for her."

"I've got no queen. Nothing for me, thanks, pal." I pressed the photo to his face. "Do you know this man or not?"

He shrugged. "You don't buy my gold, and I forget some faces."

"Look, I got robbed yesterday."

He just glared at me. So I turned around and strolled out of his shop. He cursed me in Turkish, and I waved over my shoulder.

Chapter 6

Emerging back on the thoroughfare, I dodged a blade-thin pretzel vendor. He balanced a laden tray barking out, *"Simit! Simit! Simit!"* A little further on, a heavy-set, shirtless man hawked his lottery tickets. *Sayısal Loto* was the grand jackpot. The deal was you picked 6 out of 49 numbers correctly to win. This government like Virginia's selling lottery tickets liked to gouge the little guy.

Acacias, mulberries, and beeches shaded the busy intersection I crossed before invading a tidy park, one of many dotting Ankara. A waterfall trickled into a pond. An armada of mallard ducks quacked and paddled over to me. "Sorry guys, I brought no bread scraps." The bench I sat on felt hard. Peering into the direct sunlight reddened my closed eyelids.

Red was the brilliance of mortal blood. I couldn't relax, not as long as a war raged on in the desert one country over. One percent of Americans fought for freedom while the other ninety-nine percent enjoyed it. The same kid bouncing the orange tennis ball followed a stylish, tall lady into the park. I wondered if I saw a future soldier and Gold Star mother. Amused by the ducks, they passed my bench.

I conjured an image of Mercedes on his Sunday morning stroll drifting by here to feed the ducks. I knew an MP friend, now dead, who did that early every morning at Fort Riley in Kansas. I hadn't given Maynard a thought in so long. I quit the park and swung back to the Otel Pamuk.

At the front desk the svelte girl with the cheerleader

smile yakked on the phone. Her finger flutter signaled at me. Waiting, I drafted a mental list of where I might flash Mercedes' photo: newspaper arcades, museums, and the other casinos. After a quick hang up, she swept out from behind the front desk.

"Omar went home to get some sleep. Here's his phone number. If you need to use his office, I have the door key."

"Thanks." I folded her slip of paper and crammed it in a pocket. "Use his office?"

"He mentioned a tool."

The black Luger in his desk drawer gleamed tool bright in my mind. "Got it."

"Before you go, I've got more. An American lady phoned. Omar told her you'd gone out to the hotel casino, and she grew angry."

"Mrs. Mercedes?"

"I believe so. She told Omar you better call."

"Yeah, loud and bossy sound like her."

While I talked to the girl, from the corner of my eye I saw a dapper man with a rat-tail mustache. He fit a midnight blue suit and browsed the <u>Sabah Daily</u>, a morning newspaper. His olive complexion wasn't odd, but his furtive glances slanted my way were. Before turning to leave, I thanked her.

I didn't use the corridor to my room but detoured to the cage elevator. Its front grill clanked shut behind me. I made a fuss over the panel buttons and gauged his reaction. Yawning, he tucked the <u>Sabah Daily</u> under an elbow and threaded out the revolving glass door. His casual enough exit didn't con me. He was a plainclothes cop, and I decided to turn the table and check him out.

I shimmied up in the cage elevator and hopped off at the second floor and hid behind the first corner. The lit up numerals above the cage elevator door tracked its descent to the lobby, pause, and then ascent. The front grill parted and disgorged the same dapper plainclothes cop.

Sure enough, he'd dogged me upstairs. Why the hell was he watching me?

He stroked his rat-tail mustache and craned his neck to recon the corridor, then ambled off down it. Coins jingled in his pocket with each quick step. I didn't tail him. The two knots on my head preached caution, and ill-lit corridors invited ambush. I took the stairs down to my room, fished out the slip of paper, and pecked in the number. Omar mumbled in the brogue of a disturbed sleeper.

"The desk girl gave me your message. Question. Who's the dapper runt on the second floor? He sports a rat-tail mustache."

"No idea." Omar was more alert. "Why?"

"Because he looks hinky to me. Your hotel is a thug's paradise. It used to be quiet and safe. That's why I come. Now I'm not so sure."

"Get my key. See the desk girl. The tool is where I left it."

"Not quite yet. Does Mercedes always stay here?"

"Many times. Tell her to print out the dates he stayed."

"You use the past tense. Do you know something I don't?"

"Just ask the desk girl."

"Does she have a name?"

"Damn, I need sleep."

"Fine, but -- "

My handset went dead. Omar felt that adamant on his rest. A half-dozen more questions popped to mind, but I didn't call back. The desk girl could also wait. Jet lag hit me. I laid down on the bed, propped up on the pillows, and interlaced my fingers behind my head. Bored with doing that, I ranged up and placed an international phone call.

Calling from a phone box on the street cost half what the hotels charged, but I wasn't hamstrung by a budget and paid extra for the convenience. Mrs. Mercedes was a night owl, and I updated her.

"That's it?" She paused. "This isn't a boondoggle, Mr. Johnson. I expect fast, solid results. What if I pay you nothing for the nothing I get?"

That rankled me. "If you're welshing on your bill, forget it. My work isn't pro bono."

"Robert told me you were a loose cannon but capable and tenacious. You've got no complaints at the Better Business Board and State Attorney's Office. So, I hired you."

"I never promised I could deliver overnight."

"You have to find Sylvester. I'm going out of my mind. Do it."

Mrs. Mercedes hung up in my ear. I put back the phone receiver. I'd handled other bitchy clients, but she took the cake. Again I stretched out on my bed and gaped at the ceiling. Should I keep up this wild goose chase? Who knew where Mercedes had gone in this city of 3.5 million people? Who gave a damn? I didn't. The bed squeaked.

My return airline ticket was still in the inner lining of my smaller bag. I returned the ticket, worth more than all the gold for sale in Ankara. Once fed up enough, I'd get out the ticket and flag a *taksi* to Esenboga Airport and grab the first DC-9 out to the Frankfurt hub.

I'd half a mind to cut out for the airport when Mustafa rang me from the lobby. Who quit a job on an empty gut? How did Mercedes' lady friend get up to his balcony? I took a circuitous route, using the stairs to Floor Two. No unfriendlies lurked around the corners. I worked the doorknob to Room 213, his old lair. It was locked.

Omar's key was on my nightstand. I went to the cage elevator and engaged its Down button. We stalled. The front grill clanged back open. A disheveled, bleary-eyed janitor leaning on a mop in a plastic bucket grunted in surprise at seeing me.

"Sorry. Too tight. Wait and grab the next one."

He nodded. When the cage elevator got me to the lobby, I saw Mustafa had changed from his casino uniform to wash-faded blue jeans and a Madras shirt. He was leaning an elbow on the front desk and flirting with the same girl. Smiling, she seemed to enjoy his company. My sense was she liked the company of men in general. I walked up to them. Looking at me, he spoke.

"Where do we chow down?"

"The restaurant here isn't a clip joint."

"Then that's okay by me."

The restaurant annex served a sparse lunch crowd of guests in their sixties, maybe the hotel's permanent occupants. The rearmost table by the kitchen suited us. A whipcord-thin server old enough to shave memorized our orders. Mine was basic. The server left us.

"Just rice?" A smile played across Mustafa's face. "You eat only rice for lunch?"

"Dinner, too. No knock on the Turkish cuisine, but foreign grub plays havoc with my gut. By sticking to rice I don't fall ill with the Sultan's Revenge."

No longer smiling, he observed my two goose eggs. "Where did you get those?"

I gave him the pitiful story.

"Omar needs to beef up his security."

My chin tilted in a gesture. "That gal at the front desk, who is she?"

"She's my wife, Pembe."

"You're a lucky man, Mustafa."

"Thank you very much. She works here and as a dentist." That explained her flawless teeth.

"Did she work here two Sundays ago?"

"No, Sunday is our one day off. A married couple has to tend to the home fires."

"Right, I catch your drift."

"Catch my what?"

"I mean that I understand you." Sniff.

He continued gazing at me. "Do you have a head cold?"

"No, it's just a touch of hay fever," I lied.

He raised his eyebrows. "No hay grows in Ankara."

Before I could frame a response, our server set down our lunch dishes, Mustafa's a kebab.

"A cold Efes, Frank?"

"I don't drink, but don't let that stop you."

"Are you a -- hell, what's the English term? -- a monk?"

"I'm just extra careful. Why did Mercedes drop a bundle at the casino?"

Mustafa's face lost its bright temper. Our server went into the kitchen and returned with the Efes. Mustafa rinsed out the beer stein with a splash of fizzy water and flung it on the floor.

"He always loses big because he's a lousy player. He bets on the long shots and takes too many risks." Mustafa poured his Efes into the stein.

A scosh of salt and pepper seasoned the rice how I liked it. So Mercedes was

the daredevil type, willing to take unpredictable chances. That made him a more difficult subject to get a trace on.

"So far, here's my timeline. He left your casino late Saturday night. He returned on foot here and rode up to his crib. Early Sunday a.m., he dressed in a beige suit and headed off to parts unknown, but he never returned."

"On Sundays everything closes in Ankara."

"Maybe he slipped off to see a girlfriend. He's married and wants to keep it under wraps."

"Could be." Mustafa sipped from his Efes beer. "Where did they go on a Sunday?"

I had an idea. "Are the American bars still open? One in Ulus catered to the GIs and embassy stiffs on Sundays. They poured the only bourbon in the city."

He nodded. "Sure, Enrico's Bar and Grill but a firebug torched it. The police made no arrests. So it goes."

"Right, Enrico's. Nice joint. Cheap steaks."

"Tell me again why you lived in Ankara."

"I was a military cop first based at Incirlik. Later I

got transferred for embassy duty. I used to hit Enrico's to unwind."

He nodded again.

I saw the lacy, red bra. "Do you think Mercedes has a lover?"

Mustafa bit into the kebab and spoke between chews. "I never saw him bring a lady to the casino. Omar protects his customers' privacy. Speaking of the bum, where is he?"

"He went home to get some sleep."

I followed Mustafa's gaze to Pembe on the desk phone. A tender but possessive gaze, I appraised. Laughing, she made butterfly sweeps with her hand. She chattered on and never felt the force of his eyes on her. He looked at me.

"Do you have Mercedes' photo I can use?"

"I did bring an old one his wife gave me. I'll have a few prints made of it."

"Several camera shops are up the block. We can both search and double your effort. But forget waltzing in to snoop at the casinos."

"They can afford to refuse my business?"

"But your business isn't casino business, Frank. For one thing, you don't gamble. You're nosy. That rubs people the wrong way. Let me ask around for you."

"All right. Could Mercedes have caught a train or bus?"

"Anything is possible, but I don't believe he left the city."

"Do you think he's dead?"

Mustafa shrugged. "He's my friend, but in some places Americans aren't so liked here. Did he go to one? I only hope not."

I reigned in. Homicides weren't my bag. We polished off our lunch. Standing up, I scooted back my chair from the table. "Thanks. I'm off to make some calls."

"Later, Frank."

My eyes flitting to Pembe still talking on the phone took a mental snapshot of her. She posed naked to the waist except for a lacy, red bra. She filled it out, too. Could she have been Mercedes' flame in Ankara? She looked hot enough. If so, how was she able to hide their tryst from the protective Mustafa?

I returned to my room and dug out Mercedes' old photo.

Chapter 7

The early Monday afternoon was bright and crisp like an October day in Pelham. Suburban sprawl by the lemmings with jobs in downtown Washington, D.C. or the Dulles High Tech corridor had trashed Pelham's charm, but it was my home. I kept its quaint charms locked in my memory vault. A foreboding threat of rain chilled Ankara's smoky atmosphere. I knew of a mom-and-pop arcade. It still operated around the corner.

They also still peddled the <u>Turkish Daily News</u>, the local rag in English. Its blue banner co-opted Atatürk's saying, "Peace at Home, Peace in the World." Omar had a computer kiosk in the lobby, but rather than go online for my news, I liked the crinkle of newspaper between my fingers and the odor of ink in my nose.

The <u>Turkish Daily News</u> felt thinner. Its headlines also set my blood to seethe. Another GI had died in a car bomb in Baghdad. Chalk up another Gold Star mom. Would the war ever gear down? Mustafa knew the score. Some folks here didn't like Americans, and I'd be smart to keep a low profile as I worked my case.

My wary eyes sized up the few pedestrians on the sidewalks. They came and went at will, all indifferent to my nationality, religion, or looks. Many talked on cell phones. They just didn't care if I was an American or not. Rain pattered down as I bumped through the revolving glass door still reading the <u>Turkish Daily News</u>.

Pembe had to call my name twice before I turned. Her

olive complexion by this angle of light glowed like polished jade. Her lips blossomed into a smile. She moved at a statuesque glide. Despite this beauty, I felt the cold splinters of suspicion toward her, but then it passed.

"You met my husband. Mustafa filled me in. Your stay has been eventful."

"And how. He told me Mercedes goes to the casino."

"Mr. Mercedes loves to gamble and often goes up the hill."

"Do you know where his job takes him?"

"He never mentions it to me. I assume he works out of his room. He stays in it enough."

"Do you take up stuff he might call down and want?"

She frowned at my question. "I do that for all the guests."

"I didn't mean anything by it. Just asking."

She returned to smiling. "Of course and I do."

"Can you print me a list of his stays? Omar gave it his okay. Call him, if you like."

"With pleasure, but our computer is down. Remind me later?"

"Sure and thanks."

I left my <u>Turkish Daily News</u> at the front desk and headed to my room. Relieved, I found nothing amiss. Spotting Room 213's key in the ashtray was a reminder. Omar had told me no visitors saw Mercedes. His lady friend then came and went a different way than traipsing through the public lobby.

After guzzling a half-liter of "mountain spring water" and pocketing both door keys, I left and clambered up the flight of stairs. No ruffians terrorized the corridors. My key fit Mercedes' old room, and I let myself in. On turning, I had a surprise.

The short, blade-thin man wore a kimono. A dragon across the shoulders spewed out its yellow flames. He recovered first.

"This is our room. How did you get a key?"

"My pal was staying in here," I lied off the cuff. "I came up to lend a hand with his bags. Evidently he's already split for the airport."

"Evidently."

"Did you just check in?"

"Not that it's anything to you but we did. Pat ducked out to get some ice. We've got a bottle to celebrate our anniversary."

"I think I passed her coming up."

He shook his head. "No, he. We're gay."

"Look, I'm really a private detective."

"What?"

"My client's husband stayed in here. He vanished the Sunday before last, and I'm investigating it. Besides the room door, the only way in and out is through your balcony. Do you mind if I look at it?"

"Hurry, please. To keep things civil, my name is Jerry."

"Just call me Frank."

I crossed the room and parted the monk's cloth curtains. The window used a flimsy latch and gave to a narrow balcony. Its waist-high wrought iron handrail was ornamental. The setup wasn't burglar proof.

If I lowered from the balcony, my feet would catch my fall to the pavement below without wrenching an ankle or blowing out a kneecap. But reaching the balcony from the alleyway was a different matter. A twelve-foot ladder would ace it fine. So I knew the balcony was a rear exit to Room 213. I relocked the window and thanked Jerry fidgeting in his dragon kimono.

"Say, Frank." His voice was metallic. "Leave your key, please. Extras floating around the hotel leave me skittish."

"Sure. Look sharp." The key sailed through space. "Nifty snag. Thanks again."

Jerry nodded. "Good luck on finding your missing

guy."

Out in the corridor I met the tall, lanky Pat approaching with a plastic bucket brimming over ice cubes. A crestfallen hurt creased his face. I debated whether to set his suspicions right, but he'd never believe me. This time I used the cage elevator and chuckled until I realized Jerry could've shot off the top of my head as an intruder.

Nobody manned the front desk. I went over to it and looked. No computer printouts from Pembe lay on the desktop, but I saw their computer was up again. Instead the printout was in my room's mailbox. I saw Mercedes was an old timer.

She'd dug back three years. Every three months or so, he whirled into their lobby. Including this trip, he'd stayed a dozen times. Just what or who in Ankara was the big draw? The subterranean casinos on the hill weren't titillating for a big roller used to Vegas. Did he fly in to recreate with his mysterious lady friend?

"Did you pick up your printout?" Pembe acted right at home coming out of Omar's office and pulling the door shut behind her.

I nodded. "Does Mercedes go out on Sunday mornings?"

"As I said, he goes nowhere but for his casino trips. Maybe he watches TV or reads books. Ankara has many bookstores. Maybe he bought a laptop. We use dial-up. But I don't work on Sundays. That's my one day off."

"I didn't find any books or a laptop in his stuff. Does he sit at the bar? Do any friends drop by?"

"I've never seen him with anybody except Mr. Nashwinter."

"Oh yeah? Did Mercedes give you his passport to lock in your safe? I've heard passports are hot items with thieves."

Her pinched Mediterranean features gave her a coarse look. "Talk to Omar. He'd know."

"Can you also print me out a roster of your current

guests?"

"Surely." Her smiling face reverted back to the congenial hostess. "Is this your newspaper? Shall I throw it away?"

Joining her smile, I handed her the Turkish Daily News I'd left earlier. "It's all yours. Only the headlines interest me."

"Why did your cowboy president order his armies into Iraq?"

Hot anger flushed my ears. "Believe me, I ask the same thing. Terrorists make the world a scary place, but our taking out every rogue government who might be responsible is insane."

"I agree. Do you have any family in the army?"

"No but I had a friend killed during the first days. They buried her at Arlington. It was frigid cold that morning. I sat with her family and heard 'Taps' played. Her parents cried hard. It was an all-around pisser."

"Oh my, your story is a sad one." Her high-wattage smile chased off my dark memory. "I know. Grab a *taksi*, Mr. Johnson. Go enjoy our beautiful city."

Her carpe diem idea was a good one. I deserved to take five. Besides Mercedes liked to roam Ankara to frequent its tourist haunts. I returned outdoors. The rain tattooed the pavement. At the cabstand, I hiked up a palm to flag a lemon yellow *taksi*. It swooshed up, and its rear door winged out. The cabbie grinned at me. He was Mr. Ahmet.

"Hello, Mr. Johnson. Back to Esenboga Airport? Where's your luggage?"

"It's just Frank. And no, get me to the Citadel. I left something there the last time I was in town."

He had a mystified face. "Citadel?"

"You know, *Hasir*." With Berlitz in my hip pocket, I knew my way around like a native.

"Ah, the Castle. *Kale*."

I frowned a little. "That's what I said, didn't I?"

"Get in. I'll drop you at the bottom of the hill. After that you're on your own. Be ready to do some hard climbing."

This time I didn't see the Cappadocia road map in the rear seat. Mr. Ahmet merged on Atatürk Bulvari, a north-south concourse knifing through the middle of the city. We pushed north into the heart of Old Ankara. The traffic grew maniac. The blaring horns and shrieking curses weren't taken as personal affronts. They just drove that way: controlled bedlam.

I checked out a rally of cars and trucks -- Opel, Serce, DeSoto, and Peugeot -- on the wet streets. Gasoline alley shops kept the vehicles patched up and roadworthy. Turkey had loads of real estate to cover like we did in the U.S. Erase the smog, and Atatürk Bulvari was virtually another Rodeo Drive. I gaped out the window. Since my last stay, Ankara's push to combat dirty air had been to switch from low grade coal to natural gas.

Poplars and acacias offered a shady promenade. I had a temptation to stroll in the shadows, a PI eavesdropping on the young lovers' secrets. Instead I scooted up in my seat with Mercedes' photo in my hand.

"Mr. Ahmet, does this American look familiar?"

He took his eyes off the street and studied my photo. Horns squawked at us. Locked up tires scorched rubber. I feared the near misses as he wagged his head.

"He's a stranger to me. Why do you ask?"

"His wife has lost him."

Mr. Ahmet shrugged, his grin smarmy. "Good for him. No boss, no loss. I've got no boss, no loss. You?"

"I used to but not now. I'm a detective, and his wife paid me to bring him home."

"What's his story?"

"Sylvester Mercedes checked into the Otel Pamuk. The Sunday morning before last, witnesses saw him leave it. Nobody has seen him since then."

"Why did he leave?"

"Nobody really knows. He mostly likes to stay in his room. Every so often, he ventures out and drops a ton of cash at the casinos."

"Ankara is a big city for a man to get lost in, Frank."

I nodded as the *taksi* pulled up at the bottom of the Citadel. I unlatched the door.

"Stay in touch. I'm also at the Otel Pamuk."

"You bet, Frank. Omar and I are cousins."

"Why doesn't hearing that surprise me?"

I paid him and hunched out into the drizzle. Tailpipe smoking, his *taksi* accelerated off. Mr. Ahmet didn't return my wave, but I'd a feeling he'd stay close for another fare. Ankara was like Pelham where everybody knew or was related to everybody else. I peered left to right to get my bearings.

Northward, the Turkish flag -- a white crescent moon and star on a red background -- flapped. Walking that way, I leaned into the steep ascent. Vendors from their stalls flanking me shilled their products: wicker baskets, counterfeit Levi's, and hand-beaten copper picture plates.

Then a bevy of swarthy kids converged from nowhere, peppering me with their rehearsed questions in English. "What's your name?" "How old are you?" "Are you married?" "Are you lost?" I wanted to tell them to get lost, but it was just their way to sell handmade trinkets. After I bought a dozen knitted evil eyes, they melted away and left me in peace.

The wooden drawbridge had been lowered to span the dry, shallow moat into the castle proper erected during the Crusades or something like that. It sat on three stacked tiers like the frosty layers to my wedding cake. I shuffled up the narrow steps chiseled into the green veined marble.

Maybe I was too hyper, but I sensed a stalker dogged me. After tucking into an alcove, I waited, poised to cold cock the bastard with a brick I'd picked up. When no stalker showed, feeling sheepish, I hurried on my way. At the highest rampart, breathless, I rested, sitting on a chunk of rubble, and left the knitted evil eyes in a broken concrete urn.

The diorama I took in made the hike up worthwhile. Ankara sprawled below me in its vibrancy. In the near distance, some kids flew their colorful kites in a breezy park. Further to the southwest, the fountains spewed up the plumes from a lake in Gençlik (Youth) Park. My eyes settled on the park's spindly Ferris wheel.

It chugged around like a brainless gerbil jogging on a toy wheel. The symbolism was rich. I also spun my wheels stuck here in the same place. The Ferris wheel stopped at jerky intervals to let off and take on riders. A Marlboro and an Efes would be good right about now, but I'd quit both vices. Mustafa had said I was becoming a monk. Could be, but first I was a PI.

"If Mercedes flew in every three months, then I'd say it was to escape Lois and hook up with his mystery lady."

My sigh fell into a groan. Rich people and their knotty messes galled me. I'd untangled too many of them. I touched on my first big case. A teenage girl had been allegedly trampled to death by her thoroughbred horse called Hellbent. Her mother didn't buy it and hired me to ferret out the truth. That case had taken some weird twists before it ended with a real bang. My detective work was either too dangerous or too frustrating.

I sat on the bubble of a who-gives-a-fuck moment. My return airline ticket was in my bag. First thing back home, I'd see Doctor Malamud about this infernal head cold. A fever had gripped me. My doubts flared up. What did I know on how to find the lost? Most of the time I was the one lost.

Stretching, I stood up and then tramped down the castle's three tiers. I recrossed the wooden drawbridge and trotted to the rainy street. No little thieves mobbed me. My prayer requested a cab. Mr. Ahmet tooted from the mouth of an alleyway. He waved at me to boogey over and fold in again.

Chapter 8

By the time I bopped through the Otel Pamuk's revolving glass door the showers had retreated over the mountains, and a raw wind gusted up. Gunmetal gray cloudbanks peeled away to bare the delft blue sky. My funk had also lifted.

Earlier I'd asked Pembe to print out a roster of their hotel dwellers. I'd try to get a bead on my head knocker friend. The lobby was deserted except for the doughboy striding over from the bar.

His suit, ironed and loose-fitted, was charcoal tweed. He was forty, give or take five. A tick under medium height, he treaded on the pads of his feet as if to look taller. Recognizing his ilk, right off I wanted to smash in his teeth.

"Mr. Johnson?" His official bark was a demand. "Are you Frank Johnson?"

"I could be." I glared at him. "Who's asking?"

"Felix Braintree, U.S. Embassy. You didn't register with us, sir." He flashed his photo I.D. and offered his hand. I nodded at him.

"Is that a new wrinkle in the Patriot Act?"

"Not a regulation. It's a recommendation." He licked his lips into a perfunctory smile. "As you know, post-9/11 necessitates unprecedented security precautions. We like to know who's in Ankara and their emergency contacts."

"Why is that? If I'm kidnapped, I'm at the mercy of the terrorists. Or has Big Brother made plans to occupy Turkey?"

His hands stirred, making his point. "You underestimate our resources."

"You didn't huff over to lecture me on security. What's up?"

He pursed his trout lips. "The grapevine says you're on the hunt for a missing American."

"Sylvester Mercedes. Yeah, that's right."

"I see. Well." Felix straightened a brushed silver cufflink. "We've had our tentacles out for him, you see."

"Why? Is he your spook?"

"From your own government service, you know I won't comment on that. He's a U.S. citizen who's unaccounted for, and we take that very seriously."

"Then let's compare notes. What can you tell me?"

"He's not a patient at any local hospital. We've checked."

"Did you also contact the city morgue?"

Felix nodded. "Look, this is delicate. We'll resolve it, but your meddling jeopardizes our progress."

"If you'd suggested we pool our resources, I'd agree -- "

Pleased, the smiling Felix nodded. "Excellent. You'll cease making inquiries."

" -- but this I'm hearing is jive bullshit. No dice. I'm still on my job."

"The Turkish authorities can detain you until the next plane takes off for the States."

On the ropes, I threw my Sunday punch. "My boss Robert Gatlin has some juice. His neighbor is the Assistant Secretary of State. So go tell your boss to fly his plane where the moon shines."

Felix jutted his flabby jaws at me. "You've received the official word. Leave this alone for the professionals to handle."

He pivoted and whisked through the revolving glass door, leaving me to mull over what meat hooks Uncle Sam had up Mercedes' ass. Then I had second thoughts on antagonizing Felix and the embassy staff. How many enemies could I afford to rack up here?

Pembe's printout of their hotel guests was in my mailbox behind the front desk. Apart from Nashwinter and me, all the surnames were ethnic, German and Turkish, which didn't mean a lot. I found her in the restaurant annex and asked about the gay men in Room 213, Mercedes' old lair.

"They're off the books." She fiddled with her evil eye bracelet.

"Omar offers privacy, but his guests pay extra for it?"

She nodded.

"Do you like Omar for a boss?"

She looked surprised. "Why do you ask me?"

"I'm a private detective." I smiled at her. "Asking nosy questions is what I do for a living."

"Well, I'm just a hostess. I do my job. Omar pays me. That's it. See?"

I looked at her before she gave me two slips of paper. I had orders to return calls to Gatlin and Mrs. Mercedes. The boxes by the Urgent status were checked. I balled up both slips of paper to pitch in the wastebasket. As the action figure in this movie, I decided what was urgent. I downed two cups of Turkish coffee and more pound cake before I made it back to use my room phone. Gatlin was in his office bright and early.

"I know you'd rather undergo root canal than to carry a cell phone, but this is terribly inconvenient."

The flamboyant attorney even thousands of miles away was able to curl my toenails. I caressed the tender lumps on my head.

"Nobody saw Mercedes after he left the Otel Pamuk on his Sunday jaunt."

"Is that it? If I don't give Lois something, she'll boil me alive in hot tar."

"That's it from here. Now you tell me something. Who

signs their checks, Mr. or Mrs.?"

"They're both from Old Middleburg Money. Each has their own pile. She was a Pendleton of the baby food fortune. He's the heir of a big pharmaceutical magnate. Eliminate greed as a murder motive, if that's where you're headed with this logic."

"Not if she felt a murderous yen to double her assets."

Gatlin had a sigh. "You've been issued a clear directive, Frank. Find our missing subject with your usual dogged facility. That's it. No extra frills like murder conspiracies are appreciated. Did the casinos pan out?"

"The Saturday night before Mercedes gambled away his quid. Then he returned here. All spruced up Sunday morning, he sashayed out the lobby. His fadeout beyond that point still holds."

"How late did he return?"

"Very. At least one o'clock Sunday morning, I'd say." I hesitated but then bulled ahead. "In the interest of honesty, what is your link to Mrs. Mercedes? Don't tell me she's just an old pal. That don't wash. Is she blackmailing you? Are you shagging her? With my country ass on the line over here, I better know all the angles."

Gatlin grunted. "My personal life is off-limits."

"My ticket is an open-ended flight. I'll grab a *taksi* for Esenboga Airport . . ."

"Okay, okay. What if she and I are more than friends? She's an attractive lady, and I'm a red-blooded male. Suffice it to say we enjoy each other's company."

"You're her jealous lover, a classic motive to bump off her husband."

Gatlin growled at me. "That's a flimsy motive. I already told you she and Mercedes have a open marriage where ~~ "

Our conversation got dropped. Some telecom satellite up in the blue yonder had punked out on us. Maybe a chunk of space junk had struck it. I redialed Gatlin's office and mansion, but I only roused a series of pips. A breathy lady operator got the same results. I considered firing off an email from Omar's computer in the lobby, but I was too pissed at Gatlin. Who'd be dim-witted enough to seduce their own client? So, I curled up on the bed and squeezed in a catnap to counter my jet lag.

※

I snapped awake, shivering in the cooler room. I rolled off the bed and stumbled over to shut the window. The clock said 6:30 p.m. Each heartbeat made my head throb. I looked over. Another slip of paper had appeared under my doorsill. I read the slip under the lamp. Lois "Urgent!!" Mercedes had called again. Scowling, I cradled the phone receiver I'd left off the hook.

I patched through a call to my doublewide in Pelham. My voice mail played. Good, the IRS hadn't left any nasty-grams. But an incensed Mrs. Mercedes said to get in touch with her ASAP. Good Lord, I thought. A second message came on from a guy in Rixeyville griping about a busted firing pin on his .410 Stevens Savage. I felt his pain but hung up. Mrs. Mercedes was driving me nuts with her demands for progress. Investigations didn't move that fast.

Mercedes' line of work brought him to Ankara on a regular basis. The rub was nobody had any idea what he did here. Skullduggery for our side wouldn't shock me. Felix's order that I should quit sticking my nose where it didn't belong gave that credence. A nervous rap came at the door.

"Who's there?"

"Omar. May I come in? It's important."

The desk chair I'd wedged under the doorknob for the extra security slid away before I tossed off the deadbolt and security chain. The wide-angle peephole shrank him to a munchkin. I opened the door, ushered him in, and elbowed the door shut. He breathed in spurts. His wide eyes, twin briquettes, glowed. Muted red lipstick smeared his necktie.

"Pembe is dead." He swallowed hard. "Murdered."

"Fuck." My heart swan-dived. "Did you call Mustafa? The police?"

"Should I? I mean yes, of course, I will. But first come quick. Have a look at her. I don't know what to do."

I followed him into the corridor. "Where are we headed?"

"She lies by the cage elevator."

We pounded over the carpet. His beltware chirped but, he ignored it. The lobby was ablaze like the Atlantic City boardwalk. I saw a gaggle of uniformed maids at the cage elevator, wagging their downcast heads and chattering. They parted for us. Scowling, Omar snarled in curt Turkish. They scattered, fleeing the lobby.

The cage elevator's front grill had retracted inside its slot. Pembe sat slumped against the cage elevator's back panel. A bullet through her chest had pinned a scarlet orchid to her white blouse. Take away that grisly detail, and she was glamorous as ever. I startled. Pretty corpses are rare. I had a few routine questions for Omar.

"Did you see a handgun lying around?"

"No."

"How did you discover her?"

"I was leaving the bar and happened to gaze over and saw her like this. So I ran over to her and checked her for a pulse, and I found none. I panicked, and I raced straight to your room. This is bad for the hotel."

Something struck me. "Why is she in the cage elevator? Wasn't she on the front desk full-time?"

He used a wrist to mop his sweat-lined forehead. "I don't know why she left. This is bad. Very bad. The police will come and ask their questions. Lots of hard questions I can't answer."

"Call the cops. We can't do anything else."

"The guests will see this. They'll check out."

"Maybe the cops will be fast. Just call them. Now."

As he turned, I decided to follow him to his office. Pembe wasn't apt to leave. While he dialed, I slid out the desk drawer, removed the junk, and tilted out the false bottom. I picked up the Luger smudged with my prints. A cursory sniff at it didn't pick up any whiffs of cordite. While he talked in his native tongue on the phone, I used my shirttail to clean my prints off the Luger's steel. There wasn't enough time to check the other Lugers.

Hanging up, he saw me return the Luger, put back the junk, and replace the false bottom. "The police are minutes away."

"Murder always gets their juices stewing."

"Do you want your Luger for protection from the killer?"

I shook my head. "I'm okay, thanks."

"I'll call up to the hill for Mustafa. Wait by the cage elevator and shoo off the nosy maids."

I left his office to secure the crime scene. Then I saw Nashwinter cut into the lobby from the stairway exit. The weave to his trawl over the carpet suggested his state. He halted before stepping on the corpse, his mouth falling agape. His fingers scratched his elbow. Murder even through his alcohol haze gave him pause.

"Where were you earlier?" I asked him.

He flinched at hearing me. "Asleep up in my room. Alone." He gave me a wary squint. "Why are you asking? Do you think I had something to do with this?"

"Your alibi is shaky."

"Is your alibi any better, Johnson? Where were you?"

"Never mind. Did you hear any gunshots?"

"How could I if I was asleep?"

"Just go stand by the lobby door. Holler when you see the cops. Keep quiet about what you saw here."

Nashwinter grunted. "Whatever you say, horse."

I stepped into the cage elevator, crouched down, and put my fingertips to the pulse points in her wrists and neck.

Nothing. She'd bit the dust. Her blood loss was minimal. After rolling up her torso, I frisked under her still warm corpse but raked up no purse, handgun, and spent brass casing. Moving the corpse was a CSI no-no. I didn't care.

Her missing purse indicated an armed robbery. Her sea green eyes, wide but inert, taunted my curiosity. Her legs forked out to the lobby carpet. Her stockings darkened her olive skin. She'd used no lipstick. She didn't need it. Catching the burnt cork stench from her entry wound set me to sketching out a half-plausible scenario.

Her mugger perched by the cage elevator had waited, then at point blank range put a fatal cap in her. I saw by the smile frozen on her face she'd had the final laugh. But then death always does. The top two buttons to her blouse had worked their way loose.

I reached over for a discrete look. A lacy, red bra peeked out of the vee. I also saw a pen dot mole over her left bra cup. A similar bra had surfaced in Mercedes' room. Nashwinter hollered over at me.

"The cops just pulled up, horse."

I faded a few paces, becoming a bystander as two men barging into the lobby took control. Dressed in a navy blue suit and a tie but no hat, the short, stocky homicide cop said he was Abdullah. His overdeveloped sidekick wore the sky blue uniform of the municipal police. He went by Auk.

They first grilled Omar, now tieless, by the front desk while the arriving uniforms broke out the gray sheets and rolled up a gurney. Nothing is sadder to me than watching a corpse lifted to transport on a gurney. But I credited them as pros at processing the crime scene.

Abdullah with Auk buttonholed me near the cage elevator. Auk's eyes cloudy as raki stayed pinned on me. Abdullah jotted down my statement, all three pithy sentences. When he quizzed me on why I was in town, I used my cover story.

"I'm sightseeing. Then it's off to Cappadocia."

"Troglodytes. Shit." Abdullah spat into the columnar

ashtray stand. "It's a heathenish way to live, and die, I tell you."

"Will you autopsy the dead lady?"

From the corner of my eye I saw Nashwinter slinking through the stairway exit. He was good at getting lost at the first sign of any trouble.

"In due course." Abdullah's diamond chips for eyes cast their shrewd glint at me. "Why does an American tourist ask, or even care, about a dead stranger's autopsy?"

My shrug was disarming. "Maybe I watch too many cop shows."

The two detectives traded eyebrow hikes, and I knew they didn't buy my line. Abdullah made the ruling.

"Mr. Johnson, you'll sit pat for a few days before traveling off to the land of the troglodytes."

I faked my disappointed face. "But I've given you my statement, and I've seen everything I wanted to in Ankara."

Abdullah smiled. "How'd you like to warm a bed in my prison cell?"

"I'll remain for as long as you need me."

Abdullah nodded as I retreated to my room, knowing under all the smiles was a hard-nosed cop. I flumped down on the bed. Inhaled. Waited. Exhaled. It wasn't a creepy dream, though. Murder had darkened this missing persons case and upped the stakes.

Homicides aren't what a shamus does. Most PIs can brag they've worked their entire careers without tripping over a stiff. I'm the exception. Why that was, I couldn't say. Since coming home from the Army, I'd lived under a dark star. Not a green rookie, however, I'd handled several homicides first as an MP at Fort Riley, not to mention the ones in my PI arena. What was yet another stiff?

Chapter 9

Fort Riley sits on I-70 in northeast Kansas. George Custer's 7th Cavalry trained there before galloping off to their ignoble fate on the Little Big Horn. I'd always wanted to be a cop and found a slot waiting for me once I mustered into the Army. It was during my MP stint at Fort Riley that I befriended the colorful Maynard Z. Thornburg. Mean as a snake, Maynard was a good ole boy from Tuscaloosa, Alabama.

"Maynard, my transfer orders came in today."

"No shit. Where's Uncle shipping off your cracker ass?"

We sat drinking icy cans of Schlitz in a roadhouse used by Army grunts out on Old Highway 77. The dive, once an Esso filling station, featured a cracked mirror and TV but no karaoke, my kind of joint in those days.

"Incirlik Air Base."

"Where?"

"It's in southern Turkey, east of Adana on the Mediterranean. Decent size, too. The main runway is a ten-thousand footer. They need MPs, and my number came up, I guess."

He snorted. "You better like goat yogurt."

"It's all modern with fatty food joints."

"Like I said, learn to like goat yogurt."

"Fuck it, Maynard. I'll do okay over there."

"I'm just messing with you. Hell, I'd go in a heartbeat, but you know my hitch is up next month. Until then, I suppose I'll rot here at Fort Riley."

"Big retirement plans?"

"You bet." His eyes turned dreamy. Or maybe it was the Schlitz making them glassy in the bar's stingy light. Hunching nearer to me, he used a gruff murmur. "I'm breaking into the private detective trade."

"No shit." I had some advice. "You'd better hustle harder than Pete Rose. You can't just hang out your shingle and pull your pud and wait for the work to come to you."

"It ain't a regular pay check, but I'll have my pension. Are you saying to forget it?"

"Go for it. I just mean I'd never try it."

He drained his last swig of Schlitz and smacked his lips. "Why not? You're smart enough. That's half the battle. Intelligence. Information. Investigation. That's the private eye's Holy Trinity. I see it as an extension of our MP work."

"Okay, so take a whack at it. Write me in care of Incirlik. Regale me with your big capers, and how you seduced all the femme fatales."

Yawning, he ordered us more cans of Schlitz, his treat. "Scribble down the name of that air base. It'll tax my brain trying to spell it."

"Okay but you better write unless you break both of your arms."

"Yeah, okay I will."

Fucking liar, I thought. We meant well by saying we'd stay in touch, but we never did. Why? My best explanation was that life spun us off in new, separate orbits. It was crazy really. Friends were a big deal with me since I didn't have any immediate family.

When I was a kid, a drunk CPO out of Norfolk T-boned my parents one rainy night. Both were DOAs. Later my cousin Cody Chapman took a chest load of double-ought buck from a sawed-off shotgun. So unless my own arm was in a splint, I'd drop Maynard a line. As an Irishman, I should've known better: we plan, god laughs.

Ten days later on a raw, wet afternoon in Incirlik I heard through a mutual friend that Maynard had died. His scrap with a thug pulling a knife was behind the same roadhouse. Before Maynard figured out if the thug was a slasher or stabber, the knife sank into Maynard's gut. Left face-down in the gutter, he'd bled out.

Too few friends entered our lives; too many left it. That rainy day I vowed to do one thing before I died. After I got my discharge, I'd take a hack at the PI trade. If for nothing else, I'd do it for Maynard. I'd no idea what shark pool I was diving into back then.

～

On a different rainy afternoon a few years later I was talking to Gerald Peyton. We sat staking out a titty bar over in Hybla Valley where a bail skip was hanging out. We get each other's back on our jobs. Gerald will be my best man if I ever get hitched again. He'll also be my kids' godfather if I ever get that far in life. I haven't asked him, but I know he'll do it. He's just the guy you need in the clutch.

"This Maynard sounds like a good dude." Gerald nodded at me. "Sorry I never met him."

I gazed at Gerald who always seemed cramped when sitting in a car. One recent afternoon I'd seen him bench press an eye-popping 450 pounds. He said he could hear the bones in his arms and shoulders crunching as they flexed under all the strain. Brutal.

"Yeah, Maynard was quite a character."

Wipers scraped the windshield. The bail skip hadn't waltzed out of the titty bar for us to grab up. My memories wrapped around a different friend, Old Man Maddox from Scarab, West Virginia. Old Man was a retired CIA operative. A militant clan of atheist whack jobs dubbing themselves as The Blue Cheer had teed off on us. Things had turned a little rough even before Gerald rolled into town. After that, we'd rocked Scarab to its core.

"Still going to your meetings, Frank?"

I nodded. "Religiously."

"That's a good thing. Keep it up."

"You bet, Mom. I'm on the wagon. In fact, my life has gotten pretty normal and dull."

"For now, sure it is. But life can get tricky. Sometimes the buried shit blows up in our faces like setting off the tripwire to a land mine."

I nodded. "The trouble is you don't see it coming."

"Let's go collar this asshole." Gerald had opened his car door. "I tired of waiting and, no offense Frank, talking shit."

CHAPTER 10

Every country uses an assigned prefix for their international phone calls. Turkey's is +90 while, of course, the U.S. takes +1. I thumbed in the right numbers. My signal pulsated through the icy vault of space. Then a Caribbean lady's voice poured a cultured "hello" into my ear.

"Frank Johnson returning Mrs. Mercedes' call."

"Mrs. Mercedes is occupied."

"Doing what?"

"May I take her a message?"

"Hey, she wanted to talk to me."

"I shall relay your message, Mr. Jackson."

"That's Johnson. Frank Johnson."

Click.

I wedged the desk chair back underneath my doorknob. Pembe lay toe-tagged on a slab at the Ankara morgue. A killer prowled these premises. I sat watching the war news on CNN. I disliked how Omar had herded me into his office after Abdullah had released the crime scene and left with his crew.

∽∼

"Frank, I want to hire you."

Currently not in the job market, I told Omar as much.

He wouldn't take no for an answer. "You can be my new hotel detective. You know what I mean?"

Yeah, I knew about the job. I knew it was a thankless

gig. I knew it wasn't a good fit for me. Hotel detectives still trawled the floors, elevators, and stairs to key on any pickpockets, grifters, and other criminal riff-raff. Hotel dicks bounced them out on their ears. If a hotel got a bad reputation, they went broke. These days of cell phone cameras, blogs, and messageboards reported on the security at different hotels. Who went on vacation to meet a terrorist? Our digital world was a shrinking as well as dangerous one.

There was more. At night, the hotel dicks often doubled as bouncers at the house bar or discotheque. With 48,000 PIs (think of the Metrodome in Minneap filled to capacity) scrapping for gainful work out there, I knew a hotel detective job was better than no job. The hotel dick gig also gave me a handy excuse to pry around the Otel Pamuk.

"I'm as anxious as you are to get to the bottom of Pembe's murder. So I'll keep a sharp lookout. Deal?"

"Deal. By the same token, Mercedes' whereabouts also worry me. But I can't let that news get out. Talk of abductions at the Otel Pamuk will ruin me."

"Do you have security cameras aimed at the exterior doors? Or mounted in the stairwells and corridors?"

He cringed. "Should I?"

Shrugging, I tried out something on him. "Is Mercedes' departure linked to Pembe's murder?"

Nervous, Omar at his desk shuffled a deck of playing cards. "May Allah forbid it. Can you work until late?"

"I've got to sleep some time."

"I know." He riffled the playing cards back through his palms in a deft reverse shuffle. "The news of her murder has spread. Three guests have already threatened to go stay at other hotels. What if more do the same thing? Now I can reassure them by saying my security is beefed up. They'll see you."

"Does six to midnight work for you?"

"Perfect. Be smart. Carry this." He leaned back and resurrected the Luger from inside the desk drawer.

My fingers wrapped around the Luger. Its cold, black

steel felt almost toxic. He smiled. My smile was also plastic. "Does this gun really fire? It looks older than dirt to me."

"But of course. German know-how never built a better one."

They also got their asses trounced in two big wars, I thought.

"One more thing, Frank. If you hit any trouble, deal with it but also call me."

"Where can you be reached? Your home phone?"

"No-no. I'll crash right here." His hand circled to mean the office. "Just knock on the door. I'm a light sleeper, and this chair will be my bed." He sighed. "Karin will grow angry, and life will turn to shit. Again."

"Later on, Omar."

I beat it out of his office. I'd lent a shoulder for too many guys to sob on. Their sad stories were all the same, and Omar's got sadder by the minute. I'd left him slouched over and brooding at his desk.

※

My stare now landed on the Luger on my nightstand. I got up. This was a dull room with no radio or TV. The sight of Mercedes' belongings rekindled my interest. I squatted by the pile of his clothes, but going through them I just recovered more lint. I gave up, pocketed the Luger, and ducked out into the shadowy corridor.

I tipped my lucky Kennedy half-dollar against the doorsill. Any hoodlum would grab it before stealing into my room. I also dangled out a DO NOT DISTURB sign on the doorknob. Cheesy. Sure. But it worked. No room noises came during my stroll to the lobby. The guests had settled into their sedentary night routines. That was jake by me. I searched for the most tortuous chair to sit in. Mustafa slouched in one waved at me, and I headed over to him.

"Frank, I figured you'd never show."

What do you say to a man coping with his wife's savage death? I'd no words. His casino guard uniform was disheveled. Sorrow and rage had carved up his blotchy face seeking the company of my shifty eyes. They steadied on him.

I used a thick mutter. "Sorry for your loss."

"Thank you."

"Any idea why she rode up on the elevator?"

"Maybe a guest phoned down for a bar of soap or dental floss, and she ran it up. She was helpful that way, you know."

Nodding, I recalled she'd told me the same thing. I watched his hands mash into hammer-like fists, then relax into grappling hooks.

"We'll ask the guests," I said.

"Help me get this killer. Do it for her sake."

"Use your head. What can I do for you? Detectives Abdullah and Auk are the official hands on this investigation. Lean on them for your answers."

"They're a waste of time. You can work faster."

"Not really. Why didn't you come right after Omar called the Harrington?"

"My pager was off, and I was busy."

"Busy at what?"

"Busy at making my assigned rounds. My every waking second isn't spent working the casino. My beeper going off in the corridors disturbs the guests."

The Harrington tower had many empty rooms with empty beds and many pretty maids. I stayed mum rather than whip any accusations on him. I'd no way of telling if Pembe and he were faithful. She'd struck me as a natural flirt. Whether she'd take it to next level was the key question. We listened to a vacuum cleaner droning in the corridor. Somebody had spilled a mess on the carpet.

"Tea, Frank?"

"That or Turkish coffee works for me." I felt grateful for the break in our heavy conversation.

The restaurant annex was empty. Turkish coffee smelled acrid like Espresso. I threw back three steamy cups before the caffeine's high voltage arced between my ears. Coffee was the one guilty pleasure this monk would never sacrifice. Mustafa downed the same number of cups. I tailed him back to the lobby where he found another chair, and we took a load off.

"Sticking around?" I asked him.

"No, my shift starts in an hour. We're down to a skeleton crew, and I work the dog hours. Far too many dog hours. Frank, it feels like bullshit to me. With her now ripped from my life, it's bullshit. I only wished I spent a little more time with her, and a little less time working the dog hours. But it's too late now. She's gone, and I'm still here."

"That's tough."

"Now I catch the rumors our government plans to shut down the hotel casinos. The players like Mercedes and Socrates, I suppose, will go to Cyprus. So I'm out of my wife and soon my job. Isn't that what you Americans call a 'double whammy'?"

I nodded. "A double whammy is sure bad. Did she always work at the front desk alone?"

"Mostly, yeah. At times she pitched in for the restaurant. Omar is a cheap son of a bitch. Like now he's washing dishes to save a dime."

I surveyed the half-lit lobby and recalled the shadowy corridors. Omar scrimped on the light bill. I realized he hadn't quoted me a salary as his hotel dick. I strolled over and toggled the light switches to brighten the corners where assassins liked to hide.

"Omar will growl at you."

"We've reached an understanding. Did Pembe like her job?"

"Hell, no. Omar is Allah's gift to women. But he never hit on her. Or he knew I'd come and hit on him."

Hearing that anger struck a chord in me. To get even, I'd hired a hit man named Limpet to take out my cheating ex. I wasn't thinking too straight.

"Did you make any copies of Mr. Mercedes' photo?"

"I've been too jammed for time," was my half-truthful reply. "That Saturday night what happened to Mercedes?"

"How do you mean?"

"Did he come alone to the casino? Was he in a suit? Did he reek of booze? How was his mood? Uptight or anxious?"

"All of the above, I'd say. He sweated under the hot lights and swore at his rotten luck."

"If he blows all his money, where is there any fun in it?"

"He scores a jackpot often enough to fan his vanity that he'll cash in big. It never happens. The house doles out a few bucks, but they always win. Even by going broke, he never caught on to the scam."

"Actually he's in Donald Trump's tax bracket."

Relaxing in the chair, Mustafa stretched his legs in front of him. "Then Mercedes is addicted. We've got another die-hard gambler. The fat, bald Greek -- he's Socrates like the philosopher -- camps out in our casino. Have you watched him? You should.

"Socrates hemorrhages green. I pity him, his wife and kids even more. When he flies to Ankara, he hits our casino first. He tells me he works like a fiend. What's the point in it if he can't splurge on what pleases him?"

I bit my lip. Mercedes or Socrates squandering their bankroll wasn't my affair. Once I lost five bucks at the nickel slots in Atlantic City. That night in bed at a cut-rate motel I stewed over my stupid greed and couldn't sleep a wink. Live and learn, detective.

"Frank, I better shove off." Mustafa hauled up from the chair. "By now I bet her killer has made it all the way to Samarra."

"Detective Abdullah will get him. Keep the faith. Meantime I'm here if you need me for anything."

"Thanks. Later, my man."

His bravado rang hollow. Shoulders sloped, he trudged off. He drifted through the revolving glass door as if the glass dividers didn't exist. His raised head let out a banshee howl, and then his burly silhouette faded into the street's dark margins.

Left alone with my demons, I returned to the coffee urn. Its red light was extinguished, but the cold remnants inside trickled into my cup. I let the coffee slosh over my teeth and smack against my gums before swallowing it.

Eleven-thirty and nothing stirred. Nosiness drove me to the cage elevator. I thumbed a button. The front grill shambled free to unveil Pembe's death site. Her dried blood still speckled the cab's floor. The maids had refused to scrub off the blood. Omar was left to do the dirty work.

Pembe had died hard. A trigger-happy killer smelled blood. The police had launched their manhunt. As a material witness, I'd been ordered to cool my jets here. My caffeine jolt had tapered off. Lethargic footsteps took me to the front desk.

Beyond it Omar's office door was shut. The back of my knuckles rattled three times on it. After no response on my second try, I twisted the doorknob. Inside I found him lounged back against his chair. Horror buzzed through me. Then his soft snores told me he was alive.

I shut the office door and shuffled off to retrieve my lucky Kennedy half-dollar tipped against the doorsill. Before long I also slept. In this dream, the sniper knelt on the grassy knoll except he wore a fez. He took the aim of the Marine-trained marksman. His Italian Carcano 6.5 bolt-action rifle flamed. Its thunder hit me ~~

I jacked bolt upright in bed, my ears whistling. A clammy sweat swathed me. Nightmare. I knew why, too. All of life's dark stuff clings in your head, a poison like toxic lead building up and tainting your brain.

I missed sleeping in my own bed. Then the angst over what I owed the tax man chilled me. Money punched my ticket out, but my hunt for Mercedes had choked out. I thought of ringing up Gerald and went so far as to dial his number and get his voice mail. My jaw dropped, but I didn't leave him a voice mail message.

Yet.

Chapter 11

My phone was jingling. The nightstand lamp was on. I rolled over, reached, and grunted to answer the phone. The connection was cut. I racked the dead receiver. The second ring wailed until I couldn't stand it. Mrs. Mercedes was tipsy in the wee hours. She slurred her words.

"You! You never call me. Where is my god damn husband? For a private eye, you stink. I get impatient."

As she hauled in a breath, I went to speak. Better forget it.

"Another highball, Lois? Why thank you, I don't mind if I do. Say Lois, how's your private eye over in Turkey working out? How the hell do I know? He's off loafing on my dime. He never returns my calls. He never briefs me. Damn, Lois, why do you pay him? I'm at a loss to say why. Well, Private Eye Johnson, what do you have to say for yourself?"

"You pretty much covered all the bases." My sarcasm rivaled hers.

"Where's Sylvester?"

"Your husband left the Otel Pamuk two Sunday mornings ago. The rest I haven't pieced together."

"Didn't he leave word at the front desk? What a stupid question, Lois. You leave word at the front desk, and your messages aren't answered."

"He left no word and made no international phone calls. He's not big on keeping in touch. As you say, he's a clandestine fellow."

"What does he do for his amusement?"

Dumb question. She had to know he carried on his trysts while abroad. Gatlin had told me they'd arranged a loosey-goosey marriage ruled by their individual lusts and whims. It boggled my mind. I'd gone berserk when catching ex screwing her lover and hired an assassin. That's where I was coming from on this deal.

"Mercedes is a hermit. He hunkers down in his room. I guess he sleeps or watches TV. When he does poke out, he heads to the hotel casinos up the block. He's a compulsive gambler. Witnesses say his losses stagger the mind. Does this news stun you?"

"Absolutely. I'd no idea."

She was a smooth liar. "Any recent action on his credit cards or his bank accounts?" I asked.

"Again, I've no idea. By choice, our finances are kept separate. Sylvester buys his toys while I indulge my pursuits. That tidy arrangement keeps the peace between us which is more than I can say for you and me."

This time I overlooked her barb. "Do you have any idea if Mercedes works for the embassy?"

"In what capacity?"

"Anything. I talked to a guy over there. Mercedes and Felix Braintree were buddies. But Felix is giving my questions the cold shoulder. Did Mercedes ever mention him to you?"

"No. What Sylvester does in Ankara stays in Ankara."

I'd reached my flashpoint with her. "Sorry, but you're fading out, so I'll let you go."

"Not so fast. Robert Gatlin and I rode down to Warrenton and had dinner at a café on Main Street."

"That's swell," I said, this not time not so amazed by his lack of good judgment.

She snickered in my ear. "In fact, he's lounging by me in bed. Care to chat with him?"

That was a zinger. But she was three sheets to the wind, and I didn't believe her. "Yeah, put him on."

The familiar gruff voice rang out, "Hello, Frank!"

"Have you lost your fucking marbles?"

"Simmer down, Frank."

"A lady got whacked tonight. Pembe was the front desk hostess. Murder, did you hear that?"

"That changes the picture."

"You god damn straight it does. The cops are giving me hard looks."

"You've violated no laws."

"If I get collared in Ankara, you're no use to me."

"I'll retain an effective criminal attorney there."

"This is too much. I'm here scrapping like a shithouse rat, and you're back home shagging the client. What the hell gives?"

"Good, she's off getting a refill." Gatlin dropped his voice. "She's pretty upset with you."

"Yeah well, her people skills suck, too."

"Frank, you know the client is always right."

"Not always they're not. This started as a missing persons deal. Murder ups the ante. Sorry if I'm pissed."

"You sound a lot more intense than usual."

"And you're a lot less smart with this client."

"Well, speak of the devil, here she's back again in all her glory."

"Call me later when you're alone. I'm hitting the rack."

"What a capital idea. Ta-ta, Frank."

We hung up. I mulled over in the final ticks before sleep overtook me if Gatlin's tryst went beyond his lust. Was he working an angle on her he wasn't sharing with me? Criminal attorneys loved playing their mind games. They practiced brinkmanship to see who blinked first. For the first time in months, I left the light turned on to fall asleep. The creepy vibes I felt had me that worried.

My eyelids thrashing open didn't greet Tuesday's sun nuzzling at the edges to my pulled drapes. Darkness enveloped me. My feet tangled in the sheet yanked free. I saw no sliver of light under the doorsill.

The tile floor underfoot felt tacky. My Luger was stuffed underneath the mattress. I almost elbowed over the nightstand lamp, and it didn't work. I dressed in the dark and waded over to the door. Toggling the switch also gave no light.

A blackout, a common inconvenience, had blanketed Ankara. I'd go back asleep, but I was the hotel dick. Did Omar run backup generators? He was probably too cheap. I stooped over to grope in the nightstand drawer and fished out a flashlight with fresh batteries.

I unlatched the deadbolt, dragged away the desk chair, and stepped out to join the other fireflies bobbing down the corridor to the lobby. Murmurs buzzed. Slippers scuffed. Dozens of us grouping at the front desk concentrated our beams on Omar, his face puffy and eyes baggy.

"The power is out, all. Just be calm. It's okay. Please return to your rooms."

"A loud boom jarred me awake," said a lady's quaver. "What was it?"

"Just the transformers blowing out. Accept my apologies. We'll be back online in time for breakfast. Back to bed, all."

"What was that hullabaloo earlier?" asked a tall, stoop-shouldered man in a red plaid robe.

His face bland, Omar played dumb. "Hullabaloo?"

"The scuttlebutt says a bellhop took a slug to the heart in the cage elevator. Is that so?"

"Here at the Otel Pamuk?" Omar wagged his head. "That farfetched rumor is untrue."

Red Plaid persisted. "I don't think so. Is this hotel safe?"

"This is a power outage. But everything hums along just fine. Return to your rooms."

Brace your doors with desk chairs, I mentally added. The grumbling tenants led by their flashlight beams left by the stairs and corridors. I panned my light over Omar's face.

"Who is that?"

"Me, your hotel detective."

"Frank, did you hear the crash?"

"Yeah," I lied. "What was it really?"

"The explosions went off in the direction of your embassy. Car bombs, maybe. I hope not. The terrorists after a quiet month have struck again. Probably the PKK, or the Cyprus troubles are back again."

"Terrorists rage everywhere. Pembe's murder could be their work."

"No terrorists are here. Don't breathe a word of that to any guest. She'd no links to thugs. Me either. Until today, we've had no bad things. My guests stay calm under pressure. You just saw them."

"They looked plenty scared to me."

"Your job is to calm their jitters."

"Got it. Do you run auxiliary generators?"

"I own two, but they burned up during last August's heat wave."

"Pembe's killer might hit again in this blackout."

"My guests behind their locked doors are safe. Head on back to bed. I'll stand guard until sunup."

Grunting my approval, I angled off that way. Armed with the Luger, I decided to take a romp through the place. If nothing else, I'd shadow Omar and get his back. The inoperable cage elevator forced me to go by the stairway. After giving him a head start I climbed the steps.

At every other step, stopping, I pricked up my ears. A car rattled over a loose manhole cover. Sweat greased my palms. At the second floor, with a memory of a fire extinguisher bolted to the wall, I shifted to the other side of the corridor. My eyes squinched, but I discerned no killer shadows around me.

A strand of light glinted from the doorsill to Room 213. Jerry and Pat, old pros, knew to use a battery-operated lamp during a blackout. I let them be and probed further. Twenty minutes later after casing all five floors, I hadn't met up with Omar and dipped back to the lobby. His office door was shut. I was too bushed to check in with him and headed to my room.

Still dressed, I crashed on my bed. At some point my nightstand lamp blazed back on. The electric power flowed again. Upbeat, I rolled over and dreamed of well-lit streets where the car bombs never smashed us.

Early dawn on Tuesday I awoke to find my head cold better. I diagnosed it as an allergy. If I got the hell out of Ankara, it'd clear up. A clue was in Mercedes' duffel. I just knew it. So, I pulled apart his stuff and sorted the articles into small piles on my bed. The maduro cigar scent permeated his belongings. Did his ladies enjoy his nicotine kisses?

"What's this?" A brown plastic vial was a prescription for an ED aid. The pills were the powdery blue ones. "Mercedes has to prime the old hydraulics." I plundered nothing else of any interest, repacked his duffel, and set it aside.

I jotted down several notes for my final report to Mrs. Mercedes, the one I'd sock her with before I got paid and fed the tax man. My fear of doing more slammer time drove me every minute to finish this case. I also updated my expense report.

I narrowed my thoughts, but my mind refused to focus on Mercedes. It strayed to Pembe lying flat out in the cage elevator, a slug lodged in her heart. She'd had on a lacy, red bra. I wondered if it was the same one I'd rousted from Mercedes' room. Had she slugged me over the head and taken the bra? What if she'd killed Mercedes and, in turn, was murdered by a double-crossing rat partner? Who was her rat partner? Murder wasn't in my job description, so I tried to stick to my own case.

I heard the showers blast on in the other berths as my fellow tenants slogged into their mornings. Last night at my request, Omar had sent down a color TV. I surfed to CNN.

The U.S. Embassy bomb blast in Ankara was the top news. No leads on the perps had developed, but the talking heads liked to beat a dead mule to fill the air time.

The next segment said an RPG had wiped out three Marines entering a checkpoint near Sadr City. Three new Gold Star moms had lost their souls. That left a bad taste in my mouth. I wanted to kick in the TV screen.

Instead I showered and dressed in a clean shirt and jeans. I'd better ask Omar about the laundry service. I left on my TV as a burglar deterrent. The lobby's computer was up. I logged on to my web G-mail account. The Nigerians hadn't pitched me any new, hot business deals. Before I flushed my entire inbox, a message heading -- *Hi Frank, D.A.* -- grabbed my eye. My pulse ramping up, I clicked open her message.

Hi Frank,

> *What's up with you? I pinged the doublewide, but you didn't pick up. I guess you're out of town a few days. I had a few free minutes in the lab this a.m. and decided to write you a few lines. The weather has turned nippy here for late August. I've saved up some vacation. Do you feel up for hanging out? Virginia Beach post-Labor Day is nice. How's Gerald? He's a monster. Just kidding ☐ Are you getting to all of your AA meetings? My mom is still laid off, and hunting for work. Slim pickings out there -- better stay busy in your hustle. I'm doing fine in my new job. Murders haven't cut back. It's getting late, so I better get back to the stiffs on the autopsy tables. Our diener is on maternity leave. She's expecting any day. Twins. Boys. I don't envy her. She's picked out their names, but she won't tell them until she's back home, and safe. Sorry to ramble on like this. Be well. Don't make yourself a stranger. Write me. Soon!*

xxx,
Dreema

How did I forget Dreema Atkins in Richmond? I made a mental note to call her. Curious, next I googled "Sylvester Mercedes", a semi-unusual name. No hits. I googled him using the "Image" tool. No online pictures. Frustrated, I fed in my own name and got the same result. A few of us still remained ghosts in cyberspace. I went to the coffee urn and filled a cup. The first sip corroded my tongue, and I set down the cup on a napkin.

"Is our coffee so vile?"

I turned. The man smiling behind me was Abdullah, the happy policeman hard at investigating Pembe's slaying. His compact stature didn't intimidate, but his jet eyes pierced you like a dark laser.

"Isn't that the English word? Vile? A good word for murder, too, I hasten to add."

"We had a rough night. The power conked out."

He shrugged. "Such is Ankara. But back to murder, there's been a new development. Pembe's bullet hole matches to a 9 millimeter or a Luger." His dark eyes stabbed me. "By chance, do you carry one?"

A split-screen image locked in my mind. The top screen showed that desk drawer of Lugers in Omar's office. The bottom screen locked on the Luger stuffed under my mattress. Forced to craft a wily lie wasn't how I liked to kick off my day.

"Omar lent me one. It's wedged under my mattress except -- "

"How handy. This homicide is -- what's your idiom? -- in the bag. We'll get your Luger, Pembe's murder weapon, and leave here as civilized gentlemen. No handcuffs. Then it's off to Buca Prison for you, sir."

" -- except the Luger hasn't been fired since like D-Day," I said to finish my sentence.

Abdullah's smarmy grin wilted at the corners. "Ballistics never lie."

"That's my point." I stood aside, my hand making a deferential motion. "Be my guest. Come check for yourself."

I picked up my cup of coffee. We stalked off through the corridor and into my room. I set down my cup of coffee on the nightstand.

"We're on the same team, you know," I said.

"It's a nice thought, but that's all it is."

His hand in a Latex glove frisked in the crevice between the mattress and box spring. He plucked out the Luger and unloaded it. His gloating smile sagged as he sniffed the chamber -- no cordite odor. Shrugging, he stuffed the Luger and its bullets into the evidence bags he also carried.

"Why did Omar lend you his Luger?"

Admitting now I wasn't a tourist in Abdullah's country was my first step at damage control.

"Knowing me from my Army MP days stationed here, Omar hired me to do the hotel security after Pembe's homicide." I stopped talking, raised my hand, and then froze. I'd better ask for his permission first. "Is it okay if I get out some photo ID for you?"

His 9 mil had cleared leather. "Make it a slow, easy reach, Mr. Johnson."

The license verified my claim as a Private Investigator in the Commonwealth of Virginia. Here in Ankara I knew that didn't mean jack shit. I'd given Pembe my passport to secure in the hotel safe, and I didn't show that unless he asked me.

"Mercedes' wife hired me to find him in Ankara," is how I started to reveal why I was in his city.

Digesting my tale, Abdullah rubbed his eyebrows, then knitted them into skeptical hash marks.

"Our Mr. Johnson is a private eye. Well, well. Again, why did Omar lend you his Luger?"

"He gave it to me for protection while I patrolled the hotel. A killer prowls the hotel."

"What did you see on your rounds?"

"Last night stayed pretty quiet."

"So, the killer tricked Pembe into coming upstairs, shot her on the cage elevator, and ripped off her purse like it was a robbery." He put away his 9 mil. "Clever and creative."

By now I had a firmer respect for his methodical cop style. "Detective Abdullah, I'm just doing my job here."

"I realize that." The heel of Abdullah's palm scraped across his forehead. "This is our deal. For the time being, you may work on Mercedes' disappearance and Omar's hotel security. Meanwhile Pembe's homicide is all mine."

"That's fine, but what if their cases should intersect?"

Abdullah smiled. "Then, sir, our worlds shall collide."

"She printed me out their guests list. I'll trade you it for staying in the loop on your progress."

Still amused, he wagged his blunt finger at me. "No-no. Our worlds can have no bridges. Her homicide is ours alone. If need be, I can generate my own guests list. No outside help is wanted. I hope we've reached a meeting of the minds."

What could I say? "Absolutely."

As he went to leave, he stepped back and turned, his jet eyes trying to catch me off-guard. But I only blew a breath to cool off my hot mug of coffee. It tasted like the bitter chicory blend the Fort Riley chefs used to brew on frosty Kansas mornings before I headed out on my foot patrol.

Whistling like he had all the right answers, Abdullah left by the corridor. Drinking my coffee, I had a new worry. I was beginning to like Detective Abdullah's cop style.

Chapter 12

My three knuckle raps on the office door failed to rouse Omar. I jiggled the doorknob. Locked. Where was he? From my peripheral vision, I saw a lady across the lobby give a sharp glance at my second, crisper knock.

She squared her shoulders and approached me. Her business suit -- ecru, I thought, was the shade -- included an off-white blouse and a dark skirt cropped an inch above her knees. She'd well-turned legs. Back up to her face, I smiled. She frowned. Even in her low pumps, she looked me straight in the eye. Hers were gray-hazel.

"Omar went home." She used a flat lilt.

"I figured as much. Are you Pembe's replacement?"

"More or less. But I also happen to co-own the Otel Pamuk. I'm Karin, Omar's wife. I worked the front desk as the first Pembe before we had a family."

"You sound more American than Turkish."

Karin smiled. Nice one, I thought.

"Do I now? I'm Turkish by birth, but I grew up in the middle of Brooklyn. My Turkish mother met my father in Incirlik. He was discharged, and they got married. They went to his country.

"I flew over held in my mother's arms, bawling my eyes out the whole way, I'm told. Years later, I returned to Ankara and met Omar at the university. We fell madly in love, quit school, and threw a big wedding bash. Everybody and his brother came."

"Omar told me you have a family," I said.

"We have two girls. Açelya is fun-loving while the older Zeynep is quieter and more serious like Omar. He's also told me all about our own hardboiled detective."

I didn't react to her hackneyed comparison. "Did you hear last night's car bombs?"

"We live too far on the other side of Ankara. Our maids said three bombs went off. No terrorists have come forth to claim the credit." Karin shook her head. "But who knows? Who cares? They compete in making a big bang. No longer shocking, it's all a big bore to me."

I frowned. Did she see slamming jumbo airliners into American skyscrapers as a "big bang" or a "big bore"? But I asked, "Didn't Pembe just cover the front desk?"

"Yes, she did."

"Any idea why she went upstairs?"

"I can't imagine why. If a guest rings down wanting any amenities, our maids are tasked to handle it. They make their tips money that way."

"Only the maids provide the room service?"

"Yes, they take care of everything like that. Pembe, our happy, little hostess, only flashed her winning smile. She was eye candy for our guests."

"Why do I get the impression you didn't like her?"

Karin's smile turned opaque. "I felt just the opposite. Her job here allowed me to stay home and be a mother to Açelya and Zeynep. Our life isn't all sunshine, however. Here's a tip, Mr. Johnson. Never sink your lifesavings and soul into a hotel. Running it is a misery."

"The Taj Mahals on the hill have undercut your business?"

Jutting out the pink to her bottom lip, she shrugged. "Americans with their lavish tastes stay there, not here. You're the exception. Why is that?"

"Because I'm not a Bill Gates, just a sentimental softie for the Otel Pamuk." I sniffed.

"You flatter us." Her forehead smooth as polished agate lined in puzzlement. "Do you have allergies? What in

Turkey can bother our hardboiled Mr. Johnson?"

"Beats me."

She asked about my stay, and I recounted how the American consulate wanted me to drop by. She doubted if their offices were intact, much less held any regular hours. She also said I should go sample their spice bizarre. Maybe I'd whip up a fanciful potion to unleash the evil eye dogging my health. The spice bizarre, I told her, topped my list of things to do. By now she and I were the best of pals.

She called over a portly, round-headed maid to snap our picture by the Otel Pamuk's logo of a flower on the wall near the cage elevator. Karin put her arm around my shoulder. I saw she was well-endowed, too. Then she push-pinned our Polaroid to the "Guests Hall of Honor". Now I felt flattered. She'd assembled a gallery of snapshots on the cork boards. Mercedes' portrait wasn't included, but Nashwinter's captured his drunken stupor.

"Does Mercedes court a lady pal in Ankara?"

"Why ask me?" Karin's voice crackled again. "I haven't the foggiest. He pays his bills on time and doesn't chase the maids or smoke in bed. What else does an innkeeper ask of a guest?"

She didn't like Mercedes. "Do you see him out and about?"

Hands planted on her hips. "How could I? Until now, I was a stay-at-home mom. Omar and I never talk shop unless the Otel Pamuk burns down."

I didn't press it. As with Pembe, I couldn't help but wonder if Karin also dolled up in a lacy, red bra. I nodded a smile at her and left, the revolving glass door slinging me into the morning street.

A rotten peaches stench came from the low grade coal the early risers burned in their woodstoves to knock off last night's chill. At the first corner a one-armed lady in a gypsy dress fed the warbling magpies. They strutted around her. She scattered the shelled corn held in a copper wok. Our nods were cordial. I bought Tuesday's edition of the Turkish Daily News at the arcade. The leading stories depressed me.

Insurgents had skirmished with Coalition forces in several Iraqi cities. Had the Pentagon think tanks factored in the insurgents like the WMDs? Rage quickened my gait through an alleyway shortcut. The radios pumped out schmaltzy New Age music behind the bars guarding the windows to the Turkish homes.

Geraniums, poinsettias, and coleuses lined the window ledges. I lodged my folded Turkish Daily News between two geranium pots. The street traffic was light. Ankara smelled like fried chicken to my stuffy nose before I smelled the char and smoke. Four blocks over at 110 Atatürk Bulvari, I stood gape-mouthed.

The three car bombs' detonations had been precise. The blast radius pulverized our embassy into smoldering cairns of rubble and dust. The ugly scene was shades of Oklahoma City with one big difference -- no casualties.

I breathed in the chalky grit and sneezed. The Feds had unfurled yellow vinyl tape to cordon off ground zero, now a giant crime scene. Two swarthy spectators stood with me on the sidewalk behind the wrought iron fence.

"Americans get reamed up the ass, too," said one man with a hook-shaped scar on his cheek.

His shorter, mustachioed friend nodded. "Nobody deserves it more. Nobody."

Two pairs of daggers for eyes stabbed me. A flush reddening my neck licked into my tight jaws. The urge to blow my runny nose saved me from slugging them. Laughing, they strutted off holding their hands.

A spare six-footer in a navy blue uniform and 9 mil sidearm hopped out of an Econoline van that'd pulled up. He heeled his Shepherd dog on a short leash. They worked the debris margins to register any human or incriminating scents.

My hands gripped the wrought iron pikestaffs, and my one foot rested on the bottom fence rail. Grommets in the lanyard clacked on the steel flagpole. A hand shielded my raised eyes. Old Glory still flapped in the Anatolian gusts. By God if a lump didn't knot in my throat. Maybe the Iraqi war pissed me off like it did many Yanks but, good or bad, we were all in it for the long haul.

"Horrid morning." A known face recognized me. Felix Braintree's pigeon-toed walk inflated his sense of self-importance.

I shrugged. "It could be a lot uglier."

He bridled at me. "Says who?"

"Says that cadaver dog not getting any scent hits."

He stopped just short of my shadow. "You finally made it over to see us. Good. When will you leave for Esenboga Airport?"

"Why? Did Uncle escalate the Threat Advisory?"

"We make recommendations with your welfare in mind."

"Things are tough all over." I followed his gaze back to the smoky rubble. "Any leads?"

"We've got a few solid ones to pursue."

"Car bomb?"

"Actually we believe three."

"How did three cars breach your security perimeter?"

"It was a fluke. Don't worry. The Turkish authorities are in lockstep with us on this."

"Are they now?"

A livid streak colored his double chin. "Johnson, do you enjoy getting my goat? I should revoke your passport."

Set-jawed, I lifted my chin at the smoky rubble. "Seems like you've got more important things to do."

"Funny. You've checked in with us. Duly noted. If you get into trouble, don't bother to call. We'll be too busy rebuilding."

Stuffing my breath, I kept my cool. I put my back to the morning sun and left him to oversee his big resurrection project. Murmurs in the cyber cafés buzzed, and acacias shaded the side lane I took. Bumping shoulders with the bystanders, I ignored their stony looks, most of them imagined by me, I was sure.

I tucked inside a quiet, small café where the grizzled men played dominoes, smoked on black cigars, and told big lies. The tobacco smog with my head cold made breathing a chore. The hammered tin ceiling, rough wood floors, and harsh light gave the bastion its masculine stamp.

No women, no kids, and no pets came in here. A thick-set man shorter than me fingered a *tespih*, a tasseled string of ivory prayer beads like my rosary only smaller. His lips moving, he watched me claim a ladder-back chair.

He came over asking, "*Koyu cay? Acik cay?*"

"*Elma cayi.*"

Typical for the jaded tourist, I didn't care for their strong or weak black tea but liked the apple. I stretched my sore legs and, after a little the stocky man returned with a glass cup of steaming apple tea. Two sips later, I deluded myself into thinking the world-at-large might become passably sane again, beginning right here in this quiet, small café.

The men's gruff undertones coincided with the clicks to the dominoes they played on the tabletops. I drew a few sidelong glances. My crazy thoughts put the furtive Mercedes as the mastermind behind our embassy bombing. My idea to show his photo in here didn't stir me to act. I couldn't picture him stopping to rub elbows with commoners. I plunked down a laughable sum of TLs to pay the stocky man.

Frowning, he pushed them back at me. I guessed the tea he'd served me was on the house. Not arguing, I took back my TLs and left. If a host offered coffee or tea, you were made welcome there. If coffee or tea wasn't served, it was a good idea to leave. A different side street angled into a sunny plaza. Artisans sat on their stools clanging their pointy hammers to stamp out bold designs on the copper picture plates.

A wiry man shilled me in to weigh myself on his bathroom scales out on a doormat. To humor him, I did. I'd lost three pounds. His calloused, dirty palm stuck out, and I laid the TLs on him. At the lane's end I realized I'd forgotten to show Mercedes' photo, but I pressed on. I stumbled on more of the same shops, so I backtracked to Atatürk Bulvari. Sore-footed, I hailed a *taksi*. The cabbie, a slim man with a rash of freckles, grinned at me through the open window.

"Otel Pamuk?" I asked.

"Hop in." He signaled with a hand. "We're not that far."

I folded into the rear seat with the stale cigarette aroma. The *taksi* merged into the chaos of vehicles. I looked to the side. The scaffolding -- poplar saplings lashed together using twine -- scaling a new building's shell looked rickety. I felt the cabbie's eyes flicker to his rearview mirror. He started up our patter.

"American?"

The two combative men had baited me at the embassy fence. "No. Swiss. Neutral."

"Married?"

"Once. Long ago. She left me."

"No wife, no strife, eh?"

I smiled back. "Sure, dude. No boss, no loss. No fuss, no muss."

"Hey, that last one is good."

"I've got a million of 'em."

"Good for you, wise Swiss man."

The *taksi* constructed of tin sheets and pop rivets was like my doublewide in Pelham. Homesickness dragged me down. A vague fear made me wonder if I'd locked my front door when I left it. I'd mention it to Gerald when we got in touch. The cabbie scuttled over to my hotel's entrance. I shoved a clutch of TLs at him.

"Thanks. Keep the change."

He grinned through his freckles and galloped off.

I saw through the glass panes that Omar worked in the lobby emptying ashtrays and straightening the armchairs. His frown showed he didn't enjoy seeing me. To be fair, the feeling cut both ways. I shouldered through the glass revolving door and cut for the corridor to my room.

"Frank, wait a second." He threw out his question. "Did you visit your embassy?"

"Somebody gave it the business."

"A bunch of crazies rules our streets." His eyes met mine. "Did you see Detective Abdullah?"

"You know damn well I did. He told me a Luger probably killed Pembe. Now who at the Otel Pamuk might own 'a harem' of Lugers?"

Omar pulled at his earlobe. Runnels of sweat trickled off his bald pate. "Did you mention them?"

"I just gave him the one you lent me."

"Thank you for that."

"Yeah well, I don't like suppressing evidence from the cops, especially in a homicide. I want straight talk, no bullshit. Did you kill Pembe?"

"No. Why would I? She was our most valued employee."

I could see his logic. "Did you fuck her?"

Throwing up his palms, he looked aghast. "Never. You don't know the wrath of my wife."

"I can imagine. Is she working at the front desk now?"

"For the time being, she will be, yes."

"Okay, I'll be in my room for the rest of the day." I turned to leave.

"Is Detective Abdullah coming after me?"

"I can't say. You'd better ask him. Later."

"You believe me, don't you? You don't think I gunned down poor Pembe."

"It doesn't matter. He told me her murder is a police matter, and PIs should butt out. I like taking his advice. I want to stay safe, do my job, and go home in one piece. That's all."

Chapter 13

During a morning chasing my tail, my favorite maid had claimed my bribe I'd left on my TV that was still there. The swayback bed had been made up, its linen clean. I sprawled out on it, crossed my ankles, and clasped my hands behind my head on the lumpy pillow. But I failed to doze off. My thoughts coalesced on a lady in Virginia.

Dreema Atkins was one of the few who'd escaped Pelham. She was smart in other ways, too, having graduated from Virginia Tech with top marks in her CJ degree. She went on to become an ace in her field. She'd both looks and brains and these days she was a full-figured gal and that was jake by me.

She held down a new supervisor's gig at the Virginia Department of Forensic Science's lab in Richmond. Ours was an on-again, off-again romance, though we'd remained pals through it. I guessed I sort of missed her and gave her a holler. It was early there, but as I hoped, she sounded glad and surprised to hear my voice.

"I got your email."

"Good. Where are you, Frank?" Her intonation was mountain twangy. I loved it.

"Ankara."

"Vacation?"

"No, I'm working a missing persons case."

"That's off the beaten path for you."

"Not really. I was based here in the Army."

"Right, you were an MP. How could I forget it?"

"How are things going with you?"

"Not bad. Need another favor from the lab?"

Her question derailed me for a beat. "No. I just called to talk."

"Really? You've rarely called for just that."

"Maybe I've decided to change."

She laughed. "Maybe you should. Is Gerald with you?"

"God, don't wish that on me."

"You're without your Sancho Panza?"

"I'll get in touch with him soon."

"Okay it's your dime. What's up?"

"I want to see you when I get home."

"No problem. You've got my key. I haven't changed the locks."

"Is that a backhanded invitation?"

"Frank, you know you're always welcome in Richmond."

That had to be code for she wasn't seeing anybody. Of course that was subject to change. The good ones didn't sit untaken for long. "I'm holding you to that. No wimp outs."

She laughed. "Watch it, Frank. This thing of ours might take root."

I caught my breath. "What do you mean by that?"

"You're the detective. You can figure it out."

"Just be up for my call, okay?"

"Uh-huh. Meantime you give Gerald a holler. I feel better knowing he's got your back over there."

"I will. Promise. Talk to you soon."

We dashed our signal. Then I had the oddest idea. The next time we met, I'd pop the question. Well, maybe. Seeing the bottle of mineral water got me up. I opened it and took a sip before casting a casual glance in the corner. "Huh?" Doing a double take, I almost had cardiac arrest. Mercedes' duffel had sprouted legs and walked off.

"Karin," I said into the phone. "Johnson here. Several

bags are gone from my room."

"Mr. Mercedes' baggage?"

My voice hardened. "What do you know about it?"

"I know Omar moved the bags after our maid complained. She's fussy and likes things kept in order. He plans to ship them off to Mr. Mercedes' wife in the States. We can't afford to accept any liability for the storage or loss of property."

"That's great except I need his bags here. Where are they?"

"Locked up in Omar's office. I can let you in."

"Look, I know he's well-intentioned, but he can't just do stuff like that without telling me. What happens when Mercedes returns?"

"He'll make do. Mr. Johnson, what's going on here? We're talking about a couple of suitcases stuffed with dirty clothes. Why are you so uptight?"

"His duffel is the only potential lead I have left. Just put off sending it for a few days."

"I'll pass along the word. It's not a problem. Have a pleasant afternoon nap."

Karin's hang up in my ear implied that 9-5 girls like her didn't enjoy taking siestas. Sloughing off any guilt, I phoned and got bounced around four extensions to reach Abdullah. I asked my earlier question on Pembe.

"When is her autopsy? Never, I'm afraid," he replied in an dejected monotone.

"I don't follow you."

"Resources. My bosses decide on autopsies."

"Every homicide victim is autopsied. If not, you're overrun with killers who get away with murder."

He replied with patience. "Killers don't overrun Ankara. Sooner or later we catch them. They're punished by our courts. By the way, your passport has been transferred to my office for safekeeping."

"What?" I felt an uptick in my blood pressure. Damn that Omar. "Why? Do you make me as a suspect?"

"Correction, Mr. Johnson. You're one of my prime suspects. You'd the opportunity and the right murder weapon."

"But it wasn't fired. Besides do you have a motive?"

"All in due time, sir. In the interim, you'll sit tight as the canary in my cage."

For the second time in as many phone calls, the other party cut me off. I stewed over my new status. All my movements outside, and possibly inside, the Otel Pamuk were under police surveillance. No doubt Abdullah had ordered a wiretap on this phone. My crib was bugged.

The Otel Pamuk was a nest of spies. I needed to find out a few answers myself. Boil it down to the basics, Johnson. What did I know? The lacy, red bra in Mercedes' room matched the one on Pembe's corpse. So what? Had that damn piece of lingerie become a red herring? If she killed Mercedes, then Person X had to kill her.

Who was Person X? Who hated Pembe? Omar's wife Karin had had strong words. Did her animosity boil over? Karin had to know Omar kept the Lugers in his desk where she could borrow one to use. I didn't the local police's decision to skip doing Pembe's postmortem.

My head cold hadn't improved. My two head bruises throbbed with each pulse beat. The only ice machine sat just inside the kitchen's entrance. Going there, I bumped into Pat, the gay man up in 213. He didn't recognize me, or pretended he didn't. I wrapped the ice cubes in a washcloth to baby my pair of lumps and returned to my room. The bathroom mirror revealed a new yellow skin coloring. Was yellow a sign of healing? "Aw, the hell with it." I ditched the ice compress in the sink.

My pain had dulled to a rat-gnawing ache, so I went back to work. Shoe leather was my prime asset. Starting from the revolving glass door, I handed Mercedes' photo to the shopkeepers. No dice until an old lady in a vivid headscarf at the corner arcade took Mercedes' photo.

"Speak English?"

She didn't and called over a teen-ager chomping on gum. He'd learned English, he told me, from watching episodes of Seinfeld and The Simpsons. His fingernail tapped Mercedes' photo. "I know this man. Like you, he comes each morning to buy a newspaper."

"Do you talk to him?"

The clerk nodded. "A little. Your war upsets him. Once close to tears, he said it was a waste. Maybe he's lost a son or daughter."

"His name is Sylvester Mercedes. He's gone. His wife thinks he may've been kidnapped."

The clerk resumed mauling his gum. "Has she gotten a ransom letter?"

"No, nothing yet. She's worried, and I'm helping her find him."

The clerk shrugged. "He gets the newspaper. Beyond that, he's a stranger to me. Sorry."

"If you recall anything else, I'm staying next door." I paid for his service. "I've got more, so don't forget me."

"You've given me a good reason."

My hike uphill to the posh Shannon and Harrington twins left me sweating. Mercedes' funk over the war struck me as melodramatic tripe. Who in the States gave the war a thought except the Gold Star moms, and the politicians making their flag-waving stump speeches?

My canvass along Mercedes' most probable route to the casinos was a total bust. Seven men and two ladies gave my queries either a hasty shrug or a quizzical smile. The Harrington and Shannon loomed within a baseball throw of each other. This time I'd try the Shannon. Its revolving glass door dwarfed Omar's door. The Shannon lobby's décor was big on glass, chrome, and brass. A lady glammed up in a sable stole and a cloche yawned on her languid strut by me. Faint sandalwood trailed after her. My gut twisted. My ex had worn the same perfume to bed.

The Shannon's concierge's thumb jerk indicated their casino was below us. I cuffed the only button in the dedicated elevator and swooned to the subterranean level. I darted out into the casino. Same deal here, the stolid guard at the door wanted my passport. His nametag read Berk. I told Berk the Ankara police had my passport, and I'd come armed with some questions.

Berk pointed his asp baton behind me. "Leave. Don't return without a passport or a necktie."

My TLs brought out his mercenary smile. "Now we can talk. What questions?"

"Does this guy play at your game tables?" I gave Mercedes' photo with the TLs to Berk and looked for any reaction on his face.

He nodded. "Mercedes comes too often."

"How's that so?"

After he returned Mercedes' photo, Berk tucked the TLs into his sock. "If he shows up less than sober, he acts less than a gentleman."

"You throw him out?"

"But of course. We run a civil house. My pit boss expects no trouble. When Mercedes acts up, out he goes."

"Does he get violent? Threaten people?"

"He just gets louder and hits on the ladies."

"Is this a regular thing?"

"Once or twice I've seen him that way."

"Is Mustafa on duty?"

"I saw him this morning. He only works at the Harrington. He got on my pit boss' bad side. Mustafa has had a rough time with Pembe gone."

I nodded. "That's too bad. He says Mercedes blows his bankroll. How does he get more cash to keep playing?"

Berk gave a bored shrug. "The ATM is upstairs."

"He never runs short? He never initials an IOU?"

"He knows better than to try that in here."

"Does he always come alone?"

"He does. What's with these questions?" After I summed up why, he asked, "Has his wife offered any reward?"

"Solid information has a monetary value. But it has to

be solid, see?"

"What a shame that I know nothing more."

After thanking Berk, I grabbed the lift back up to the lobby. The hydraulics whirred as the cab shimmied. I'd paid for worthless information. I'd worn blisters from chasing down ghost leads. I'd run into dead ends. Once at the lobby, I quit the luxury Shannon, my usual gumshoe frustrations intact.

Chapter 14

I took a roundabout way back to the Otel Pamuk. Late afternoon heavier in shadows made me shiver. I stopped by the duck pond in the same park and realized Abdullah might roll up at any moment to arrest me. I'd go sweat in his interrogation stall. A Caucasian, I didn't blend in as a chameleon here. What I needed was a quick-witted, loyal Turk. But who did I tap?

I plunked down on the park bench. Omar had to be a suspect for Pembe's homicide, so he was out. His shrewish wife Karin was a lousy bet. Given his security background, Mustafa was a natural choice, but he was too beat up over Pembe's death.

A magpie alit in a sticker bush near the pond. A trickster bird, it was also a moocher. But I'd no potato chips, and it took off. Right, I thought. Quick mobility was the key. Who could zip me around this town? Who knew the obscure streets and seedy hangouts that Mercedes liked to go?

Mr. Ahmet had ferried me from Esenboga Airport to the Otel Pamuk. The problem there, as I saw it, was Mr. Ahmet as Omar's cousin. That didn't mean they were close. For instance, my own cousin, Rod Bellwether, was a lifer without parole at Red Onion, the max security tucked away in Virginia's mountains.

The psychopath Rod had shot his wife Kathy in the eye to get his sick jollies. I wouldn't cross the street to speak to Rod. Quite by accident, I might shove him into the path of an oncoming Mack truck. These days Rod lived in a state-owned cell no larger than a coat closet. Once or twice, he'd written me, and I'd sent him a few bucks for cigarettes. I had to be double sure Mr. Ahmet wasn't a backstabber. I'd better test his loyalty before I tried to recruit him as my Watson.

As soon as I made the street corner before the Otel Pamuk, a lemon yellow *taksi* hissed to a stop. I bent in the knees and peered through the windows and wasn't disappointed. Mr. Ahmet gave a finger salute off his temple. His passenger door flapped out. Draping my arms across the car roof, I leaned in the door.

"You're just the man I wanted to see."

"Glad to be at your service, Frank."

"I've got a business deal for you."

Mr. Ahmet grinned. "Hop in, sir." This time I sat up front with him, not in the back. "Business deal?"

Before I could open my mouth, a sharp right at a red traffic light threw us into Atatürk Bulvari's heavy traffic stream. Mr. Ahmet thumped his palm on the top arc of his steering wheel. Greasy auto and bus emissions choked us.

We rolled under a gold leaf archway, dead dabs for the rack of antlers on Bullwinkle Moose. Testy drivers squawked their horns. Mr. Ahmet yelped. The other drivers matched his outbursts, scream for scream.

The glowing orange *Eczane* signs were the pharmacies. They sold aspirin tablets and antibiotics. Such a regimen might reboot me. My sinuses burned with each breath. Mr. Ahmet spurted down a side lane and tracked through a rat maze of alleyways. It was time to run my test. Rolling up my window, I used a crafty murmur.

"I think Omar deals drugs."

His eyes widening, Mr. Ahmet glared at me. "What?"

"Sure, it's a cool setup. Mercedes flew in, made his drug sales, and then left town before things heated up," I said, spinning the lie. "But he's out of the picture. So I've got it figured I'll take his place, and you can drive me to the buyers. We'll split the sales profits down the middle. What do you say?"

"Not a word of that is true." His lean face darkening with anger, Mr. Ahmet's lips shrank into a gash.

"The Otel Pamuk has to be Omar's front. He sells the narcotics while pretending to run a hotel."

"You're wrong. He isn't so stupid. As his cousin, I should know. Do you know the punishment for that? Unless you're lunatic no man deals drugs in my country."

I backpedaled. "Maybe I've been too hasty in my thinking. But the signs are clear. Shady characters stay there. Take that Nashwinter. He's a beer peddler from the States. Yeah right. He and Mercedes top my list of shady characters."

"Your list stinks. Where do you get the balls to climb into my *taksi* and accuse Omar of all this?"

Mr. Ahmet had shown his true colors. He wasn't my man. I put out my hands. "Hey, lighten up, okay? I'm really just pulling your leg. Omar is okay."

"That's a sick joke. Omar won't laugh either. I'll take you to the Otel Pamuk," said Mr. Ahmet, his words still sharp. "Next time you need a *taksi*, don't wave at me, or I'll mow you down."

The glass façade of the Otel Pamuk came up. Cutting the steering wheel in a jerk, Mr. Ahmet chewed his tire into the curb. "Get out, you."

I bounded from my door and watched him etch a U-turn and fly up the hill. I felt okay on how it'd played out. The familial bond between Mr. Ahmet and Omar was a strong one. What I'd said would leak back to Omar and might fan a wild fire. Hoping for as much to break this case wide open, I shouldered through the revolving glass door.

Four Turkish businessmen crowded at the computer kiosk. Aside from them, the lobby was a ghost town. Hunger drove me back to the restaurant annex. When the server, a gangly youth speaking with a smoker's rasp, jotted down my order, I went with the usual.

"Yes, I know. You're our Rice Man."

"Is that a problem?"

"Your loss, not mine. Today's specials are smoky ox-tongue, pulpy fava beans, and peppery aubergines ~~ "

"Those are fine for others, but not for me. Bring me rice and ice water. Nothing more, nothing less. Do that, and I'll double your tip."

"Coming right up, sir."

Chopping sounds hauled out of the kitchen's batwing doors. The chef muscled like a bodybuilder had to be tenderizing the dinner's meat. The pounding stopped. I chuckled. Then the whacks erupted again, and I realized there was the meat's opposite side.

The four Turkish businessmen wandered into the restaurant. The server bustled through the batwing doors toting an aluminum tray holding a ceramic bowl of dirty rice and a glass of ice water. He set both items down in front of me.

"*Bon appetit*, Mr. Johnson."

"Stick it plus your tip on my tab. But just that, nothing else."

"Yes sir," he replied over a shoulder. "Enjoy your rice, sir."

Salting and peppering the warm rice, I felt the eyes surveying me. Eating my rice, I was the object of the Turkish businessmen's curiosity. Their amusement grew. I chewed a forkful of rice. The server drifted by their table, and they jabbered in Turkish. Laughs went up. The tips of my ears turned red, but I didn't react. The novelty of my rice-only diet wore off, and they left me alone. I finished my rice and water but left the table still hungry.

Back in my room, I watched TV. With no legitimate lead, I was in the foul mood to bag it. Punch my ticket, kiss off Turkey, and jet straight home. Cooler thoughts prevailed. The best course of action was to hang tough and finish what I'd committed to do. Being branded as a quitter was bad news with the other 43,000 PIs hustling out there to snap up the jobs. Yawning, I shifted on the bed for better comfort. My heavy eyelids drooped, and I fell asleep.

CHAPTER 15

"Frank? Were you in bed? After hearing no word, I decided to call you."

"Never mind. Where are you? If that Mercedes lady is around, we ain't talking," I told Gatlin.

It was early Wednesday morning, and I'd jolted awake to the phone braying in my ear.

"I'm alone. Lois and I haven't seen each other since we last spoke."

"Good. You'd do us both a favor by ditching her."

New anger gave Gatlin's voice an edge. "She's a sophisticated, outspoken lady. I have my reasons for taking my actions. Enough said. Have you picked up Mercedes' trail?"

"No, but this war has me figuring a new slant. You know how Americans get abducted on Iraqi streets? I wonder if our man fell into a similar trap.

"Track this with me. Sunday a.m. Mercedes ambles out into the street for a stroll, and up the block a nondescript van careens up to him. Masked brutes vault out. Armed with automatic pistols, they grab him. They fly off to a secret compound and hold him for ransom."

"We've fielded no ransom demand. Besides who knows he's loaded? The Otel Pamuk isn't a four-star hotel. Lois tells me it's a hole-in-the-wall."

"She's just about right. Does Pembe's murder tie in with his disappearance?"

"Yeah, I haven't forgotten her," said Gatlin, annoyed.

"Don't get off on that tangent. Mercedes is our scope. The Ankara authorities are capable of closing their own homicides."

As always, Gatlin liked to issue his long distance edicts.

"Too late. I'm already involved. The cops are probably tailing me. This phone is probably bugged so watch it."

"We've said nothing incriminating."

We traded beefs on the weather here (unsettled) and there (muggy). He told me the Redskins had opened training camp and better sign a bruiser running back, or it'd be a long season. I didn't care. We signed off.

I unscrewed the mouth and ear pieces to the phone's handset just like the wily PIs did in the movies. Then I dug out the listening device, the size of a dime. I flushed the device. Then I swept the room as best I could and found nothing.

In the shower a thought struck me. Both Mustafa and Berk had said Mercedes lost big at the casinos. Maybe the news had gone out that a fat mark stayed at the Otel Pamuk. If I was a hungry shark, Mercedes made for prime chum. A kidnapping or mugging grew in probability.

Toweling off and dressing, I shaped up my plans, starting with a post-breakfast visit to the Taj Mahals on the hill. Mindful of their dress code, I searched in vain for a necktie. My blue Aloha shirt and another bribe had to do.

I bumped into my favorite maid trundling her linen cart. I paid her not to pilfer my color TV. Agreeing, she stuffed my TLs in her fanny pack. She wore lipstick, I saw, the same mute red shade as the smear I'd seen on Omar's necktie. Such coincidences were rare. So, he liked to bang the help. It was easy to see him putting the moves on Pembe. Lust was a precursor to murder.

A steamy mug of Turkish coffee thawed my blood. While I scarfed up pound cake and more coffee, I kept glancing at the shut door to Omar's office, and then I realized why. I wanted to toss Mercedes' stuff again. My favorite maid for a second fee disclosed Karin's hideout. Her door was the first crib on my corridor. No knock, I strolled in. Flinching at my noise, she awoke.

Our eyes locked, hers stunned and mine just curious. She lounged in the armchair with her bare feet -- her toenails painted mint green -- propped up on the bed. CNN's talking heads neighed on the TV. A ginger jar lamp burned at a dim setting. Annoyance set her jaw.

"Did you mix up your room number?"

"Nope." I sat uninvited on the end of the bed next to her.

"Then why are you charging in here?"

I didn't reply, just got an eyeful. Her dress suit still fresh despite its long night of service rustled as she moved her legs. Long, bare legs, I saw. With her face turned to a brighter angle, I saw her taking stock of me, and I returned the favor. One blouse button than usual was undone. She used no cosmetics.

Or had our hectic night rubbed them off? A soft makeup brush and a lipstick tube sat by the empty Efes bottle on the nightstand. Her hair tamed in a bun gleamed an exotic cider brown. Had this beautiful murderess left a beautiful corpse in the cage elevator? Karin's sharper leg movement conveyed a large cat's restlessness.

"I came for the key to Omar's office. I need Mercedes' duffel."

"Ha. You're a day late."

"How so?"

"Omar stormed in last night, grabbed Mr. Mercedes' bags, and shipped them out as overseas freight. I repeated your message, but Omar was on one of his tears. Were the bags so important?"

"Hopefully not." My anger flared, then faded. Mercedes' duffel was now out of my reach. Who did I chew out, Omar or Karin? I had to wonder about his impulsive act, and she picked up on my thoughts.

"Look, we can't afford to incur any liability to store

our guests' stuff. Now before you leave maybe you can clear up something for me." Her eyes darted to the TV screen. The camera panned over American soldiers, combat ready, patrolling a rubble strewn alleyway in a Baghdad ghetto.

"You better forget that."

She smiled. "You oppose the war?"

"No comment. When will Omar be in this morning?"

"Why?"

"How did he know where to send Mercedes' duffel?"

"He attached the address tags to his suitcases. Also, we keep his contact information on file. We've got a file on all guests, even our hardboiled Mr. Johnson." She smiled again. Her gray-hazel eyes danced in the light.

My read: a coquettish smile.

Her mint green toenails caught my eye. She wiggled them at me. So, kitten was playful. I liked to share my toys. I made the next move. Her bare calves felt smooth as jade. Her muscles rippled under my palms. She didn't slap me. Her smile didn't fade.

So I advanced to her knees. That same inviting smile met my eyes. My thumbs lifted the hem to her skirt. Still she didn't stop me.

Her thigh muscles under my hands flexed, then went soft. My fingertips grazed third base, the fabric to her panties. My fingers parted the elastic and --

She crossed her legs and broke my heart. "I think not." Her voice had a hitch.

"My hardboiled reputation is at stake."

"I know. But remember, no means no."

Smiling, I glanced up to greet the black snout to the Luger she trained on me. Have you ever looked straight into a howitzer? She'd kept it stuffed behind her. I went limp all over.

"I take your point."

"I knew that you could. Please remove your fingers from my lingerie."

My hands drew out from under her skirt.

"I'm a married lady. That still means something here. You'd better leave now." The waving Luger showed me to the door.

Shutting the door to her day room, I forced down the bile in my throat. Wasn't my day off to a rip-roaring start? My best clue, Mercedes' duffel, had shipped out while I'd slept.

But then my acting the role of a cad had made my landlady tip her cards. She possessed a Luger. Had she fired it to kill Pembe? Murder wasn't in my bailiwick, but I took away my bargaining chip -- knowing of Karin's Luger -- to trade Abdullah, say, for my liberty, if necessary.

I returned to my room and updated the notes for my final report. The heading on a new page read: *** <u>Suspects in Mercedes' Homicide</u> ***. Under it, I compiled my short list.

Omar (Otel Pamuk owner)
Karin (Omar's wife)
Joel Nashwinter (U.S. beer salesman)
Mr. Ahmet (Turkish cabbie & Omar's cousin)

My slate of suspects didn't cover a wide field. The process of elimination should whittle it down, but I realized that I didn't have enough information. Who was the least known to me? That'd be Number Three, Mr. Nashwinter, the U.S. beer peddler.

I wondered if he had a rap sheet. My phone signal caromed off the satellites orbiting our gray planet. Counting the rings, I pushed off my doubts if this call was a smart idea. Friends kept you grounded, and I'd few, if any, friends in Ankara.

"Peyton here," said the rumble of an insomniac. "Bail Enforcer Extraordinaire."

"Gerald, Frank. I need a hand, bro."

"It figures. Where the fuzzy fuck did you go? I get your answering machine. No yahoo has seen you around

Pelham."

"I'm in Ankara."

Pause. "Say what?"

"Ankara."

"What the fuck for?"

"Missing persons case."

"Shit. What do you need?"

"Use your state cop pal and run background checks."

"You got a name?"

"Joel Nashwinter. N-A-S-H-W-I-N-T-E-R. Also, Sylvester Mercedes. M-E-R-C-E-D-E-S."

"Got it. Give me a legit number."

I gave it, and he hung up. Three breaths later, my phone blatted. Sighing, I engaged. "Yeah Gerald, I'm really at this number."

"Gotta be sure. Hey, if you need any help, just sing out. Things are slow and boring. Where the fuck is Ankara? I've got a full tank of gas."

"Uh, you better google it."

"Will do. I'll run this Nashwinter and Mercedes. Give me a few hours. Then I'm out of here."

"I'm really on the home stretch."

"Uh-huh. You sound downbeat. What's wrong?"

"Blame Gatlin. He got me this lousy gig."

"So? Fuck it. Money is money."

"I don't give a damn if I track down this chump."

"It's a job, Frank. Catch? Don't let the bastards grind you down."

"I'll be okay."

"No, you're sucking wind. I can tell. I'm off."

"Just run these two chumps."

"Be up for my holler. Later."

We disconnected. Getting a workout, my phone again jangled. It was my cranky client who also never slept. By now I knew she was one of the rare few who could get under my skin. I didn't like the bad blood between us. She was my best source of information on Mercedes if I was ever to find him.

"Sylvester still hasn't called me," she said.

"This isn't his usual behavior?"

"Most certainly not. We always know where the other is. For complex reasons I won't go into here, our marriage is unorthodox, but our communication never breaks down like it has now."

"You don't sound too torn up over it."

"Of course I am. Why else did I hire you?"

"His duffel is on the way home."

"Why?"

"The hotel owners said they can't keep it. I didn't find his passport. Does he carry it on him?"

"I imagine so. We haven't traveled together in ages. Ironically, we honeymooned in Istanbul. The old city was glorious. Our return some day was in the works. Why am I babbling on like so? Give me one reason, if you can." She only stopped to catch her breath.

"Because I'm paid to be your doormat?"

"Ha, but you're an argumentative doormat. For now, I've finished wiping my feet. You have my private number. Quicker results, hear?"

"Loud and clear."

Click.

I felt drained. I was fed up sparring with her. I dozed off and a little later, Gerald rang me back.

"Joel Nashwinter and Sylvester Mercedes show no priors."

"Another brilliant idea goes up in smoke."

"You owe me fifty."

"I'll bury it under Miscellaneous Expenses"

"Yeah, bribes aren't reimbursable."

"I just got off the phone with my client. She's a piece of work, Gerald."

"Look, I bust scum every day. Then I go home, take a shower, and kick back with a brew. I've got a job and a life and I remember the difference. See?"

"Yeah and thanks. Are you still coming?"

"I gotta go scoop up a bail skip in Amissville, then I'm on a fucking plane."

"Do me a favor. Bring a few bluegrass CDs."

"Uptown or downtown?"

"I miss Dr. Ralph and Alison."

"Got it."

"Later, Gerald."

"You just fucking hold it together until I can get over there."

After our talk, I felt better and riffled the banknotes in my wallet. The mirror's reflection of the paperback on the bureau top didn't interest me. Glancing over, I saw a shadow slipping under my doorsill. That did interest me. How long had my eavesdropper hovered there? I crept over and whisked out my door. My favorite maid, her raised hand clasped in a fist, was in the act of knocking.

Her hand fluttered at me. "Come."

"Why?"

She smiled, nodded. "Come."

We filed out. Passing by the door to Karin's day room, I heard the TV bleating with the talking heads wasting our oxygen. My first sight in the lobby fell on the four Turkish businessmen in the wicker chairs. One saw me. His grin widened. An elbow nudged his neighbor in the ribs, and I soon had an audience, but I ignored them. The maid left me.

Abdullah did a scooping hand gesture the Turks like to use to signal me to the front desk. Eager to aid the police since I was an ex-cop, I did. He wore a Turkish flag pin on his narrow lapel. Some law enforcement customs were universal.

Chapter 16

"Is your head cold better?" Abdullah asked me.

"I guess I'll live, thanks."

"Let's hope so. I've got a new development on Pembe's homicide. Out in the city streets, it's nice and noisy, not nosy like I find it in here. Let's take a little walk."

I realized his walk in the street was to pump me for information. Of course that worked both ways. We decamped from the Otel Pamuk, one spin at a time through its revolving glass door into the late morning sun. Hands stuffed in his baggy pants pockets, he shambled along the uncrowded sidewalk with me as though we were old pals. I opened our conversation.

"Omar mailed Mercedes' duffel home."

Abdullah's face showed surprise. "His wife in the States will be grateful."

"I doubt it. She's not so easy to please."

Abdullah shepherded us down the hill away from the two ritzy hotels, and we headed toward the Castle. The breeze I felt cooling my cheeks made the Turkish flag snap on the stony parapets. It was an impressive flag, too.

"Now you give. What new development?"

"Politics. My boss may approve our doing Pembe's autopsy. He's leaning that way, and I'm keeping up the pressure."

"Good. I'd like to be there."

"Precisely my best argument to do the autopsy. Have you visited our *Kocatepe Camii*? We're almost there."

I liked his idea. At the very least it gave me another place to flash around Mercedes' photo. An eyewitness like a guard or official there might recall seeing him.

"Lead on. What's the latest on the embassy bombing?"

He shook his head. "Nothing solid is what I hear." He stopped walking and looked at me. "Mr. Johnson, what would you say if I told you Pembe wasn't killed in the cage elevator?"

"It's crossed my mind. But here's the kicker. How did her killer buy enough time to stage her murder like a robbery?"

"The Otel Pamuk's lobby at that hour has little or no activity. I've staked it out and checked."

"Where did she get killed?"

"The killer shot her upstairs. Then he moved her corpse to the cage elevator. At the bottom, the elevator opened, and she tumbled out. The killer stepped over her and left through the lobby."

"What a cold-blooded bastard. According to Karin, Pembe never went upstairs. The maids run any errands for the guests and make their tips money."

Walking again, Abdullah grunted. "The killer used some pretense to lure her up. Mustafa has a shaky alibi. When Omar phoned him about her murder, he was out of contact. Claims he was making his security rounds at the Harrington, and his cell phone wasn't on."

"He seems pretty ripped up over it."

"We've questioned both families -- his and hers -- at length. By all accounts, they enjoyed a solid marriage. We're assured they never had fights. He doesn't get any life insurance payout, so it wasn't for the money."

"Omar found her dead. When he came and got me, he acted distraught enough."

"But of course." Abdullah patted his shirt pocket. A pack of Barclays non-filters appeared. He tapped out one and, wrinkling his forehead, tipped the pack at me. When in Rome: I accepted one.

Thumbing the flint wheel to the vintage Dunhill lighter, he cupped the cigarette to its fiery tuft. I lit up in turn, and he spoke after a puff.

"If I eliminate Mustafa for the lack of a motive, I then have to look at Omar who'd plenty of opportunity."

"But as her employer, Omar also had motive." Abdullah had a blank expression, so I sketched it out for him. "Omar has a wandering eye. She was young and pretty, and he was in a position of power over her. Suppose he copped some feels, but got his face slapped for his trouble? Her rejection might've angered him enough to smoke her."

"Married to Karin, he wouldn't dare cheat. She'd crucify him if she got any hint of it."

"Okay so that's motive for her. The jealous, violent wife killed her husband's lover."

"Several possibilities exist."

A disgusted Abdullah flicked away the once-puffed cigarette to just miss nailing a magpie strutting under a parked car's tailpipe. Actually an ex-smoker, I let my cigarette drop and crushed its embers under my shoe.

"There are too many handguns in Ankara," said Abdullah.

"I know Omar owns a bunch of Lugers."

An iron-muscled forearm flew up to club my chest. Abdullah was curt. "What Lugers?"

"I already told you. I got mine from Omar. He collects them."

"Tell me again." Abdullah's eyes hard as obsidian didn't waver. "Where?"

"They're under the false bottom to a desk drawer in his office."

Abdullah grabbing my shoulders jostled me. "Show me. Now."

His meat hooks for fingers bit into my muscles. I didn't share his excitement. "They haven't been fired since D-Day. Doing ballistics on them will only delay your investigation.

It's a dead end."

"I'll decide that." He squeezed with impatient force. "I want those Lugers."

Jerking away, I escaped his grip. "Round them up on your own. I've got to stay at the hotel."

He knotted his fist and shook it at me. "I've been a cop for eighteen years. Buca Prison in Izmir holds more than a few men I've sent there. One more is nothing to me."

"All right, we'll go back."

We hiked to Otel Pamuk as he jabbered on his cell phone. We sailed through the revolving glass door. Behind the front desk, Karin was sorting a pile of tourist brochures. She heard my story as told by Abdullah.

Her face set in refusal as she protected Omar's domain. She'd no key. Auk and two burly detectives pounced in from the street. They grabbed her by the arms and dislodged her from in front of Omar's office door.

Abdullah's bullish shoulder lowered and rammed the locked door, splintering its brass hinges from the wood jamb. The smashed door fell free. Auk and one detective poured in behind Abdullah. Livid with rage, she cursed. Her guard's deadpan look accepted her outburst as all in a day's work.

"Mr. Johnson, I count seven Lugers," Abdullah called out from Omar's office.

"Seven Lugers, yeah, that's what I saw."

Flaring her vindictive eyes, she turned on me. "Get out. Pack your bags. Leave at once."

"Nobody is going anywhere." Abdullah strode over and using his native tongue amended her thinking before he looked at me. "She agrees you'll remain here. That's how I'll keep tabs on you both."

I went for broke. "You'll return my passport?"

Striding into the doorless office, Abdullah hefted an empty milk crate Auk had brought over to carry out the Lugers. "I hardly think so."

She phoned from the front desk and barked at Omar.

Who needed a translator? Posted at the office doorway, Auk had an impassive expression. Just as stony faced, Abdullah cataloged the Lugers while she vented.

Omar on the other end couldn't pacify her. As the detectives angled out of the lobby, her curses lashed at them. Nobody reacted. The cops, one by one, slotted through the revolving glass door and piled into their squad cars.

"Mr. Johnson, I don't have to like you staying at my hotel."

I just shrugged and backed off. The squad cars, their roof bar lights flashing, accelerated away to headquarters. A tactical withdrawal also struck me as a wise move until she'd a chance to cool off. She yelled as I whisked through the revolving glass door into the street. That's how I came to the Atatürk Mausoleum.

CHAPTER 17

A beige stone edifice, it squats on a prominent knoll in south Ankara, a chip shot down the street from what was left of the U.S. Embassy. I viewed Atatürk's touring car (a ding in its rear bumper), his personal library (sadly, no Spillane, Chandler, or Hammett), and his collection of canes (a trick one fired a .22 slug).

I showed around Mercedes' photo. No dice. An armed guard's suspicious glance my way had me cool it. Every clock on display I checked had its hands frozen at 9:05, Atatürk's time of death. Giggling grade schoolers in their uniforms cantered through the staid rooms. I dodged the kids and left the mausoleum. Out front, the goose-stepping soldiers did a changing of the guard.

I hustled by the recumbent bronze lions preening at the mausoleum's gate. Compacts blatting their horns and jitterbugging for an extra inch clotted Atatürk Bulvari. The soles of my feet burned, but I didn't slow down until I scooted into the Harrington's opulent lobby. The hostess I slinked by had tawny blonde hair. I picked up my pace before she could yell at me.

The middle of the five elevators yawned open. I got in and lowered to the gambling mecca that was out-of-bounds for the Turks. I drew a blank if Mustafa or Berk worked the security at the Harrington. Who had I first met? Right, Mustafa kept the Harrington's casino shipshape. His wife Pembe awaited dissection on the morgue slab. I was descending to chat with him again.

The Saturday evening before his fadeout, Mercedes flush with cash had used this elevator. Later that night he chugged back up, broke but happy. I had an idea. My palm jabbed the Stop button, then the Lobby, and I craned back up.

When the elevator doors whirred free, I saw the tawny blonde hostess perched at her station. She watched me crossing the lobby. Why did fear cloud her pretty face? Did my lumps look so thuggish? She spoke English, and I played it straight telling her my story.

"Is this thing real?" Her inflection was throaty.

Ignoring a twinge of irritation, I extracted my PI ticket from her fingers. "As real as they come. Was this man was a casino regular?" Mercedes' photo slipped into her fingers. "Two Sundays ago he was spotted leaving his hotel down the hill. He hasn't been observed since, and his wife sent me searching for him."

"Like for real?"

Second thoughts warned me this was a waste. "Do you recognize him?"

Then she threw me a surprise. "Oh sure I do. Mr. Mercedes always has a friendly wave and smile. Everybody knows and likes him. Too bad our game tables are his kryptonite. He likes to keep plugging, I guess. Is he in trouble?"

"What makes you ask that?"

The tawny blonde smiled. She wore braces. Maybe she was younger than I'd first thought. "You seem anxious to find him."

"Yes I am. For good reason." My pause was for effect. "Possibly terrorists have kidnapped him."

"Terrorists?" Her mouth shriveled into a pink bow. She talked faster. "B~b~but I didn't work then. My sister and I went shopping."

"I need to buy a gift for my wife," Now I lied to divert our conversation and put her at better ease. "An article of clothing might work. See, she wears a different outfit each day, but I'm bad at picking out stuff. Any ideas?"

"Buy her a *yemini*. It's a square headscarf for ladies." My idea worked as she returned to our original topic. "Mr. Mercedes came in once or twice with the same lady. She had on these big, yellow sunglasses, and I didn't see her face, but I'm pretty sure she was Turkish."

A hot wire of nerves tingled down my back. After asking a slew of questions, what good PIs are trained to do, my first real break gave me an electric charge.

"Did they get on the elevator together?"

"Maybe so. I didn't watch them all that much." An unseen phone's ringing turned the tawny blonde away from me. "Ask Mustafa. He's the casino guard. He should know."

I thanked her before hurrying over and waiting on another elevator. I rode down alone and found Mustafa in an alcove. Cavalier on the smoking ban, he sparked a Bic to fire up a weed. He took a long toke. The fruity whiffs of marijuana hit my nose.

Seeing a different man shocked me. The grief had sapped the health out of him. The sallow skin molded to his skull gave him a heroin chic look. Eyes from his acid holes saw but didn't acknowledge me. His words sounded feral and hoarse.

"Frank, I can see the gambling bug has bitten you. It strikes the best of us. No ID is required. Step right in. The piranhas will pick your bones. Hear their little chomps? Why the frown? Face it. You can't beat the house. Too many don't get that. But who cares? Betting is what heats the blood. Go ask Mercedes. He'll tell you how the gambling fever preys on your sanity."

"Mustafa, you look like hell."

"But Berk sold me a joint and, whoa, I feel no pain."

"Berk, what an asshole. Where are Socrates and the other players?"

Mustafa just smiled. Poking my head inside the casino, I had a look-see. Shafts of the task lighting gave form to the old swirls of blue cigarette smoke. Ghosts playing at the black jack tables never lost. Over there the Grim Reaper counted up the lost souls in the cashier's cage. Video poker screens invited me to sit in and lose. The mirrored ceiling, potted coconuts, and leopard-dotted shag carpet added to the Vegas sleaze.

"This is our slow hour." Mumbling, he swallowed his words.

"You're high as a kite. Snuff that damn joint. Let's go grab some air."

"Lead on, Frank."

The Emergency door at the top of the stairs used a locking device I monkeyed with but couldn't trip. My lowered shoulder pummeled the door, but it didn't budge. I shepherded Mustafa ahead of me down to the elevator. Once upstairs, I cut into the lobby and screened him from prying eyes. Feeling the warmth from the sun inspired my next move.

"A city park is two blocks down. We'll go there. You can clear your head. Then I've got some questions for you."

"What questions?"

"They can wait. But you have to quit this moping around."

"Do you think I killed Pembe? The police do."

"I don't and they don't either. You're too busted up to be her killer."

The pedestrians we brushed by on Atatürk Bulvari looked as harried as we felt. The park shaded by the acacias had few other takers although the trash overflowed in the receptacles. The first bench was our rest spot.

"Okay Frank, what are your questions?"

"The lobby hostess said she saw Mercedes come in with a Turkish lady."

Mustafa flicked a gnat away from his ear. "This is news to me."

"There's more. Mercedes went up to a room with her. Later he came down alone and hit the casino."

"Makes sense. She's Turkish and can't use the casino."

"Is his mystery lady a prostitute?"

"That's a safe assumption. But I never saw her."

"Are you certain Omar didn't hit on Pembe?"

"There isn't a bed in the Otel Pamuk he hasn't used. He's the boss. But with my wife, he never tried a thing. If he looked twice at her, I'd break his neck."

"Did you threaten him?"

"He knew to always keep his hands off her. Or else."

If I was Omar, I'd keep glancing back for a new widower coming for me. "All right then, we'll sit."

Mustafa gazed off at the pond. "What's the fucking use?"

After grabbing his uniform at the shoulders, I gave him a good shake. "Man, you've got to pull it together. Hear me?"

"What do you know about anything?"

"My point is basic. Shit happens. But life goes on."

"Frank, just shut the fuck up."

"All right then, we'll sit here until you clear your head."

"As long as you shut up, okay, I will."

I said nothing, and we sat in the shade.

Chapter 18

I was feasting on my rice lunch after one o'clock at the Otel Pamuk. After recouping in the park, Mustafa had reported back to the casino, but I hadn't tagged along. While I felt sorry for the guy, I couldn't skip my PI work to baby-sit him. I'd overheard the maids giggling in corridor and figured Karin, their dragon lady for a boss, had left for the day.

The same gangly server had learned my all-rice diet. In fact, he'd emerged from the batwing doors, gave me one look seated at the table, and turned back to the kitchen. By my next glance he swept out balancing a tray holding a ceramic bowl brimming over with dirty rice. I sent him back for the glass of ice water to complete my power lunch.

"Sir, will that be all?"

"No, not quite." I tugged out my wallet. A raft of TLs flopped out of it on the table corner nearest to him. The server's bird bright eyes glued to it. Good, I'd hooked his attention. "I need a written report of interviews with the hotel staff."

"A written report?"

"Yeah, that's right." I arched an eyebrow at him. "Are you the man I see?"

"Maybe. My name is Hamza. I can read and write English. What's your report about?" He fingered the lank hair out of his eyes still buttoned on the TLs.

"Do you know about the American who disappeared two Sundays ago?"

"Yeah, and I also heard you're searching for him."

"That's right. I want you to ask each maid about him. You speak Turkish, and you can set down their answers in passable English."

"What are you after?"

"Ask them questions like did he get any visitors, especially ladies? Where did he go during the day and at night? What was his job? You get the idea, right?"

"I'm a fast learner." Hamza's fingernail tapped on the Turkish banknotes. "When do I get my money?"

"That's yours, so take it." He did. I went on. "That's one quarter of your payment. Once I get your written report, I'll pay you the rest. It's the easiest money you'll ever earn."

"Boy I'll say."

"But be discrete. Omar knows what I'm after, but there's no reason to stir up things."

"I understand."

"I figured I could count on you. Can you write it all up for me by tomorrow morning, say, when I sit down to my first cup of coffee?"

"Piece of cake." He blinked at me. "Why are you doing this?"

"I'm a private detective who Mr. Mercedes' wife hired to locate him. But I need more information to get it done."

"Yeah, I've seen you guys in the movies." Hamza smiled and nodded. "Doing this will be cool."

He doubled over the sheath of banknotes to pinch into his shirt pocket. Even hampered by the language barrier, I felt lazy for not doing the interviews. I wasn't sold on their value, but who knew? A nugget among the colorful exaggerations, half-truths, and sketchy memories might shine out. My job was to cull out the facts from the fiction.

My hungry gut still pinched as I went into my room. Yawning, I yanked on the cord to draw open the window drapes. Ankara's brittle sun didn't warm my crib, but I liked peering up into a patch of blue sky. I flaked out on the bed, my ass slumping as if I was lying in a hammock. I'd no sooner relaxed than the phone sang out. It was Gerald.

"These overseas calls will tap you out."

"Huh? Ain't this on your dime?"

"Yeah, I got you covered. What's you got?"

"I checked some more on your boy Nashwinter."

"What's the skinny?"

"I nicked my Fed pal for a favor. He fed Nashwinter through NCIC. Guess what? Bingo, a hit."

"What's the database hit?"

"He pulled some hard time. Felonious assault."

"What a stand up guy."

"Your other boy Mercedes got no hits."

"I can believe it. He's a ghost. One theory says he's a spook for Uncle."

"I can believe it. 9/11 changed a lot things."

"I wonder if some goon squad scooped him up."

"Wouldn't surprise me. Any demands for ransom money?"

"No and that's why I'm not chasing that angle too hard."

"Sounds like lots of questions, few answers."

"Welcome to my Ankara."

"Listen Frank, I'm free. It's a new day here. I can zip up to Dulles Airport and hop on a plane in a few hours."

"First I need you to do something else for me."

"Just name it."

"Aren't running stakeouts up your alley?"

Gerald snorted. "I taught you how, didn't I?"

"You did. It's my client Lois Mercedes."

"What makes you nervous about her?"

I tried to explain. "For one thing, she's making noises on stiffing me. Man, I ain't doing this for my health. For another she and Gatlin have got a thing going. Do me a favor and go sit on her place and see what's up."

"Gatlin is stupid, and getting stiffed bites ass."

"You damn straight. The IRS is all over me. I can't

settle with them using my good looks. I better get paid, or I go to jail."

"Enough said. Consider it done."

I gave him the particulars on her, and we rang off. If anybody could keep tabs on Mrs. Mercedes, I'd put my faith in Gerald every time. He was a pro's pro. Then I thought of the teenage girl in Middleburg whose horse had trampled her to death. Her mother had also been good at barking out her demands. Back then I was also stone-cold broke. Christ, the grubby jobs we did trying to turn an honest buck.

Chapter 19

The glowing orange *Eczane* signs were the pharmacies. The one I visited didn't offer the sick either head cold nostrums or allergy meds. I kicked through the revolving glass door as the lobby's overhead lights flickered on. Omar fussed behind the front desk. From the look of things, he'd survived Karin's earlier ass tear over the phone. He gazed up as I set a course for my room.

His shout hailed me. "Frank, a quick word, please." He angled across the lobby to head me off. I cringed.

"Did you hear word from Detective Abdullah?" I asked.

"On my Lugers, no, I didn't. I'll tell you this. Detective Abdullah has a dark heart." Omar stopped in front of me. The spicy aroma of cloves from the kitchen came with him. "You also have a dark heart, Frank. You screwed me. I should throw you out. Only Detective Abdullah's orders you should remain stand in my way. I can't cross him and hope to run the Otel Pamuk."

"He kept pressuring me, and I couldn't lie. He has my passport, and I want to get back home. Besides, why sweat it? Your Lugers will sail through. Ballistics will prove they were never fired. Then you're home free."

The craggy lines on Omar's forehead smoothed away. "Will I get back my Lugers?"

I'd no idea, but I said, "Detective Abdullah will return them."

"That's a blessing. Why do I fret? But I tell you with a

broken heart Pembe will be missed. Hands down, she was my best worker." He paused, his face darkening again, this time in more anger. "My cousin Ahmet had quite the yarn to tell me. How I'm this big-time drug dealer using the Otel Pamuk as my cover."

"He fell for that bullshit?" I forced a dry chuckle. "We were joking around, and I was messing with him. He knows that, too."

Omar frowned at me. "Everything is a joke. Your last stay was crazy, too, wasn't it? Didn't you go to jail for a bar fight?"

"Those brawls are in the past. I quit drinking, and my life got a lot tamer."

"You do seem to act calmer."

"You trusted me enough to work as your hotel detective."

Omar shook his head. "Maybe I don't need a hotel detective."

Still wanting an excuse to poke around here, I looked stunned. "Have you lost your mind? Your hotel is a hotbed of crime. First, Mercedes vanishes. Second, I get beaned over the skull. Then you find Pembe shot dead. Detective Abdullah is breathing down your neck. One more foul up, and he'll shut you down. That's where I can help you."

"That's all true. It's better for you to stay on. There can be no more foul ups."

"Something else. My pay. How much is this security worth?"

"What if I waive your room and board?"

"My client already covers those expenses. Waive my laundry fee, and we'll call it even. I'll patrol from sundown until after midnight. Then I'll crash until dawn. Agreed?"

"Agreed. And thank you. This mess will straighten itself out. Life will be a bowl of cherries again."

"Sure it will. When Mercedes left here, did he take his room key and passport?"

"He must have."

I revised my timeline. "Early Sunday morning he pockets his passport and room key. Dressed in a jacket and tie, he leaves behind his other stuff. He leaves no word at the front desk. I'd say he intended to return on the same day, only he didn't."

"Was he kidnapped?"

"I've considered that except in broad daylight his captors ran the risk of eyewitnesses. I'm not certain they would. Suppose he agreed to meet a party at a bench in the secluded corner of a park?"

"Sunday afternoons everybody flocks to the parks. If he caught a *taksi* or used the subway, he could be anywhere in the city within minutes. Something I don't understand. Why did he go alone? Mr. Nashwinter was available."

"Would you take a boozehound like Nashwinter into the city? You'd be watching out for him, not the other way around." I paused and stared Omar in the eye. "Why did you ship Mercedes' stuff home?"

Scratching his neck, Omar shrugged. "I'd no choice. Mr. Mercedes' wife phoned us. She was angry. His suitcases didn't belong to us, and she wanted what was hers. We told her we'd no interest in stealing them. Accusing us of theft was insulting. We also told her you wanted them kept here. She screamed that she was in charge, not you."

"That's her all right. What happens when Mercedes returns?"

"I asked her that. She said he always buys his suits new while in Ankara."

She'd never brought up her decision to ship his duffel home with me. Gatlin hadn't either. My cryptic boss and client across the pond doling out selective bits of information wasn't how I liked to operate. I had to consider what else they'd held back from me. Gatlin had lost his sense of propriety. We seemed to work at cross-purposes, and while maybe that wasn't a new insight, it sure as hell chaffed me now.

"Never mind on Mercedes' bags. You did the right thing

by carrying out her wishes."

Omar smiled in relief. "After all, she's the boss."

She is but only up to a point, I thought. And she's damn close to crossing it.

"During your patrols tonight, will you sweep the upstairs corridors? That's where Pembe was shot. Detective Abdullah harps on it. An innocent guest might fall as the next victim. Let's all stay safe."

More amped than I'd ever seen him, Omar, swiping off his perspiring bald pate on his hand, walked away. I was a little hacked over his telling me how to do my job. I retreated to my room and switched on an all-news cable channel. Talking heads -- for the most part white men in their 50s with bad haircuts and pointy beards -- blabbed past each other. Their shtick was to compete in blurting out the most outrageous thing.

I pinged Gatlin's Middleburg office. Busy. My next signal hit Gerald's cell. I got just rings. I hoped he was checking on Mrs. Mercedes. My redial snagged Gatlin.

"Mrs. Mercedes told the hotel to ship home Mercedes' duffel. I was still using it. What's the deal?"

"Where else would it go?"

"I asked her to leave it alone. Aw hell, what's done is done." I had it in mind to tell him about Gerald's tail job on Mrs. Mercedes but held off. Instead, I said, "You're always her big defender. I'd say you're hooked on her."

Our long distance connection poured that spacey, white noise into my ear.

"Franklin, I don't see how that's your affair," he said with stiff formality. "You better accord her more respect. Return her messages in a timely fashion and quit picking a fight with her when you talk. She's a reasonable lady if you give her a chance."

The heat flushed the tips of my ears. "I won't wear a fucking cell phone if that's where this is headed."

"I may well recommend that to her."

"Yeah well, here's what I recommend. Quit banging my

client. You're putting us in an adversarial position. Personal feelings cloud your thinking. This is a business deal, not the latest filly to frolic with in your stud paddock."

"Why are you sore? Why don't you trust her?"

"How can I? I'm busting my conk trying to find her husband, and you're off romancing her. How do I know you didn't want Mercedes out of the picture? You've got the classic motive for murder. It's a love triangle straight out of James M. Cain. Meantime I play your PI stooge in Ankara to give it a legitimate sheen."

"We're both concerned for Sylvester. You can put your client's heart at ease and earn a few bucks if you ever get it cranking over there."

Among a few other things, it bristled on the tip on my tongue to ask if Mrs. Mercedes had a heart.

"Don't forget the IRS wants their pound of flesh."

"That's the only thing keeping me here."

"Look, everything is going fine. Just find Sylvester."

"I'm not making a lot of headway in case you hadn't noticed. Now level with me? Are you balling the client?"

Gatlin said nothing. I felt my gut grinding away. Butting horns with him was a waste of breath. True to a lawyer's form, he took a conciliatory note.

"All right, Frank, I'll admit that I tender intimate feelings for Lois. Do they make me less effective as a criminal lawyer? Absolutely not. But I do get my Irish up when she's unfairly maligned. You understand, I'm sure."

"Not really." My rage had ebbed to a controlled burn. "Have you planned ahead? What will you do when I find Mercedes? Go in halves with him over her? That's perverse even by Middleburg's standards."

"That won't upset the status quo. Lois and Sylvester go their separate ways in their marriage."

"You harp on that fact. When you stare down a .44's borehole as big as the Holland Tunnel, tell me a man doesn't care if you ball his old lady."

"I'll take your point under advisement. To get back on

task, what are you doing tonight?"

"Omar hired me for hotel security protecting us from the local evildoers."

"Don't let it interfere with your investigation. I'm late for a meeting. Bye."

I hung up as a scratch came at my door. My favorite maid indicated Omar wanted to see me in the lobby. I checked the clock on the nightstand: six o'clock. Hotel Detective Frank Johnson stepped out into the corridor reporting for his debut shift. I didn't go armed. Abdullah had taken my Luger for ballistic testing. Meanwhile a killer roved in our midst.

Chapter 20

I sat in a brocade chair old as the Crusades that Omar had moved down from a suite on the top floor. The twilit lobby lay quiet. Poor Omar. He'd pitched in washing the dishes. Coming behind the server, he'd vacuumed the restaurant floors again.

It dawned on me his make-busy work put off his going home to face Karin. As he swiped out the ashtrays, the desk phone chortled in its European ring tone. I caught it. Karin asked for Omar. I called him over.

He pleaded a litany of duties left to finish here. She didn't buy it. After grabbing a cold Efes from the bar's fridge, he waved, scuttled through the revolving glass door, and whistled for a *taksi*. Maybe the cabbie was his cousin Mr. Ahmet. I allowed a chuckle.

Omar had shown why marriage is overrated. Not until going up the steps did I realize Karin was his relief tonight. If I stayed out of the lobby, maybe we'd never clash. I walked along the third floor. Arms outstretched, my fingertips grazed the walls. Passage was that narrow.

A band of light glimmered at the doorsill to Room 213, Mercedes' former digs. My soft knock roused the beanpole Pat. He gave me the fish eye over the brass security chain. A jazzy sax riff inside came from Charlie Parker's "Yardbird Suite". Vintage jazz after bluegrass pleasured my ears.

"Johnson, hotel security."

He quirked his lips. "I know who you are. What do you want?"

"To talk."

"What about?"

"The last guy renting this room."

"How might we know him?"

"I'll be upfront. It's Pat, right? Pat, I'm also a detective, and my job is to find the guy. His name is Sylvester Mercedes, and he's gone missing. I've got reason to believe somebody not too nice ran an electronic surveillance on him in here."

As Pat swallowed, his Adam's apple quivered. "Are you saying our room is bugged?"

"That's it. Visual as well as audio is possible."

"Dreadful. We'll move tonight." Pat pushed in the door, unhooked its brass security chain, and stepped away. Glancing at me, Jerry retied his kimono with the flame-breathing dragon across the back. He nudged down the CD player's volume.

"Do you carry any ID, Frank?"

I flashed them my PI photo ID.

"The photo is fuzzy like the ones taken of Sasquatch."

"Pat, don't be rude. Amateurs work in the camera shops."

He glanced at me. "Did you look for Mr. Mercedes in our room earlier?"

"Right."

He let out a sigh. "That's why I saw you skulk out of here."

Jerry bristled. "Like I'd seduce a lover boy while you fetched the ice? Why, that's insulting."

Pat ignored him. "Is this electronic bug well hidden?"

Gazing about, I'd the same concern. Room 213 had plaster of Paris walls. I saw no stray nail holes to mount a mini-camera behind. A laptop was out on their desk.

"Do you guys have a smoke detector?"

"None is in here." Jerry cinched the belt to his dragon

kimono tighter. "We're safe."

Pat disagreed. "I'm getting us a better room."

"Pat, set down the phone. If Frank says we're bug free, I'm happy. My back can't take the trauma of lugging our crap to a different room."

"How convenient your trick back acts up just now."

"Keep it up, and I'll go book a single at the Harrington."

Hearing that made me curious. "Why didn't you stay there to begin with?"

Jerry sniffed. "We had to pare back our travel budget."

Pat glanced over at the laptop. "We'd be flush again if you'd ever finish your book. That's money in the bank."

"I'm writing my fingers to the bone, Pat."

Meanwhile I scanned for other places to hang any bugs. Furniture blocked the wall receptacles. The overhead light fixture was out of reach. Pat and Jerry continued to snipe at each other. After bringing over a ladder-backed chair, I climbed to stand on its cane-bottomed seat. The nut attaching the light fixture unscrewed as if it'd been just taken off. That kicked up my pulse, but I examined the sockets holding the two sixty-watt bulbs and spotted nothing. I put the light fixture back.

"False alarm, guys. My apologies to bother you."

"That's a load off my mind."

"Pat, your insensitivity appalls me. Frank needs a clue, and all you can think of is a Peeping Tom."

"No big deal, guys."

"We both thank you." Jerry frowned at Pat. "Don't we?"

"Whatever you say, Jerry."

I left them feuding behind their closed door, but not before a check of their clock-radio showed it was five hours until midnight, my quitting time. Resuming my hotel walk-through, I was left prey to my thoughts. Working security details had never jazzed me. I'd guarded a few bank lobbies, no stick-ups attempted and no shots fired. That was a creditable record compared to my summer fiasco at the heir finder agency. It'd sounded so easy until I couldn't trace down any heirs. Maybe my heart wasn't in it.

I dwelled on home. I knew that Gerald enjoyed flush times. Bail skips figured it made better sense to take a shot and book than to pony up the dough for bail. Gerald went after them. It occurred to me he was up to his neck in work, and he'd lied to me. Or maybe he couldn't stand to miss out on the high jinks here. Later we'd laugh about it over T-bone steaks, my treat.

My beat sent me through a semi-dark labyrinth of corners and turns. Several paces from the cage elevator, I shivered. The drafty Otel Pamuk had five floors, thirty berths on each tier. One hundred and fifty doors for me to bang on was a daunting challenge. But I was gut-certain a guest knew something on Mercedes.

The cage elevator creaked me up to "5", and I hopped off. My first door knock raised a fast response. A wizened Oriental man in an ankle-length robe appraised me through his cracked door's outspill of brightness. He was a bundle of shakes. I also saw his facial tremors and rigidity as if from the outset of Parkinson's. One of my aunts had died from it.

"Y-y-yes?"

"Johnson, hotel security. I'm looking for this man. Have you seen him lately or know anything about him?"

Inhaling, the Oriental man buttressed his vibrating shoulder against the doorjamb. The tremors slowed. "Hold up the photo to the light . . . that's fine . . . no, I don't recognize him, but then I rarely go out."

"Thanks. Sorry to disturb your evening."

"No stress, sir. Is he in any trouble?"

"All I know is he left and never returned for his stuff here."

"American like you?"

"Yeah, that's right."

"I've been studying your inscrutable war on CNN."
"Let's pray it winds down soon."
"Are you living in a lotus kingdom? Say hello to your new Vietnam."

I winced at the truth's sting in what he'd said before I left his closing door. The prospect of doing this at one hundred forty-nine doors was maddening. I went to the next door where my knocks got no takers. Moving on to the third door, I made an executive decision.

I'd move my canvass to the Floor Two. It stood to reason anybody knowing Mercedes probably stayed on the same floor he did. I scampered down the three flights of stairs to the corridor and cutting the corner by the cage elevator, I almost collided with Pat.

"The lady at the front desk just called us. She thought you'd be by Mr. Mercedes' old room. Anyway, Jerry and I wanted to warn you. Christ, how did you piss her off?"

"Go on back. It's okay."

Pat made himself scarce. I'd no desire to catch a ration of shit from Karin snarling in the lobby. So I drifted like smoke along the second floor. Otel Pamuk offered more berths with shared baths than private units. Omar (or now Karin) rode herd on the staff, making them go chop-chop.

He didn't allow pets in the rooms including guests like the well-to-do ladies with their whippets. That made sense. Turks didn't keep household cats or dogs. As I policed the corridors, no more car bombs or faulty electrical grids ravaged Ankara's night. But I didn't let myself relax too much.

I slipped down three steps in the stairway where my hackles stood on end. One more step down, and I felt my pulse go haywire. Evil poised near me, but I couldn't pinpoint just where.

At the landing, I froze. My senses flashed on red alert. Doors above me clanged. A baby whimpered. The elevator cables chirred. Tension also coiled the muscles along my spine. My eyes kept peeled, I moved in a tiger crouch, set to spring.

My shadow flowed to the first floor where I planted against the wall at the nearest corner. A heartbeat later, a man-form prowled into my sightline. Smelling his gamey BO wrenched my stomach. Fear galvanized me to act. I loaded up and slung a hard fist at the head shape.

My knuckles hammered bone. Teeth crunched. To counter a retaliatory strike, I reloaded. But not in attack mode, he pivoted and raced down the corridor. Ice picks of pain stabbing my hand cooled my adrenaline to give chase. Ten years ago, you bet, but now I stood pat. A heat gun at full blast scorched my knuckles. They shrieked out in pain. I knew where to get some relief.

Ignoring Karin's glare, I lumbered into the lobby and shouldered through the batwing doors to the kitchen's ice machine. I pawed open its Plexi-glass door. My mangled fist dug into the ice cubes. My teeth unclenched as the Arctic cold deadened the fiery licks of my agony.

The tattoo of heeltaps on the tile floor brought Karin into the kitchen. The fuzzy, pink shawl was tied in a knot below her neck. Her cider brown bun looked a little frizzy. Her gray-hazel eyes burned in their intensity.

"Why is your hand stuck in my ice machine?"

"It's by necessity, not choice."

"I see." She her folded arms under her ripe breasts. "What happened to you?"

After hauling my mangled hand out of the ice cubes, I unbuttoned the cuff and rolled up my shirtsleeve. "I slugged a creep by the stairs. Probably a thief, he came your way. What did you see?"

"Nobody but thanks for chasing off the prowler. I don't know what's going on here. Come sit by the front desk. It's less dangerous there."

"No, I'm set to bag it for the night. I'll walk my beat once more. Chances are he left through an open window and won't be back tonight."

"Good. Tomorrow I hope you'll see Detective Abdullah. Omar has been a pill without his Lugers."

"I told him after they pass ballistics, the police should return his property. Did he get an itemized receipt?"

"I suppose he did."

I shook out my numb fist. "Your hotel is violent place."

Heaving out a sigh, she lifted the fuzzy, pink shawl off her shoulders. "What's to be done?"

One primal idea hit me. Strip that fuzzy, pink shawl off her shoulders and tear open her blouse and hike up her skirt and do her up against the ice machine and howl over her moans as her hot, wet sex enveloped mine. But it'd get bloody if she brought out that Luger. So I grumbled "good night" and left her to marvel at the nail points for eyes to the hardboiled Mr. Johnson.

Chapter 21

A chilly breeze whipped my face as I hung out on the Otel Pamuk's rooftop terrace. My cigarette -- the first smoked in four-and-a-half years -- glowered in the pre-dawn's chiaroscuro. The roll-your-own used an aromatic tobacco, the brand with the kicking zebra logo. Its tinfoil pouch included the rolling papers and a matchbook.

Television antennas, radio aerials, and satellite dishes studded the terra-cotta roofs across the street and up the block. I inhaled another puff and watched the salmon pink splinters of bright crack the eastern horizon. Wednesday had arrived. I emptied my lungs of smoke and wished Ankara a good morning.

My final drag burned down the roll-your-own to a roach. An old habit, I held in the smoke, ran a slow count to three, and then let the smoke gush out. I'd forgotten how sweet tobacco was the first thing in the day. After stubbing out the roach on the wrought iron rail, I let the residual pieces of tobacco flitter off on the breeze. A cough unclogged my throat.

I knew I was drowning in deep shit. Coming to Ankara had unhitched me from my psychic moorings in Pelham. But I always stayed in control, or kidded myself enough that I did. Returning to Turkey had almost undone me. I moved to the rear of the roof terrace and leaned my arms on the wrought iron railing and peered down the five stories into the alleyway. This was an ideal spot for a security camera, but I saw none. Omar was too cheap.

A bare-chested, one-legged cabbie was scrubbing down his lemon yellow *taksi* in the alleyway He sloshed more water from a spigot into a green plastic bucket, and then he scoured off the white wall tires. His brush tapped out a jingle on the baby moon hubcaps. Then he stood up and popped the *taksi*'s hood to delve into the engine's dark, greasy mysteries.

He unsheathed the dipstick and wiped it on a rag. To check the oil, I figured out. Unhappy, he used a cane and hobbled back to key open the trunk. He used a screwdriver to pock the top holes in a quart can of oil and poured it into the crankcase. When he tinkered where I guessed the carburetor was, he lost me.

I relied on Gerald to keep my rackety Prizm on the road. Come to think of it, he did a lot more for me, too. I wondered how his stakeout on Mrs. Mercedes was going in Middleburg. I'd buzz him for a status later in the morning.

Then I spotted an aluminum ladder stacked lengthwise against the hotel wall. Could the ladder at its fullest extension reach to the second floor? Could an athletic sort scale the ladder to get on the balcony? It looked doable to me. Intrigued, I left my watchtower.

My eyes acclimated to the stairwell's streaky light as I cantered down the steps to the lobby. The breakfast crowd had queued up at the buffet tables. Karin bent over the desk inside Omar's office. I did a double take and schemed again how to get past her Luger and under that fuzzy, pink shawl.

Instead the revolving glass door spewed me into the street. I cornered the hotel to the alleyway. The same one-legged cabbie leaned against the *taksi*'s fender. He pulled a hearty drag off his cigarette. His safetypinned pants leg fluttered in the wind. I caught his eye, and he smiled.

"Is that ladder yours?"

The cabbie nodded. He didn't get my question, but he stood eager to please a potential fare. "We go?" His hand unlatched both doors and invited my visual inspection. "Very clean. We go? Very soon?" I glanced inside and saw a chrome Thermos on the front seat.

"No, I don't need a *taksi*." I walked over and toed the aluminum ladder. "Is this yours or does it belong to the hotel?"

He shrugged. "We go soon? Okay? Very clean. Okay? Very cheap. We go, sir."

"Okay." I turned from the aluminum ladder. "Soon."

"Good. Pay in American dollars?"

"Sure, whatever you say. Pay in American dollars."

I left the thrilled cabbie, returning to the lobby and hustling up to the front desk.

"Is the *taksi* still parked in the alleyway?" Karin shouldered the straps to her purse. "Did you happen to see him?"

"He's ready to go for the day. There's also a ladder. Is it yours?"

Ruffling her shoulders, she readjusted the fuzzy, pink shawl to project the rising contours of her breasts. Her gray-hazel eyes almost caught me looking.

"Yes, Omar stows his junk back there. I bitch at him. Then he moves it somewhere else. The ladder is only the latest thing in our ongoing squabbles. Will you be dining here?"

"It's the only place I eat."

Her lips tamped down a smile. "I hear you're our big rice eater."

"That's only two-thirds true. For breakfast, I devour your Turkish coffee with the great pound cake."

"Omar will soon return." A half step moved her to the revolving glass door. "I'll hold you to your promise. Please talk to Detective Abdullah. Those Lugers are Omar's pride and joy. More than me, I sometimes think."

"I'll do what I can."

I figured Omar should give his wife a little more attention. Or did she hold him at bay by pulling out that

Luger on him?

"Be sure to report last night's prowler to Omar."

"Will do." I waved at her. "See you."

A few minutes later through the front glass I saw her climb into the lemon yellow *taksi*. The one-legged cabbie now wearing a red soccer jersey smirked at her. Were they illicit lovers? PIs always suspect the worst in people. They hurtled off toward the Citadel as if late for something big.

The four Turkish businessmen enthralled by my all-rice cuisine straggled in and sat at their table. This time their thick-set shoulders didn't go unnoticed. My bruises reminded me how muscles increased a sap's bat speed swatted at a target's head. No grins flashed. Grim faces said their trip wasn't coming up roses. For a refreshing change I didn't feel so damn alone in my own professional setbacks.

Appearing a little shell-shocked, Nashwinter shambled out of the cage elevator. Unshaven, he wore the same suit. He put on the brakes at the bar and perched on a barstool. His beefy shoulders called to mind Gerald's report on Nashwinter's slammer time for felonious assault.

I walked over. "What's shaking, Nashwinter?"

"Huh? Oh, it's you Johnson. All I know is no money is shaking in my pocket." His bloodshot eyes saw me. His chin wasn't scabbed over from my knuckle sandwich. "How's that PI gig working out for you?"

I took a barstool. "With a bit here and a bit there, I can get by okay. Did you bunk in your room all night? You didn't explore the hotel corridors and plow into anything nasty?"

"I dozed off watching the tube. What's so nasty?"

"Never mind. You answered my question. You're not scraping up much business?"

"In this economy, how can I?"

"Too bad, Nashwinter."

"I stopped to enjoy a snort, and I like to drink alone."

"In a second, sure. A couple more questions. I'm guessing Mercedes is really your barroom pal. I'm also guessing you have a spotty memory. Am I guessing right?"

Nashwinter scratched a thumbnail across his chin stubble. He glared up, then down the untended bar. A dry noise croaked in his throat.

"Yeah okay, we shoot the breeze while we're drinking. He pays, and I sort of listen. What can I tell you? At the end of the day, he's one the saddest men I've ever known."

"Lots of guys cry in their beer."

"I've bent elbows with a lot of them, too. But Mercedes is stuck in a funk bordering on clinical depression. I'm no shrink, mind you. Just my read on the guy."

"Depressed? What about?"

Nashwinter stopped scratching his stubble. "Life is a bitch for him. Can I get a Tom Collins here?"

"Omar will be in soon. First round is on me, too. What's weighing on Mercedes' mind?"

"Decent of you. A morning gin restores my equilibrium."

I smiled. "Happy I can help out. On Mercedes -- "

"He beefs about his old lady."

"She's made his life a living hell?"

"And how."

"If she galls him so much, just divorce her."

Nashwinter brooded at the clean shot glasses arrayed beneath the bar's mirror. "It's not that simple. She's got her hooks deep into him somehow."

"Man, marriage. Who the fuck needs it?"

"Tell me. That's why I fly solo. Sure I gave it a whirl. Got a minute?"

I didn't but nodded. My shoulder was a big one to cry on only if I steered this conversation back to Mercedes.

Nodding his chin stubble, Nashwinter warmed to his back story. "Miss Cary Ides was an ash blonde beautician from a coal town just off the Interstate. We were high school sweethearts. Soon we got a mortgage, a rust-bucket Volvo, and a brass bed large enough to land F-14s on. Then one sunny afternoon a plumber checked out Mrs. Nashwinter's plumbing. Too bad I caught them red-handed. End of tale except to add that asshole won't lay much pipe again."

"Didn't you get busted for doing that?"

"That hard lesson came later. Nowadays I keep my nose clean."

"Tell Omar to put your first on my tab. Just that one, though. I ain't made of money like you."

Laughing, Nashwinter slapped the bartop. "Who's rich? Next time, it's on me, Johnson."

I left the bar hoping there'd be no next time for us.

CHAPTER 22

I heard the phone ringing at the front desk. The disgruntled guests calling down wanted their mouthwash, shampoo, and clean towels. The maids were hustling. I loitered at the breakfast buffet. The whacking noises erupted from behind the batwing doors. I chuckled. The muscular chef was getting an early start on tenderizing the night's dinner steaks.

The four jabbering, gesturing Turkish businessmen left en masse to climb the stairs. I felt sorry for the Oriental gentleman with Parkinson's, a prisoner up in his room. Or maybe he preferred his solitude isolated on the top floor.

My favorite maid hadn't picked up in my room. A nicotine craving tortured my brain, but not as much as finding the elusive Mercedes did. A talking head gracing the TV screen made for lousy company. After muting the volume, I showered and shaved.

Three more GIs (or "troops" as the media now liked to call them) had been killed in action, two from a roadside IED and the third from a RPG. That left three more Gold Star moms in the States. I wanted to howl. Another terrorists' hostage had been decapitated. The video of her slaughter was a free Internet download. I had a mind how we did live in The Last Days, the Antichrist biding his or her time to pull the plug.

I did my paperwork, taking notes on my chat with Nashwinter at the bar. Mrs. Mercedes would get it all wrapped up in a pretty bow at the end. Then I'd get my money from her. A civil rap sounded at my door.

"Yo, come in. It's unlocked."

When my caller cleared the threshold, he asked me, "Why are you holding that lamp?"

"The better to brain you with if need be." I closed the door and returned the lamp to the nightstand.

As Hamza, the gangly server, digested my cynical reply, he took out a folded sheet of paper from his pocket. His nervous fingers undid its edges.

"I put your questions to the staff like we talked about. First I should tell you Mr. Mercedes is like a mouse. He doesn't call a lot of attention to himself."

"When does Mercedes come out of his room?"

"Hardly ever. He never eats in our restaurant. I heard him once quarreling with the other American guest."

"Nashwinter?"

Hamza nodded. "That's him, yeah."

"Where and when was this?"

"A couple of weeks ago I saw them in our Guests Hall of Honor. You know, the photos tacked up near the kitchen? Mr. Nashwinter grew angry. Mr. Mercedes had made a crack about his beer."

"That's interesting. Any idea where Mercedes goes if he leaves the Otel Pamuk?"

"He's a big gambler."

"Yeah, his casino jaunts are famous. Anywhere else?"

"Every morning he buys a newspaper at the arcade around the corner." Hamza handed me the folded sheet of paper. "Do I get the rest of my money?"

"First something else. Does your boss likes to chase the ladies?"

"We don't call Omar The Groper for nothing."

"Did he have an affair with Pembe?"

"Put it this way. He talked to her differently than the rest of the staff. He'd lots of smiles for her."

"Did they take it further than flirting?"

"I've heard stuff. But I don't know, especially since

Karin now has a shorter fuse."

"Shorter fuse, why?"

"Last year she had cancer and got a mastectomy."

"Damn." I took a pause. "She's so young for that shit."

Hamza shrugged. "My money, please."

I stacked our agreed upon sum of TLs in three piles on the bureau top. Karin's disease had thrown me. My glamorous femme fatale's body scars were real. Hamza snatched up the money piles, murmuring "thanks". He darted out the door and lit off to the lobby. Still distracted, I spread out Hamza's sheet of paper to read it under the nightstand lamp.

"Huh?"

The sheet of paper was blank. Nothing was scribbled on the front or back. He'd gamed me. Furious, I vaulted up from the bed and ran to the door. Then just as fast I cooled off. The greedy bite came out of Mrs. Mercedes' pie, not mine. Balling up the useless sheet of paper, I laughed and threw it in the wastebasket.

But Hamza had told me something valuable. Mercedes and Nashwinter had jawed. I wondered if their heated words had led to a vengeful shooting. Stupid men liked to carry grudges, pick their spots, and even their scores. I'd brace Nashwinter again, and maybe Hamza to get back the money if he ever showed here again.

The revolving glass door spat me into the morning haze. My eyes teared up. Cinders on the wind also gritted between my teeth. I touched on a memory of the dirty smokestacks to Pelham's wire factory that'd shut down and moved to China during the Clinton regime. Fewer local jobs put more commuters on the already gridlocked roads. I saw the wet spot in the alleyway where the one-legged cabbie had scrubbed down his *taksi*.

The aluminum ladder felt lightweight. I extended the two halves and secured it against the hotel. The top of the ladder cleared the second-story balcony, six inches to spare.

I peered up at it. Climbing from the alleyway into Mercedes' old lair was doable, but it took a bit of effort.

From the top rung, my attacker could've grabbed the balcony railing and wrested himself over it. I didn't mount the ladder to test my theory. From the corner of my eye, I saw the cops swooshing up in a squad car. The ladder went back, and I eased to the front and into the lobby. Abdullah sat in the brocade chair where the happy warrior smiled at me. I failed to catch the moment's humor. He stood up.

"Mr. Johnson, you've got a knack for vanishing."

"Hardly since you took my passport. Did you bring it?"

"Why? Is your business in Ankara done? I think not. We haven't granted you waivers to fly home. You'll be our guest under house arrest until we've cleared up Pembe's homicide."

"House arrest? Where's your evidence?"

As his smile widened, I regretted ever trusting a cop like Abdullah.

"Circumstantial evidence but it grows like the lotus vine. Have you consulted with a criminal attorney? Several English-speaking lawyers practice in Ankara. I can refer you to one."

"If you're stacking a homicide case against me, your short list for my defense counsel no doubt scrapes the bottom of the barrel."

Abdullah laughed.

"Did you finish running ballistics on Omar's Lugers?"

"We did. Omar scored a smashing victory."

"What about the Luger I gave you?"

"Same deal, Mr. Johnson. You discharged no shots from it. That's the reason why I don't haul you off to jail this morning."

I didn't say I told you so. "Without Pembe's murder weapon, your case is circumstantial."

"For now, true enough. But don't cook up any ideas on

leaving town and don't interfere with my detectives. That includes putting ladders against the hotel balconies to check out your harebrained ideas. Leave the investigation to the professionals. Is that clear?"

"You don't leave me a lot of choice."

"That's the general idea, Mr. Johnson."

Chapter 23

Abdullah's new orders putting me under house arrest grated. While I rotted at the Otel Pamuk, Auk and his detectives twisted a set of facts to strap my ass to Old Sparky. No, that wasn't right. They'd abolished the death penalty here. Texas and my native Virginia still topped the leader board for the most penal executions in a year. Just the same, I didn't like to see myself as a jailbird locked up in anybody's cage.

"What's my motive? How do I benefit from her death?"

Abdullah's heavy-lidded eyes glowered. "You assume her homicide was premeditated. A crime of passion is more likely. Or her being at the wrong place at the wrong time. Don't worry. We'll untangle the truth. How goes the hunt for your lost Mr. Mercedes?"

"It's dead in the water. I'm too busy scheming how to bump off Turkish babes like Pembe."

"Sarcasm isn't a sign of cooperation."

"Neither is your watchdog always on my ass." I nodded to the dapper plainclothes cop with the rat-tail mustache crossing the street from the corner arcade.

"You're right on his beat. He watches the hotels. His orders are to stick on you. Day and night, where you go, he goes. Think of him as your second shadow. Better stay near the Otel Pamuk, or I'll clip your wings."

"I've got nothing to hide."

"The negative ballistics on your Luger is a good start.

Let's hope it stays that way. Good morning, Mr. Johnson."

Smiling, Abdullah strolled through the lobby like he sat on the top of his game. Maybe he did. From his standpoint, it was too early to arrest and put me in police custody. He knew I'd never skip town or go hide out. My Irish looks didn't blend in with most faces here. Any try to board a plane with no passport bordered on brain-dead. Setbacks like the negative ballistics on the Lugers didn't rankle him. I'd known my share of bulldog cops like him in the MPs.

Abdullah's plodding style didn't fit a career policeman out to impress his boss. Whether the homicide solve rate was up or down didn't faze him. Working the cases was his all. He probably kept no family snapshots on his desktop or in his wallet. I bet his exes reviled him. His offspring hardly knew him.

Intractable homicide cops wired like Abdullah could go for years before picking up the thread again on a cold case. But the particulars to any old homicide went on glimmering in his memory vault. Shaking my head in begrudging awe, I had a cup of coffee, stuffed down some pound cake, and beat it to my room.

My favorite maid had tidied up. My bag of dirty clothes had gone to the laundry downstairs. The cost of that amenity jacked up my bill, but the free laundry came with my job as Omar's hotel dick. I checked my scabby, swollen knuckles. Some fool out there walked around with fewer teeth. The sight of the ice bucket on the TV reminded me how to doctor my busted hand.

Omar came on as I pulled my room door shut. "Walk with me," he said. "Karin came home, and we buried the hatchet. The world is back to good. My girls went to school, and Karin is all smiles."

"You got laid this morning. Good for you. Last night I slugged a prowler in the mouth."

I told him about my fisticuffs with the shadow skulking down the stairwell.

"Who it was?"

"With not enough light I couldn't make out his face."

"But that's your job." Omar's forehead beaded up with sweat. His eyes bulged out. He balled up a fist to mash it into a palm. "No creeps can terrorize the Otel Pamuk."

It wasn't a stretch to point out how some of his guests qualified for creeps, but I kept my mouth shut. After a staredown, he spoke in a low voice.

"The guests in Mr. Mercedes' old room said you stopped by there."

"Pat and Jerry let me in to have a look. Either Mercedes' kidnapper isn't computer savvy, or he's decommissioned the bug. My sweep turned up empty."

"Or the third possibility says there is no kidnapper at all. Could it be Mr. Mercedes decided to walk out of my hotel and just drop out of sight?"

"Sorry, I don't follow you."

Omar smiled. "It's not so bizarre. Men do it all the time. Perhaps he melted into the crowd. He'll pop back up at a time of his choosing. Until then, he prefers to live in secrecy. He does what he pleases when he pleases and answers to nobody. There's something to be said for that."

"Then Mercedes went to elaborate lengths to do it."

"Not really. We tell the story about the Khoja."

"Say what?"

"The Khoja was a clever fellow much like your Paul Bunyan always dealing with his pack of troubles. One moonlit night the Khoja went to the well to draw up a pail of water. Peering down in the well, he was shocked to find the full moon was floating at the bottom. The moon, he thought, had tumbled from the sky and into the well.

"Scared out of his wits, the Khoja hitched the pail to the rope and lowered it. He scooped up the moon to rescue it in the pail. He cranked the handle to winch up the rope. At the top, the pail of water bumped against the stone wall and spilled out. The Khoja also slipped and fell flat on his back. He looked up to see the moon, delighted it was back in the sky where it belonged."

"Cute story. Your point, Omar?"

"Isn't it obvious? Mr. Mercedes is like the Khoja. A whim also sent Mr. Mercedes to the well. Once he feels ready to winch up the pail of water, he'll fall back into his old life and return here."

"He packed too light to take off on a frivolous trip."

"So he uses his wits to get by. Just leave him alone. He'll return home when he's ready."

"So I sit around the Otel Pamuk until he strolls into the lobby. We'll concoct a cover story for his absence, and I'll be the hero of the day."

"Brilliant, Frank. It shouldn't be long. Tell his wife to relax."

"She's pretty intense about me finding him soon."

Omar threw up his hands. "Women. Look, couldn't Pembe's murder just be a random act of violence?"

Pembe's lacy, red bra matched the one I'd fished out of Mercedes' duffel. That was still a doubtful clue, and I didn't bring it up.

"Anything is possible. But Detective Abdullah told me to butt out of his homicide investigation. That's solid advice by me."

"Then just keep your eyes open for any more trouble." Omar went into his office and shut the door.

I wanted some fresh air and left through the revolving glass door.

Chapter 24

License plates bearing the letters "A" and "AA" were the Turkish cops. Traffic police wore the white hats while the beat cops had green hats. None carried handguns, but the security squads at the different nations' embassy gates had automatic assault rifles. All the guards looked button-downed and ready if hell broke loose. I struck off at a jaunty clip, and Abdullah's plainclothes cop always trailed some fifty paces behind me.

At the leveled U.S. embassy, I saw no further bombsite investigation underway. A Kubota backhoe scraped the chunks of brick and cinderblock into rough piles. A second Kubota backhoe shoveled up the rubble and tipped it crashing into the bed of a dump truck.

The diesel engines brayed. Other dump trucks hauled the debris out the embassy gate. Greasy, black plumes belched from the heavy equipment's exhaust stacks. Gritty dust choked us. My coughing didn't help to clear my throat. Only the foreman holding a clipboard wore a brain bucket.

On the sidelines by the pikestaff fence, Felix Braintree, his navy blue suit and matching tie pressed, put a Zippo's fire to a cigarette drooping from his thick lips. He waved the smoke out of his face and surveyed the cleanup's progress. I jaywalked the other way, but he'd drawn a bead on me.

"Hey, Johnson! Wait up."

I stopped and turned. A self-important waddle brought him over to me.

"Have you seen a bigger mess? We took it on the chin."

"Somebody doesn't like us. Better watch your back."

His shoulders stiffened. "The Turkish officials reassured my superiors we'll be safe from hereon."

"But your superiors didn't take it on the chin. You did."

An American flag pin served as his tie tack. "Not for long I won't. My overseas assignments are winding down. By next spring I'll be sitting pretty in a D.C. office. I've started a realtor scoping out choice properties in Potomac and McLean."

You'll fit right in there. "Any clues or suspects?"

"None that I'll discuss out here."

"Okay, you wanted to talk. What's on your mind?"

"How's your search for Mercedes progressing?"

"Aren't your own tentacles out for him?"

"This incident has moved him to the back burner."

"Well, I'm stuck for any leads. Any casualties here?"

"Thankfully, no. Well, Asok, our night custodian, is unaccounted for. We haven't yet confirmed with his wife if he was still at work or not."

"So then, there's one probable casualty."

Felix had a dirty look. "My tally is of the staff, all Americans."

"The terrorists strike more than once. Next time they'll take out a few Americans."

"The Jersey walls and Marine security checkpoints will keep us secure enough."

Tempted but I didn't roll my eyes. "Who claims responsibility?"

"We're pursuing several angles. I'm optimistic that arrests are imminent."

"Your investigation of the bomb blast was a quickie."

"Brief but intense. A pile of rubble sitting here is a black eye for the perpetrators to gloat over. We'll rebuild fast. That's important to do in the war on terror."

I changed gears. "Do you and Mercedes pal around much?"

"Not so much anymore. He has his fun, and I have my work. Unlike you, he always checks in once he hits town." Felix vented cigarette smoke out of his nostrils.

I ignored his dig. "What was his mood last time?"

The cigarette smoke wreathed Felix. "Easygoing, friendly. Just his usual self, I'd say."

"Any idea why he dressed up for a Sunday morning stroll? Did he hook up with a lady downtown?"

"No doubt he wanted to use the casinos."

Wanting to blow the dust and gunk out of my stuffy nose, I waited for the next dump truck to rumble by us.

"He'd lost his shirt there the night before. Besides the casinos are closed on Sunday. An eyewitness saw him leave the Otel Pamuk. After that, where he went is anybody's guess. Don't you know all this?"

"Pretty much." Furrowing his brows, Felix gnawed on his cheek lining. "Did he grab a *taksi* or take the subway?"

"A cabstand is close to the Otel Pamuk, but my eyewitness didn't watch him once on the street. My leading assumption is he didn't flag down a *taksi*. No local cabbie I talked to recalls picking him up. His rendezvous spot with anybody had to fall within walking distance of the Otel Pamuk."

"Sunday is comatose here." Felix paused, thinking. Deeper wrinkles creased his forehead. A thumb rubbed his double chin. "Maybe he caught a prearranged ride to points unknown."

"You're on the same track as my abduction theory."

"Sadly Americans get shanghaied off the streets. We do our best at negotiating their release, but the outcome is often grisly."

"Just for the record, did Mercedes do spook work for Uncle?"

"You've read too much Le Carré. Anyway I'm unable

to confirm or deny that. With no good clues left to follow, will you be leaving Ankara?"

"No."

I left the scowling Felix to gag on his diesel fumes from the dump trucks carting off the embassy's ruins. A crack team of masons could raise a new one in a jiff. Across the shady side of the street I saw the news vultures in their vans -- CNN, Fox News, CBS, BBC, and Al-Jazeera -- had gathered. They didn't give me a second look while I blew my nose.

Cutting down the next side lane and tailed by Abdullah's plainclothes cop, I ran into a self-effacing, compact man. He wore fringed dungarees, T-shirt, and leather sandals. He worked his patter, shilling in a few marks under a pomegranate tree shedding its red petals. His bathroom scales sat on a square piece of pasteboard.

He eyed me and clicked his stubby fingers. I went over, he finger-flashed his price, and I paid him in TLs. His bathroom scales had to be made of gold. I'd dropped four pounds since my last street corner weigh-in. My all-rice diet had brought unforeseen benefits. I overtipped him.

On the off-chance they'd met, I took out Mercedes' photo. The man's nod said, yes, Mercedes had also used his scales. How long ago? I asked. The compact man jabbed up the right number of stubby fingers to mean two Sundays back when Mercedes had been last seen alive.

"This man." I held up the photo. "How was he dressed?" My question got a "huh?" look. I tugged at my sleeve, saying, "Clothes."

The compact man's oily thumbprint stamped Mercedes' formal photo. So wearing a suit he'd walked this way. That part was believable. Had he returned to the U.S. Embassy to see Felix? I rewarded the compact man a second tip.

I left him bowing, but I was the grateful one. My next lead hadn't come from a nifty piece of police work, but from a random encounter with a street hustler and his rusty bathroom scales.

A few ticks shy of Wednesday noon, Ankara's outdoors grew more oppressive from the increasing traffic jams. I rubbed my gritty eyes and passed under a copse of willows on Atatürk Bulvari. Then I executed a few deft backtrack maneuvers in the alleyways to shake Abdullah's plainclothes cop.

On the next block a tavern sat by a pharmacy. The plasma TV under the karaoke machine beamed in a soccer match. A welter of cheers filled the place. A coppery, fleet player flashing a telegenic grin had just nailed a sensational goal. I was back to being a MLB fan now that most of the steroids idols had quit the sport. The tavern's menu showed most dishes came with fish.

"Efes Pilsner, sir?"

The trim, young blonde didn't see my blush as I shook my head and ordered my old standby. "Dirty rice."

"You just want rice?" Annoyed, she tapped the serving tray against her thigh. "Is this a joke?"

"No joke. That and a glass of ice water will do me."

"Rice and water. You're a simple man."

"Doctor's orders. That's how I stay healthy."

She left for the kitchen, and I drifted over to a vacant barstool. My elbows leaned on the shellacked cedar top. The barkeep -- the mature version of my trim, blonde server had to be her mother -- never blinked through my question. Studying Mercedes' photo didn't alter her firm-set, peasant face.

I felt stupid. "Do you get me? Do you speak English?"

"Fluently. Who are you?"

Her jade green eyes darkened a shade while squinting at my PI ticket. "Okay, run this guy's story by me again."

"Sylvester Mercedes is an American businessman. He stayed at a budget hotel six or seven blocks from here. Two Sundays ago early in the morning he put on a suit and left the lobby. That was the last time anybody had any contact with him."

"He left his hotel alone? Dumb move. Nobody leaves our flat without an escort and a cell phone. A bad situation but that's how it is."

"I grant you he used bad judgment, but my job is to locate him. Can you help me or not?"

"Mr. Johnson, I hate to say it, but your man probably lies in a gutter, his throat slit open. Maybe I'm too lurid and cynical, but that's how the reckless Americans end up here. That's what they say."

"They? Who are they?"

"One out of every other Turk. Your war is unpopular."

"I'm not too crazy about it myself."

She pealed out a laugh. "Okay, I believe you. But it's like this. You're here. So you're the face of America the Turks see. A few will get nasty with you."

"I look no different than you." Defensiveness honed an edge to my words.

"I'll give you that. But I don't go around repeating my hard luck tale on every street corner. You're the American private eye searching for a lost countryman. Word gets around." Caginess now made her jade green eyes glint. "Do you take precautions?"

"Apparently not enough," was my brusque reply. The placid street outside her windows and door belied the hostility she described. I wondered if Ankara was as dangerous for me as she claimed it was.

"Are you against the war? Would you fight if you were called up?"

I shrugged. "I put in my time, but if the orders came, yeah, I'd go."

"Well, good luck on finding your AWOL friend."

I looked at her. "We're not friends. It's my job."

"Your lunch has arrived. Rice." She winked. "Eat hearty, sir. No patriot leaves us hungry."

Her quirky sense of humor didn't amuse me. I left the half-eaten dirty rice and some TLs tucked under my plate. But I'd be more careful.

Chapter 25

Flexing my bruised knuckles, I ruled out taking any neighborhood cut-throughs and stuck to the main drag. The traffic on Atatürk Bulvari had thinned out to lemon yellow *taksis* and cube trucks chugging out diesel smoke. My gait quickened. A pair of cops riding in a squad car blared out a proclamation in Turkish over its PA system. It didn't rile my fellow pedestrians, and I also played it cool. At the turn-off to my hotel, I continued on up the hill.

The sister pinnacles, the Shannon and Harrington Hotels, gleamed in their amber-tinted glory against a metallic, blue sky. I ducked inside the Harrington where the light bounced off its polished brass and chrome, and the acres of tinted glass. The tawny blonde hostess I'd charmed before was away from her kiosk.

Her words, however, rang a bell in me. She'd said she'd seen Mercedes escort the same lady into their lobby. The hostess was unable to identify the lady, only that she was probably Turkish. Mustafa had told me the lady was a prostitute. Mercedes had packed his trusty ED aid. No wonder he flew into Ankara every three months to get his sex fix.

I reasoned a sly concierge who did paid favors for the Harrington guests like Mercedes might sell me information. I borrowed an English-Turkish dictionary from off the front desk. The Turkish translation I found for the word "pimp" left me chuckling. Right. I'd never pronounce it.

Several guests lolling in the lobby chairs helped me to hunt up Phillip the concierge at the hotel's upscale restaurant. As I approached the short Phillip in a dark suit standing by the restaurant's marble pillars, he pointed an arm amputated at the elbow.

"No-no, sir, that just won't do."

He took exception to my apparel. Their strict dress code required all gentlemen attired in neckties. If I didn't adhere to their strict dress code, an usher answering to "Hans" would show me to the front door. Hans struck me as more of a bouncer than an usher.

Phillip refused to take any of my questions until I was up to snuff. He kept spare neckties in his locker, and he'd make me legal for "a modest fee". It sounded silly and pointless, but I liked his idea more than dealing with Hans. Phillip sold me a clip-on necktie. He smiled his approval after I put it on.

"May I see the missing gentleman's photo?"

I brought out Mercedes' portrait with a wad of TLs. After pocketing the gratuity, Phillip took the photo to study under the small brass lamp on the rostrum holding their reservations book. He said nothing and gave me an expression blank as a piece of tin. A pang of disappointment came before my anger for shelling out the money.

"Do you recognize him or not?" I asked.

"Yeah okay I do now. But this gentleman is a day guest. We've had several conversations. You're right. He brings no luggage except the same lady on his arm."

"Go back two Saturdays. He escorted a tall lady. She wore big, yellow sunglasses."

Phillip smiled. "Sure, she's his favorite. Yagmur. It's Turkish for rain. It's her working name, I'm sure."

"Y-A-G-M-U-R?" I printed it on the back of my business card.

"That's right. I've no idea what her actual name is."

"You call up Yagmur when Mercedes makes a request?"

"Yes but we keep it discrete. This is the Harrington, after all."

"For another 'modest fee', can you put me in touch with her? I'd like to ask her some questions on her last visit with Mercedes."

"She stays near the Citadel, I believe."

"Can you get in touch with her?"

"Tell you what. I'll leave her a voice mail. When she calls me back, I'll explain your request. She'll decide if she wants to see you."

"I guess I can't do much better."

"Come back tomorrow. You better go now." Phillip pointed his stubby arm. "You can use the atrium for a shortcut."

Cutting into the sunny atrium, I ducked under a grove of silk banana palms where I yanked off the much hated clip-on necktie. Who in their sane minds could choke on one every day at their 9-5? I ditched the clip-on necktie in a potted palm. Later Phillip would troll by and recycle it for his locker.

Then I heard a bearish tread lumbering up behind me. I pivoted. On first sight I knew who he was. Hans's beige gabardine suit, narrow tie, and pointy black leather shoes failed to hide the giant ape in him. I got a whiff of his gamey BO. He was a stickler for the rules, and he saw how I was flaunting them by going tieless.

"Just you stay cool," I told him in a level voice. "This is no big deal."

My words sailed through Hans' empty skull. His knuckles consolidated into a pair of sledge hammers. But I didn't backpedal an inch. That was a sign of weakness to this carnivore. We'd stand toe to toe and duke it out. My frenzied mind plotted any possible escape routes out of the atrium. None showed any promise.

Hans shuffled into the shaft of sun, and I saw a stitched up chin on his meaty face. I'd popped him in Otel Pamuk's murky stairway. If he scared then, chances were a show of force might save me again. His shark eyes gleamed, seeming to recognize me as he crouched in a mauler's stance.

Knifing in, he uncorked the first haymaker. Jerking my head, I felt the swish of air, and the top of my ear clipped. A split instant later my right cross exploded on his jaw. He grunted. His chunky head recoiled under my blow. Fight adrenaline was my pain killer. My twice-banged knuckles oozed blood. Every bone in my body felt jarred.

Using a weapon evened up the odds. My eyes flicking over saw one. The columnar ashtray stand was a half-dozen inches away. As Hans cleared away the cobwebs from his skull, I stretched down to grab up the ashtray stand. My slice at him sped up. The crimped steel edge to the ashtray stand clouted his chin stitches. They flayed apart. Blood spurted out everywhere like a hand-squeezed tomato.

Clutching his chin, he shrieked. My weapon backed up. My next salvo aimed to crush his skull. But I hurried -- my luck this good had to be a fluke.

Just then, a sheet of icy, blue light danced before my eyes. A z-z-z-z noise resonated under the silk banana palms and throughout the atrium. Staring, I backed off. The electrical jolt had zapped Hans to fall down. His shakes on the floor were the most grotesque DTs I'd ever seen.

"Set down the ashtray stand." The Taser gun Phillip clutched had paralyzed Hans to lay quivering between us. "Then get. This wears off fast."

"Thanks."

"It's a good thing I was here. The others weren't so lucky."

I took off in an open field sprint across the lobby's carpet and didn't stop hauling ass downhill until I spun through the Otel Pamuk's revolving glass door. Pounding footsteps didn't hound me. I'd made a clean getaway.

Chapter 26

I tried to relax, but it was time to get on the stick and earn a pay check. My two international phone calls beamed off the satellites back to the U.S. Neither Gatlin nor Gerald picked up, and I recorded no messages. Voice mail was stupid. That left me to deal with the spiny Mrs. Mercedes. Not big on totally ruining my day, I passed. Her open marriage had encouraged Mercedes to wander off and explained why I now played her bloodhound.

I fixed on Mercedes' lady friend Yagmur. I realized Phillip wasn't going to reach out to her for me. I knew where Ankara's tenderloin district was in Ulus from my MP days. But how did I see my way around the Ulus nightlife? A Yank waving a fistful of greenbacks and specifying a lady by name might entice out Yagmur.

I mulled over how to weasel out of my hotel detective shift tonight. It was two o'clock. Soon Omar would come to remind me, and I'd balk. He'd demand to know why. Ulus, I'd reply. Ah, I understand, he'd say through his smirk.

My fingertips drummed on the TV console. CNN ran a sad commentary. Vets, their blasted off legs and arms left as shreds in the Iraqi sand, returned home to face bankruptcy court. I scowled. This one GI who'd laid carpet before the war and now without any hands had a tough go of making it. Our active combat soldiers' benefits, it seemed, didn't include long term disability. What the fuck?

I shut off CNN. Run the basics, Johnson. What did I know? Abdullah's ballistics on Omar's Lugers had ruled them out for killing Pembe. But Omar owned enough Lugers to outfit a Panzer division. What was one more squirreled away here or at his apartment? What's more, Karin carried her own Luger. I'd seen its hurting end. But I didn't feel up to tangle with Abdullah over their jurisdiction in a homicide investigation.

So I put my missing persons case front and center. Maybe I could rush to the Citadel and find Yagmur, ask her my questions on Mercedes, and beat it back here before dark when Omar came to get me. My door snicked to catch.

Stopping at the mouth to the corridor, I scoped out the lobby. Omar sat slumped over at his office desk. His even breathing was a sleeping man's. The revolving glass door kicked me out into the muggy afternoon. A burnt orange *taksi* popped up at my gesturing hand. "Citadel," I said, diving into the rear seat. "Step on it."

The beagle-faced cabbie chuckled. Nodding, he took out the gold toothpick with a leering gaze back at me. "Okie-dokie. You young. Get hootchie-kootchie."

He floored the gas pedal, lurching me back into the upholstery. "No, I'm just

off to see the Citadel."

"Sure, sure. I know. Okie-dokie, we go there."

We barreled through Ankara proper, and my backward glances didn't make Abdullah's plainclothes cop tailing us in another *taksi*. We invaded the Ulus sector at the center of Ankara and scooted up to the base of the Citadel's knoll. I paid him.

"I wait for you?"

But I didn't like him. "No, I'll be here a while. You better go on."

Pulling away, he tooted his horn. The alleyway brats scurrying out from nowhere clambered up to me.

"*Turist! Turist!*"

I bribed them each a dollar of Mrs. Mercedes' loot to disappear. That stunt caused more to come at me. Before I knew it, the sawed-off thieves had cleaned me out of thirty bucks. Then they left me alone. The strong oniony aroma from the flat, brown *pastirma* baking in the ovens smelled good.

At a switchback of shanties along the Citadel's lower ramparts I stopped to get better oriented. Stranded in this tumbledown ghetto left me nervous. My striding legs moved around the next corner. Three willowy ladies in faded jeans and peasant blouses sat on the low wood benches basking in the afternoon sun. Near my age, they looked to be sisters. They stopped chattering before the tallest one's smile dazzled me.

"Help you?" she asked in mechanical English.

"I hope so. I've looked everywhere for Yagmur. Do you know her?"

"Yagmur? Yagmur who?"

"Many Yagmurs live in Ulus."

"Our younger cousin is Yagmur."

"No, not her." I put on my best smile for them. "I want Sylvester's Yagmur."

"Oh Sylvester."

"We know Sylvester."

"Sure, everybody knows Sylvester."

I had to wait for a sleek, black Army helicopter's *chop-chop* to fly over us in the cloudless sky. The chopper looked like one of ours. "Sylvester's Yagmur interests me. To talk to her is all."

"But of course Yagmur lives with her father."

"Go to the top of the hill."

"Right before the Citadel gates, he keeps a small shop."

I tried to pay them, but they acted insulted. So I thanked them, took in a hearty breath, and tackled climbing the switchbacks leading up to the Citadel gates. A three-legged, russet dog gimped across the lane's uneven cobblestones. My legs stretched into longer strides as I wended my way between the knots of tourists taking it all in. Merchants set up in their rustic kiosks hawked everything from Turkish towels to zinc wash basins to bronze coffeegrinders.

The breezes wicked off the sweat beaded on my forehead. The late afternoon shadows obscured the right nook when I found it just before the Citadel gates. I ducked inside the nook. The crouched swarthy merchant's ball-peen hammer rained down on a copper picture plate large as a Frisbee.

The template under the copper picture plate was a flame-throwing dragon pitted against St. George. My "hello, there" didn't slow his hammer strokes. I poked him. His shoulder felt bony. Scowling at me, he set down the ball-peen hammer and stood up. He was a head shorter than me.

"I do much work." He spoke in a smoker's baritone.
"What?"
"Yagmur is what. Where is she?"
"Yagmur now live in streets. She bad girl."
"She knows Mercedes."
"Mercedes bad man. You his friend?"

That was a tricky question. Though having never met him, I didn't find much to like about him. "He's vanished. Gone. I've been paid to track him down. Yagmur was last seen with him at a hotel."

The merchant spat on the hard ground by the copper picture plate. "Yeah, fancy hotel. I know it. American hotel. You American?"

"No. Swiss. Neutral."

"Swiss. Really. You like, Swiss man?" A withered hand circled us advertising his coppersmith wares -- amulets, pots, plates -- displayed on the shelves and pegs. His entrepreneurial slyness had caught me flat-footed.

"Maybe. Sure I might like it." I nodded once at him. "But I buy more than what I see here. You'll give on Yagmur and this bad man. I want to hear everything you know."

"Deal, Swiss man."

I selected three copper amulets on a wall peg. I fished out the new wad of TLs, and the merchant snatched it away.

I waited as his wet thumb counted the bills. His greedy hand thrust out, and I gave him a helpless shrug, saying, "That's it, friend. Now you give."

"Yagmur a dancer. The fancy hotel man know where she go. Not me."

"The one-armed man? Phillip the concierge?"

The vendor nodded, taking up his ball-peen hammer. "Yeah. He bad man. Now go. I busy man."

The bastard had lied to me. He knew where to find her. I took one of the merchant's business cards out on display and scuttled down the switchbacks from the Citadel gates. This time no sawed-off beggars swarmed me. The three sisters still sitting on their low wood benches luxuriating in the sun saw me and waved. I thanked them with the three copper amulets. All smiles, they accepted my nominal gifts.

Chapter 27

The one-armed concierge Phillip at the Harrington had lied on knowing where to look up Yagmur. I'd no choice but to go back and brace him. Not until I'd asked for directions from a cyclist and circled the same block did I run into a major artery. Dried chewing gum jammed the *taksi* button I thumbed on the lamppost.

I picked up my gait. At the next busy intersection a sky blue Renault *taksi* spotted my frenetic waves and squealed over to me. Barking out "Harrington Hotell!", I dived in to land on its rear seat.

We funneled into Ankara's traffic stream. My cabbie -- mustachioed, five-four, gaunt as the Oz scarecrow -- pinned the gas pedal to the fire wall. We overtook and whipped by a red and yellow *otobüs*. The riders' lock-jawed faces pressed like wet, dark tulip petals to its row of windows. Steaming up on our right was one of Ankara's gasoline alleys.

Various car gurus had propped up their signs. *Oto Lastik* was the tire guy. *Oto Elektrik* fixed the electrical systems. *Oto Eksoz* did the muffler repairs. The sciatic nerve tingled in my leg. Did Yani warble his New Age on the *taksi*'s radio? Dr. Ralph had a better range, I thought. We snaked under the Bullwinkle Moose archway. A small bus they call a *dolmus* cut us off to veer down a side lane.

Growling, my cabbie flipped the *dolmus* driver the double bird. "Son of a bitch."

"You know English?"

"But of course." He acted dumbstruck that I'd ask him.

"Are you an American?"

"I am."

"What's your line of work?"

"Private detective. Frank Johnson."

"You must be at the casinos. Is the pay good?" The cabbie's eyes blazed their blue in the rearview mirror at me.

"No, I've been hired to locate an American businessman. He left his hotel two weeks ago, and nobody has seen him since then."

"Who?"

"His name is Sylvester Mercedes. Americans are always stepping in it. That's why I'm in Ankara."

"I see. You're a fixer. I'm half-American. My mom is from Milwaukee. A native of Kayseri, my dad met and married her on a business trip himself. I'm the souvenir of their Poconos honeymoon. Have you gone there?"

Recalling the violence to my big blowout with the Blue Cheer in the West Virginia mountains petrified my heart for a beat. "I'm not a big fan of the mountains right now."

My cabbie blitzed through a red light. I liked his ballsy style.

"And you are?" I asked him.

"Sorry, Frank. I'm Selami like the sandwich. Selami Hanim."

We rocketed by the monolithic broadcast studios to *Radyo Ev*, Turkey's state radio. Maybe I'd leave them my Dr. Ralph CD and launch the bluegrass music invasion of Turkey. We'd exported worse things.

"You may know of Kayseri's Whirling Dervishes."

My mouth dropped to reply but something flagged my eye. The marquee outside the *Büyük Tiyatro*, Ankara's state opera hall, advertised in both English and Turkish John Steinbeck's <u>Of Mice and Men</u> (*Fareler ve Insanlar*). I knew the play centered on two friends where small, clever George looked out for big, slow Lennie. I could number my friends on one hand: Old Man Maddox, Maynard Z. Thornburg, and Gerald Peyton. I missed them. Was Gerald in the wind right now?

"Have you seen this dervish?" I asked Selami.

"No. Have you seen Graceland?"

"No, but I take your point. Elvis ain't my cup. I'm a bluegrass music fan."

"Right: banjos, dobros, mandolins, and fiddles."

"Close enough."

"Good stuff. I love it."

I looked up at Selami. "No damn kidding."

Establishing a rapport with him, I warmed up to his good musical tastes. I was more than ready to bring in a Turkish assistant. Willing to take the calculated risk and trust him, I laid bare the details to my case, and what I needed. He listened with polite attentiveness.

"Here we are at the Harrington." He downshifted, and the *taksi* nosing to the curb stopped at the luxury hotel's portico. "Do I wait for you, Frank?"

"Just keep your meter running. I'll be right back."

"Take all the time you need. I'll mull over your offer."

"Does it grab you at all?"

"I've loved reading about you PIs since I was a kid."

"Then I hope you're here when I get back."

"You worry too much." He winked at me. "Go take care of your stuff."

I left his *taksi* and barged into the Harrington. At this hour its lobby was like meal time at the zoo. The well-heeled guests, all late risers, hectored the bellhops for service. A cart bulging with overstuffed, expensive luggage steaming over the carpet almost sideswiped me. I turned to avoid another cart bearing down on me.

My neck craned, but I didn't key on Phillip at the restaurant. The tawny blonde hostess, mussed and harried, dodged me before I could get out a word. After making it to the elevator, I got on, sank one floor, and plowed into a second mêlée. Grouchy players glutted the casino's smoke-choked entrance. Indignant elbows jabbed my ribs to block me from cutting in line.

"Wait your turn, sir," said the squat lady.

"What's all the excitement?"

"Didn't you hear? Socrates hit the bonanza jackpot."

The hatchet-faced man in front of us turned around. "Lucky bastard. I've played every day for the past eleven years and never hit the big one."

"Mustafa just came out and said they'll be tied up for the rest of the hour. All the winnings are counted and recorded. You won't see him until then."

"Have you seen Phillip the concierge?"

The hatchet-faced man jabbed his thumb to mean above us. "Try upstairs in the restaurant. Just watch your wallet around him."

Waving, I left them and ducked into the men's room. I peeled off three folds of TP and relieved my stuffy nose. My head cold was fizzling out. I skipped taking on the zoo upstairs in the lobby again to find Phillip. Leaving more frustrated than when I came, I conquered the stairs and exited through an emergency door. My trot was to the front of the Harrington.

Back at the Renault *taksi*, Selami dozed under a newspaper. My clutching the door handle to open it snapped him awake. He fumbled the newspaper and grabbed the steering wheel.

"Is everything okay, Frank?"

"It's a damn zoo in there."

"Well, I've decided to help you."

"That's some good news I can use." I had a thought. "If I was a gambling nut like Mercedes is, I'd stay here at the casino's hotel. But he always uses the Otel Pamuk, a real roach trap. I have to ask why. You got any ideas?"

"He prizes the anonymity."

"I agree he's flaky as hell. For openers, he has this open marriage. They each take their own lovers."

"Is that a bad thing?"

"Well, I'd say his footloose ways have finally caught

up with him."

Selami made a wry face. His Renault's squealing tires left burn marks as we shot off.

"Are handguns easy to buy in the city?"

He cut the steering wheel and skirted a pothole. "If you know the right people, yes. But I don't own one. Handguns are stupid."

Karin might know those right people to buy the Luger she'd waved in my face. Or maybe her Luger had come from Omar's private armory.

"Run us by what's left of the U.S. Embassy," I said.

Five minutes later as we swerved up to the embassy, I saw the debris was still getting trucked off to wherever they got rid of debris in Ankara. The lot was more cleared for the quick restoration to its former luster. Felix Braintree, his hands entwined behind his back, watched from the shadowy margins. Smug glee stamped his doughy face. I got out.

"Cool your heels. This guy might now tell me something."

"Make him answer your questions, Frank."

I closed the car door. The mix of dirt and char filled my nose. I could feel my rage at getting all the runaround had reached its combustion point. Felix hearing my scuffing tread faced me.

"Johnson, what brings you back? Lose your passport?"

"What did Mercedes tell you when he came?"

"I've got nothing to add to what I told you."

"Just lay it out again." My words sounded unstable, always dangerous.

"Set up an appointment. My Admin will schedule it."

His reply was just stupid enough to flip my hot switch. My last drop of good humor evaporated. My hasty scan didn't spot any Marines. Why guard a stinking pile of rubble? The embassy files had been carted away for safekeeping. The cleanup crews had finished their grunt labor for the day.

Both my hands blurred out. Felix's suit bunched up in my fists. I gave him a banging shove against the pikestaff fence. I heard the *taksi*'s engine crank. Selami gunned it up to screen me from any rubberneckers stopping on the street.

Felix didn't give in. His forearms jacked up and out to break my grip on his suit. His lucky jab speared my Adam's apple. I gagged. Tears wrung out from my eyes. A car door thudded shut.

"Stand back, Frank," I heard Selami say.

A short man, Selami packed a sweet, low center of gravity. I heard his left-right combo pummel Felix. Yelling, he grabbed his bloodied cauliflower for a nose.

"You had enough?"

"I'll bury you two," Felix managed to sputter behind his hands cupped over his injured face.

"In Turkey, that's not your call." Selami lowered his voice. "Just get Frank's questions, and I won't pound you like your embassy here." To drive his point home, he sank a left hook into Felix. Clutching at his guts, he doubled over. Arms folded, Selami backed off. "Ready to talk?"

Felix nodded, yes, he was.

"Good. Ask away, Frank."

"Did Mercedes come alone to the embassy?"

This time Felix wagged his head. "No."

He'd lied to me. "This is important," I said. "Who came with him?"

"He didn't introduce her. She was Turkish. He called her 'his belly dancer'."

"Yagmur," I said.

"I don't know. She never said a word."

Selami tugged at my elbow. "Come on, we'll find her."

Leaving Felix to take care of his busted nose and embassy, we left in Selami's *taksi*.

"I was holding my own back there," I said. "Why did you help me?"

His thumb pad slicked down his bushy, jet mustache that Atatürk had made fashionable in his nation. "Simple, Frank. I couldn't let you get hurt. You haven't paid me yet."

"Getting paid is important." I nodded. "We'll get along just great."

Chapter 28

Selami smiled his appreciation at our server. "I asked her to put on national Turkish TV. It gives the best news coverage."

Our server struck a tall, curvy figure in her snug designer jeans and peasant blouse. Sighing in annoyance, she aimed the remote and surfed to NTV Turkey. The beetle-browed announcer was reporting the Turkish authorities had captured thirteen Islamic militants. Their bomb-making materials had also been seized. They had known ties to al-Qaida active inside of war-torn Iraq. The beetle-browed announcer didn't make a link to the embassy bombing, but I sure as hell did. Selami scowled a little, but he offered no comment, good or bad, on the war.

"Sorry but I can't pay you much, Selami."

"No problem. I also need the action. I go soft and lazy stuck driving a *taksi* twelve hours a day."

"Your cut comes out of my piece. Twenty-five, maybe thirty dollars per diem is my best offer. Still interested?"

"Shake, partner."

We did.

He nodded at me. "Belly dancers like Yagmur work in the floor shows to entertain the tourists. Most dancers I've seen should become dentists, but the show must go on. The Germans and Englishmen use the beach resorts while the French and Dutch go to Cappadocia. But they all clamor for the belly dancers."

That exotic name -- Cappadocia -- had cropped up

again. "Do you mean the mole people? The underground cities of the troglodytes?"

"There's nothing on earth like it, Frank. Cappadocia is magnificent."

"I'm a little tied up here to go down there."

The ice chips rattled in my water glass. Our server flirting with a swarthy man several tables away ignored my hope to get a refill.

"I'd be a bad host if I didn't show you Cappadocia."

"Thanks but after I round up Mercedes, I better get back home. I left a bunch of stuff hanging out."

"But that might not be for some time. You'll need a break. Think it over before you decide. I'd love an excuse to go visit my family. I've only seen my niece's baby pictures in their emails."

Our indifferent server pocketing her latest tip from the swarthy man sauntered by our table. Selami gestured his fingers at her. "My friend is bone dry," he said. "More water, Frank?"

"No, I'm okay now, thanks."

"Good, good. He's fine. You may leave us. We're talking." She slapped down our check. Her bossy manner reminded me of my ex. I paid her, minus any tip, from my stash. She left us with an acerbic look.

"Where are you staying, Frank?"

"I'm at the Otel Pamuk."

"Oh . . . you might rethink that. It's a firetrap."

"But it's centrally located. Taking a spin out to the Citadel might be worthwhile."

We left the restaurant and headed to the side lane where his *taksi* waited.

"The Citadel you say?" Selami canted his eyebrows at me.

"Yagmur's father makes copper picture plates in a kiosk by the Citadel gates. I've spoken to him. We'll need her photo or physical description, not so easy to do since he's disowned her for her risqué lifestyle."

"Then here's a better idea. Ask Omar. He knows the right contacts for the performers in the floor shows."

We maneuvered through the narrow streets to an open-air bazaar. My head cold better, I'd skip stopping at the spice market. Merchants in motley head garb and pointy slippers toked on their water pipes more for pretense than pleasure, I suspected. They sold everything in their cluttered stalls. I saw candlesticks, braziers, and a musical instrument resembling a mandolin they call a *saz*.

"Junk." Selami waved at the products in the merchants' stalls. "The foolish tourists come to part with their cash for junk."

"Aw, let them have their fun. It's only money, and they're on holiday."

"See those statuettes that old lady is holding?" Selami tipped his chin to guide my eyes out the car window. "She buys them from China and soaks them in mineral water to give them that mossy green. Why? Greed. Doctoring the statuettes to be antiques puts more cash in her purse."

"Her buyers going away with their treasures happy will never be the wiser."

"She has no shame." He jammed on the brakes. After rolling down his car window, he yelled in guttural Turkish at her. Her bronze, leathery face, seamed as a sandlot hardball, didn't flinch. In fact, she may've smiled a little.

"Do you feel better?" I asked as we moved on.

"I do. She's dishonest. I told her she's no better than a crook. I am punishing her."

"She acts as if she could care less."

"I know. She always does." He laughed. "By the way, the old lady is my aunt. She loves it."

Wednesday's deepening shadows engulfed us braking in front of the Otel Pamuk. The silhouettes moved behind the illuminated lobby windows. The neon tubes outlining the revolving glass door gleamed orange. The driver of a *taksi* scooting off from the nearby cabstand may've been Mr. Ahmet. Finding no parking slots forced us to U-turn at the end of the block. A second driveby didn't better our luck.

Selami stopped. "We'll double park here."

"Omar will throw a duck fit over my not working security tonight."

"I'll speak to him in Turkish. Speaking the same language is better."

"All I ask is don't blow it."

We emerged from the *taksi,* and Selami blew through the revolving glass door, sweeping me in behind him. At the front desk, I saw inside Omar's office the hotel safe without my passport. Abdullah still had it. Wiping his hands on a dish towel, Omar bustled through the batwing doors and waved at us.

"Hello Frank and Selami."

"Mercedes likes a lady named Yagmur. She belly dances in the floor shows," I told him.

"She doesn't at the Otel Pamuk. No sir, I don't go in for that sort of thing."

"That's a smooth lie," said Selami. "You're only sneakier than the other hotels. Ladies go up to the paying gentlemen's rooms. Your palm gets tickled. Before you start up with the denials, I'll warn you my *taksi* drops off the ladies at your front door."

Omar glared at Selami. "So we cater to a few gentlemen's wants. But I keep it under wraps. I've had no hassles with our police or complaints from my guests. Everybody wins."

"Your soul is unblemished," said Selami before lapsing into Turkish. They traded eye rolls and hand chops with their snappy dialogue as I waited.

"Omar knows your Yagmur, after all," Selami told me.

"But I'd no idea she's with Mr. Mercedes. She's never danced or come to the Otel Pamuk."

I knew from my MP days prostitution in Turkey was legal but outlawed for outsiders like the American servicemen I used to go round up. State-run brothels offered licensed prostitutes in "Public Houses" or *Genelevs*, but using a call girl service was frowned upon. On the other hand, Omar might grease a palm. Police graft here wasn't any different than in the States. I didn't throw out any bribe accusation just yet.

"Mercedes must reserve them a day room at the Harrington for the casino rates," I said. "Eyewitnesses confirm he came in with Yagmur. Later, he left his passport at the casino door, but he went in alone. The casino is taboo for Yagmur, but she's the key to my tracking down Mercedes."

Selami glowered at Omar. "Tell us where she is. Now."

"The last I heard she lives with her father somewhere by the Citadel gates."

"I talked to her father," I said. "He's disowned her. She doesn't live there anymore."

Omar shrugged. "He must have some idea where to find her. What father stops loving his daughter?"

"We can try reaching out to him again," I said.

Back to smiling, Selami glanced at Omar and then at the bar. "Is your Efes cold?"

"And it's free," said the solicitous Omar.

"Go ahead, guys." I made for the corridor. "Meantime I'll go use my phone."

But my room was probably bugged again, and I didn't have the time to sweep it. After clearing the corridor's corner, I found each room door before mine locked. Picking a lock wasn't my forte. It took the years of practice, and I didn't have patience. A hooligan bar or a slot-head screwdriver was my tool of choice. Easier still was to turn the doorknob that some naive hotel guest had left unlocked. I sidled into the room.

The guest's tweed suitcase spilled out its sloppy contents -- socks, belts, T-shirts -- over the foot of the bed. A wrinkled suit hung in the closet. Keeping an eye on the door, I used the phone on the nightstand. I pecked in the numbers, screwed it up, and slowing down, tried again. Mrs. Mercedes jumped on my second ring.

"You finally deign to contact me. Well, give me a status."

"Does Mercedes bring up his Turkish lady friends?"

"His liaisons are his private affair and vice versa."

"I'll record that as a no. Do you know a Yagmur?"

"My chihuahua is named Dagmar. Is this Yagmur another dog?"

"Another no, I'd say. Okay, has Mercedes' duffel made it home yet?"

"I didn't pay extra to expedite the shipment. His crap probably lies in the cargo hold of a Venezuelan tramp steamer. But it's mine, and I want it back. Now it's my turn. You haven't returned my calls. Why?"

"No time. Did Mercedes report his passport missing to the U.S. Consulate?"

"His passport is lost? Find it. Then find him."

"Finding a lost man takes time."

"I've run out of time. Do I need to come over there?"

Her radical idea left my head to swim. "I sense a breakthrough is very near."

"Excellent. So keep me better appraised of it."

Click.

The receiver whined like a gnat's wing in my ear. I racked the handset. I was back to sitting on the bubble of a who-gives-a-fuck moment. How many rich ladies' doormat had I played? Why did the batty ones glom to me? It was tougher to force a rich client to pay up. Too many freeloaders had never coughed up a nickel. Wasn't that how they kept all their money? Gatlin had recouped some of my lost revenue. On that upbeat note, I raised him at his Middleburg office.

"Are you with her?"

"No, and I getting fed up with you criticizing us."

"Where are your ethics, Counselor?"

He snorted. "My ethics are fine."

"All right, truce then. Can you check Mercedes' bank accounts and credit cards for any activity in the last two weeks since he disappeared?"

"Good idea. I'll talk to Lois."

"She says she has no access to his financial records. Better tap your online sources."

"If it helps, I'll get right on it."

"I need something over here."

"This case is harder than I thought it'd be."

I looked up at a scratching noise. "Somebody's at the door. I gotta go."

After his awkward rattles fiddling with the lock, Joel Nashwinter opened the door and hobbled into the room. He kicked the door shut and flipped the key to the ashtray on the bureau top. The key rimmed out and flew to the carpet. At three paces, he blinked at me standing between the two beds.

"Johnson? Why are you in my room?"

"Yours?" I snapped back my head in disbelief. "I thought you stayed upstairs. You've busted into my crib."

"The crapper backed up in it, so I moved down. This is one-four-three." He stalked over, stooped to retrieve his key, and pointed to the number stamped in its copper tag. "How can we both have the same key to the same room?"

"Oh. Mine's one-four-eight. I misread it. Sorry. I just pushed on the door and came inside."

"Well, beat it. Or else I'll beat you."

"Speaking of fights, I heard Mercedes and you got into a jawing match near the kitchen. What was that about?"

"He shot off his big mouth, and I almost decked him which I feel like doing now."

"If I sneezed, you'd fall over."

"I've had few snorts, but that's my business, ain't it? Yours is to scram before I blow my stack at you."

Both his hands wrapped into fists, and a vein popped up from his forehead. I wanted to laugh as I sidestepped him. His glare followed me out the door. After double-timing it to the lobby, I saw Omar and Selami talking over at the bar. They used Turkish.

Spotting me, Selami hand gestured to the barstool by him. Omar's mirror behind the bar caught a bewildered, scruffy shamus I didn't recognize. He looked as if he'd scrounged in the cargo hold of Venezuelan tramp steamer for too long. Selami addressed this same man in the mirror.

"Omar says Yagmur sees Mercedes at the Harrington."

"Omar has always known this, and he's been blowing smoke at me." I gave him a surly look fed by my angry frustrations.

"Frank, let's move on and do some good here," said Selami.

Nodding, I revamped the timeline. "We know Mercedes goes up to the Harrington on Saturday afternoon. He rendezvouses with Yagmur. Then alone, he takes the elevator down to the casino. But that still leaves us with her. Didn't the maids spot her stealing out?"

"She knows how to slip around easily enough," said Selami.

"Who set up their meeting?" Just then Omar got distracted mopping a towel over the bartop. I went on. "Who could arrange such a meeting?"

"Omar." Selami glared at him. "Did you call Yagmur for Mr. Mercedes?"

He quit his bartop ministrations. "All right, yes, I called her. She gave me her latest number. It's safer that way."

"Isn't Phillip at the Harrington her pimp?" I asked.

"Cutting out the middle man is cheaper. Anyway I relayed Mr. Mercedes' wishes. He's generous. Yagmur cheered her luck. She's always happy to make some money."

"Then you tack on your fee," said Selami.

Omar lowered his eyelids, an admission of guilt. "The Otel Pamuk is always a business, Selami, just like your driving a *taksi* is."

I horned in. "Where's Yagmur staying now?"

A know-nothing shrug was Omar's response. "If her father kicked her out, for all I know she lives in the streets."

"She's now out on the streets in Ulus? But where do I go look there?"

Selami nodded at me. "I know just the place."

CHAPTER 29

A crescent moon the color of taffy beamed in the Wednesday night sky over Ulus. Selami and I sat on our stakeout. The most effective stakeouts seldom last over two hours, and we were fast approaching that deadline.

Selami had moored his *taksi* moored on the murky side of the street. We hunkered down, knees jammed into the dashboard. I hoped we didn't get carjacked or mugged. Just down the block, a security lamp sprayed its brilliance down on a red door. Behind it, a brothel did a lucrative flesh trade, according to Selami.

"Are you sure this is the right place?"

"I'm here all the time letting off johns."

"Tonight is a slow one."

"Patience, Frank."

"They take in homeless girls?"

"They all use young girls. Didn't you use one in your wild days?"

"My job was to steer our GIs away from the cat-houses."

"You should know I used Omar's phone."

"What for?"

"The way I figure it is Mr. Mercedes had to use a *taksi*. So I called and put out the word. A cabbie might know who picked him up and where they went."

"Good show. Thanks."

A cat scampering off a trash can made us flinch. The coppery fog settling in haloed the security lamp. Selami chomped on a wad of gum. This hurry up and wait frayed my nerves. I gnawed on a torn thumbnail.

"You're all-sold Yagmur will be there?"

Squirming, he groped for a pack of cigarettes on the dashboard, then thought better of it. We couldn't relax. "Left on the streets, she knows this is her last haven."

"Only the Cro-Magnon bouncer has showed."

"First the johns get fortified on liquid courage. Any sleazy bar will do. Don't get in an uproar. They'll come as sure as the steel filings are drawn to a magnet."

"Your *taksi* is a good camouflage vehicle. I see them everywhere."

Back at home the teal or champagne, nondescript four doors blended in the best. I liked to rent one to use on my stakeouts if my clients could afford it.

"I won't be a *taksi* driver much longer. Next month I start my new job as a tech writer in Istanbul. My command of English can give me a bigger pay check."

"Your new job sounds boring to me."

He nodded. "But the hours are better than a *taksi* driver's."

"An older man's body isn't up for the night work."

"I just saw a john go up and rap on the red door. It's time, Frank. Do you know your play?"

"We've gone through it enough. At the red door I knock ~~ "

"No, Frank! Rap three times like this." He demonstrated the signal on the dashboard. "The bouncer will greet you. Tell him a friend sent you. He'll ask what you want. Say you'd like tonight's Turkish Delight. That's important: Turkish Delight. Are you with me?"

My nod was slight. "Turkish Delight. It's like a code word. Next I go into the room with the blacked-out windows. Three or more girls will file out. I look them over to spot Yagmur."

"No, Frank. Use your head. First you pay the madam. Keep in mind this is a business deal. You have to pay to use a service they offer."

I repeated it. "First I pay the madam. Do I tip her?"

He wagged his head. "No, only tip the prostitute. Now if Yagmur isn't in that lineup, say you prefer something else. But be polite. This is their show. Do this until Yagmur comes out on the stage.

"Then pay what they ask. No dickering. This is no time to be stingy. Hear me, Frank? Good. Once you're alone with Yagmur, ask her where Mr. Mercedes is. Bribe her to stay quiet. Questions?"

"What if my saying no angers the madam or bouncer?"

"If you get jammed up, flash me the high sign."

"That's a problem if I'm knocked out."

"If it all runs to shit, I'll know. Trust me."

"Did you bring a Luger?"

"No Luger, Frank. Handguns are stupid."

"One last thing. How long do I pay for Yagmur?"

Turning thoughtful, he ran his tongue across his teeth. "No less than ten minutes but no more than a half-hour. Talk fast. Try to muffle your voice. Remember, the walls have ears."

"Sure, the bouncer likes to monitor the johns," I said, undoing the door latch.

"Off you go. I'll fly in orbit around the brothel."

"Keep your radar on red alert," I said, outside the *taksi*.

He nodded at me. "You'll do great."

I eased shut the car door. My slapping footfall across the tarmac echoed off the smut pit's façade. The coppery fog licked my face as I sized up the three stories. Pinkish light guttered at the window edges. The madam had tugged down her blinds. Burglar bars guarded the windows. Caged behind steel bars gave me the willies.

The damn cat screamed by my ankles, almost tripping me. My heart locked in mid-pulse, but my feet went on. The red door was heavy-gauge sheet metal riveted together.

Closer up, it was scabrous and blood-red like in a Poe tale. Scanning up and down the lane, I noted Selami had bugged out. I was on my own. My three raps were his code. Then just quiet came. "Fuck." Sweating droplets of blood, I tried the code again.

Swinging outward, the red door, whining on its hinges, brushed me back. My heart plunged. The interior light had flooded a face I recognized. The bouncer was Hans. We'd met in the atrium at the Harrington. My nostrils flared -- he still hadn't bathed.

"Yeah?"

Hanging back in the street shadows, I muttered.

"A friend sent me."

"So."

"Turkish Delight?"

"Huh?"

"Turkish Delight!"

"Yeah, okay." Now on the same script, he jerked his meaty head. I saw the new stitches from my chopping him on the chin. "Follow me."

My chin tucked low, and my eyes downcast, I scooted by him. The corridor I used was short. The whiff of burnt incense I got was like attending Easter Mass.

"Go right."

I cornered at the first doorway.

"Wait here." He left me.

Where was I? A twenty-watt light bulb swaying from the low ceiling gave off a red incandescence. My eyes adjusted. The windows looked blotted out. That checked. The air redolent with incense made me sneeze. My stare picked out the boxy shapes to a sofa behind me and a stage in front of me. That also checked. I wondered if I'd run into Phillip. Hearing a cloddish tread, I faced the doorway.

"Don't I know you?"

Hans's question put me in brain freeze until the hot blood hammering through my ears thawed out my thoughts.

"Yeah, I do," he went on.

"Hey, we do this now, or I'm gone."

My abrupt impatience jolted Hans back on the right script. "Wait here."

"Not for very long I won't."

His tromp faded down the corridor. My ears picked up their play. The traffic thrummed by on the street. I hoped one was Selami in his *taksi*. My hand raised to my eyes was skeletal. Then a lady above me screamed like a stuck banshee. I flinched in my skin.

My bones melted inside me. Right then I felt that tired. Tired of roaching around in Ankara. Tired of rich drama queens for clients. Tired of a glory-hound lawyer for a boss. Tired of the tax man's hassles. Dark urges hit me. I'd torch this joint. I'd break some bones. I'd get home. But I stayed rooted. Why? Because I had to get paid.

Snick.

The harsh lights flared on overhead. My cowering eyes greeted the small, raised stage. Wrinkly, green baize carpeted it. A row of cup lamps mounted across the stage bottom streamed up light on the folds to the black velveteen curtains. Elevator music crackled and played on the Bose speakers bracketing the stage. Finger-cymbals clacked, a cue.

Hans tramped into view, but my eyes were glued to the stage. Three ladies -- girls, really -- trooped out, two from stage left and one at my right. Their pimply flesh and zombie eyes horrified me. All wore Dutch boy coifs but little else. I could count their ribs. Their shoulders dipped as if inviting and provocative, but it was more sad and heartbreaking.

"Sir, you like?"

I half-turned. The small, stocky madam wore a beige suit with a narrow, red necktie. Shrewd malice toughened her bulldog features. She was Mrs. Hans. A laugh bubbled low in my gut, but I didn't crack a smile or wise. Her nod channeled my sight to the playmates she'd trotted out for rent.

"Sir, you like?"

"Nope, sorry, not for me." I tilted my head at her. "An older lady?"

"A most wise decision."

Mrs. Hans clacked her finger-cymbals. As soon as the three ladies had filed offstage, a second trio waiting in the wings skulked over the green baize. At first sight I knew they were veteran streetwalkers.

Pretending to deliberate, I stalled over a problem. Having never met Yagmur, it was hard to pick her out. Maybe she'd vamped in the first chorus line.

"You see, my friend knows this special girl. She's Yagmur, and she sounds nice."

The tallest girl, the slim beauty in the middle, skewered me with her eyes. "Who's this damn friend of yours?"

"Yagmur!" Mrs. Hans lashed out. "Enough. Silence."

Yagmur flicked a hand at us. "Who's your friend? Who are you?"

Mrs. Hans was sharper. "Quiet, Yagmur. Referrals are okay."

"Call me Frank. Sylvester Mercedes is my friend." Her lips tweaking to smile encouraged me. "He spoke highly of you."

"Sylvester. I know him, sure."

"We go back a ways in the States. Have you known him long?"

"Oh my yes."

Her catlike pounce off the stage released her sisters to dart behind the black velveteen curtains. With the deal closed, Mrs. Hans beamed on us.

"When he flies in, we visit."

"Well, if you're not busy, I'd like to spend some time with you." Acting confused, I scratched my chin. "Do I pay now or afterward?"

Mrs. Hans stated a fee. Too steep but I grinned like an eager john and anted up. My U.S. dead presidents, not TLs, sweetened the deal.

"Enjoy," said Mrs. Hans.

Yagmur wrapped an afghan around her bare shoulders. "Quick, through here, Frank."

I edged by Hans. He was straining to peg my face to our dust-up in the Harrington's atrium. I dogged Yagmur's heels. The staircase we mounted was shoulder-width and grungy with spent Trojans, hypo syringes, and cigar butts discarded on the steps.

This was nasty. I sweated. My shirt matted to my armpits. At my say-so, we grabbed a breather at the landing. Leaning against the banister, I strained to see if Hans followed us. No shadows slipped up. We scaled the stairs as she mewed over her shoulder.

"Okay, Frank, you bought up thirty minutes. Using the stairs took five. That leaves you with twenty-five. What did you have in mind for tonight?"

"Just to ask you about Sylvester."

"Are you messing with me?"

"Not at all. He vanished the Sunday morning after you two met at the Harrington."

She halted in her crib's doorway. "Huh? I've told nobody about the Harrington."

"Look, I'll come clean. His wife paid me to find him. I got a lead. That's why I came tonight."

"She paid you? Why? Who are you?" Yagmur gave me a cold glare. If I flunked her litmus test, I knew the meat-eater Hans slobbered below us. My wallet came out.

"I'm a private eye. Here's my license."

She gazed down at it. "I see now. All right, come in." Her tense body english relaxed. I ducked into her crib and sat on the end of a narrow bed. She hit a button, and brightness raped my blinking eyes. I'd rotted in bigger jail cells. "Sylvester is missing?"

"Two Sundays ago, he left the Otel Pamuk. From there, his trail turns into vapor. Did he stop by here?"

"Not on Sunday. Doesn't he go to church?"

"I haven't checked that," I said, hiding my disappointment. Somehow I couldn't get with Mercedes' expression of piety.

"Sylvester is married?"

"To Lois Mercedes. They live in Middleburg, Virginia. You didn't know?"

"I suspected. But Lois doesn't love him. I do. He's special. Generous and kind." She unhooked a poplin robe off the door and sheathed her potent nudity. The mental Polaroid of her stayed burned on my retinas. "We'll leave this pig sty and go live the good life. I'll return to London, this time not to work as a nanny, but I'll hire my own."

She didn't miss the doubts gouging my brow.

"Do you use the Otel Pamuk?"

She blurted out a laugh. "That dump? Never. Omar is a jerk. Sylvester is all class. We're always at the Harrington's suite. Why not? He has money to burn. Phillip arranges it."

"Did Sylvester act distracted or seem anxious the last time you saw him?"

"Yes." She rebelted the poplin robe. "His shaky hands sloshed his coffee. He turned pale as a ghost. I almost got up the nerve to ask him what was wrong, but I chickened out."

"He never dropped a hint or let something slip?"

"He isn't the chatty type."

"Something frightened him?"

"It was more like something excited him."

A scream ripped out below us, shivering the floorboards. I put it with a lady's orgiastic glee, no doubt hyped for her john's vanity.

Yagmur smiled at my jumpy nerves. "You get used to it."

"Doubtful. I'm roasting like a peanut in here."

My wrist swiped a film of sweat off my brow. The ventilation duct above us spewed down a flush of hot air on us. Stretching on tiptoe, I reached up and flipped the switch to shut off the vent's flap.

"Ouch!"

The prick in my right thigh felt like a hornet's sting -- then, *poof,* nothing.

Chapter 30

Confusion tore away from my eyes, and I squinted up into nothing but the inky darkness spilling down on my eyes. Several blinks didn't clear it up. The stinger jab in my thigh replayed and then the span of blankness until now.

"Fuck." My voice rasped out. My tongue was glued to my teeth. "Where am I? What time is it?"

The concrete floor under my hands felt gritty as if covered by sand. My hands were hogtied. The bedpan odor lay rank in my nostrils. I ached all over as if I'd been tossed under a zamboni or something big. I thrashed my ankles, but they were also bound. Spasms of terror raked over me. But my slower breaths and willpower stuffed the panic attack.

"You're okay?" The lilt was Yagmur's. That surprised me. She was off to my right.

"Zonked out, but I'll live."

"We're prisoners."

"The last thing I recall was a hornet's sting in my leg."

"Hans stabbed you with a dope syringe."

"What sort of dope?"

"The sort that zonks you out. Then they tied us up."

"Me, yeah okay. But why you?"

"Phillip and Hans are pissed I met Sylvester at the Harrington. Gypping your pimp is a bad idea." I recalled it'd been Omar who'd arranged their last rendezvous. "Hans overheard us talking in my room."

Selami's warning the walls have ears came back to me but too late. "Where are we?"

"They tossed us into the cellar."

"Shit." I hated such a tight, dark place and pictured how the troglodytes had gutted it out cramped together in their catacombs. "What comes next?" I realized it'd been a stupid question.

"Nothing good. My wrists and ankles are lashed together."

"Mine, too. Can you wiggle like a worm?"

"I'll try . . . okay, a little bit. Careful about the walls."

"We'll risk it. Otherwise we're worm food."

"Keep talking so I can worm over to you."

"Christ, could it get any darker?" Shaping thoughts, then saying them took a major effort. My head throbbed. Dope mixed with fear did a number on me.

"I'm behind you. Now what?"

"Gimme a second, will you?" After pausing to clear away the moss upstairs, I asked her, "Any slack in your wrists? Try it."

Her scuffle on the concrete floor was a spit away from me. "The knots are too tight."

"Spiffy. Feet?"

She stirred further down. "Same way, I'm afraid."

"Damn. Can we untie each others knots?"

"I can't feel my fingers. They're too numb."

"Same here. Any other entrances?"

"The hatchway door opens to the rear alleyway. From my window I watch Hans go out for a smoke there. The door is padlocked."

"Ah, padlocks can be busted. A tire iron will crack it."

"Do you have a tire iron?"

Her sardonic tone grated on me, but it also crystallized an insight. "My guy is in his *taksi*."

Even in the dark I could see her roll her eyes. I caught

her dry sigh. "He must've gone home."

"No, he hasn't gotten paid."

"Then Hans took out your guy."

"Don't think so. My guy is smarter than Hans." I kicked my feet a few times. My ankle bonds loosened by an inch. Progress, I thrilled. "I'm snaking to that hatchway door. Which way?"

"Go straight behind me, I think."

Like a sidewinder, I scrabbled my way over the gritty concrete and bumped into a wall. I coughed on the raised dust and knocked along the wall until I hit the steps she'd recalled.

By tilting my head and propelling my feet now like a caterpillar, I squiggled up three steps to crest the top one, situating me inches from the hatchway door -- and freedom.

My chest heaved to gulp in air through my mouth to my lungs. Sweat pasted my crusty shirt to my skin. Vertigo confused me. But getting us out of this pesthole was job one.

After squirming to wedge flat out on the top step, my shoe tip moved just enough to thud into the hatchway door. This went on until I my head felt like an ice pick had been driven through my ear.

Pant. Thud. Pant. Thud. Pant . . .

"Frank!" Her sharp voice broke my routine. "Your guy is out there. Hear his return knock?"

She was right. Three raps came from the other side. Selami. Gritting my teeth, I responded with a thud.

"Well . . . Frank?"

"He knows it's us. It shouldn't be long."

"Does he work fast?"

Rattling the hatchway door answered her. I hollered out instructions. "Crack the padlock. Use a tire iron."

"Okay," I heard shouted through the hatchway door. Then the silence grew ominous.

"He's gone to get the tire iron," I said.

"Meantime I'll snake over to you."

"God, it reeks like a stockyard."

"I hope they're no corpses." She sniffed. "Like ours."

She scraped over the concrete floor, crawling to reach the steps. Lighter framed, she was also quicker.

"How did you get into this rotten business?" I asked her.

"First I was an exotic dancer. Phillip knew ways to get more cash. I was young. Naive. Foolish."

I digested that part. "When we break out, I'd say find a new trade."

"That's my plan. Sylvester and I will get out of Turkey."

"Forget Sylvester. He's just a rich bum."

She screamed at me. "You don't know him. I do."

"Wrong. I'm a detective. I know he screws around. I know he runs out on people. I know he lies. He's a bum."

She shut up, stewing in anger. I didn't care. We ignored each other and waited on Selami. Soon hammering punished our ears. Hans and Phillip had to be deaf. Selami hacked the padlock from different angles. They also used a cheap padlock. His final flurry cracked this one apart.

He scraped away the bracing bar and winged out the hatchway doors. The fresh, cool night air plunged in, chilling my face. A thin cone of light spilled down into our eyes.

"Frank, how did you manage to . . . oh, never mind. They used rope. Good, my knife can cut through that."

"Did Hans hear you?" asked Yagmur as Selami freed her first.

"Who?"

"The big ape guarding the door," I said.

"Oh, him." Selami brandished the tire iron in his fist. "He fell asleep in his chair. The butch lady also took a little nap."

I grinned a little. Payback felt sweet. Selami slit off my rope bonds. Grateful, I rubbed my wrists and ankles.

Getting the blood moving gave back their feeling. Yagmur also stood up on wobbly pins. Slanting over the flashlight beam, I saw she wore mechanic's overalls. Hans's dope still in my system left me groggy.

"Do you have a lighter on you?" I asked Selami.

He fished out a Zippo and handed it to me. "I don't have any smokes, Frank. But we better scram."

I strummed up the Zippo's flame. Fire was good. Fire burned. Fire purged. I headed down the steps through hatchway doors. A sharp tug came on my shirt.

"What the fuck are you doing?" asked Selami.

"I'm torching this joint."

"You can't be serious."

"Just find me some tinder, and it's burn, baby burn."

Yagmur gripped to my forearm. "That will bring the police."

"You're acting goofy," said Selami.

He was right. I snuffed the Zippo. Their heads were screwed on straighter and tighter than mine crazed by the dope.

Selami took charge. "My *taksi* is parked one block over."

Yagmur gave a thumbs up. "We'll make it."

Our hike to his *taksi* involved a lot of leaning on him, two rests, and a few curses. Once buckled in, he put the *taksi* in gear, and we sped off. He did a flyby of the brothel, our former prison. We saw the lights blazed in every barred window on all three floors.

Our late night jailbreak had stirred a general alarm. The spectacle of Hans I saw slumped over unconscious in his chair by the red door tickled me. Selami joined in my laughter, but Yagmur frowned at us as if we'd slipped a few gears.

Chapter 31

The red neon said: *Otel Pamuk*, and we trooped into the lobby. Selami chose to crash on his prayer mat in my room over going home to face his cranky, half-asleep wife. At the front desk, I caught myself staring at Karin's breasts and wondering which one had gone under the scalpel. What the fuck is wrong with you? I next thought.

"Did you bring any bags?" asked Karin in a frosty tone. She looked at Yagmur.

I cut in. "We'll bring in her bags from the *taksi* first thing tomorrow."

Nodding, Selami agreed. "Yes."

The bald-face lie left everybody but Karin hiding their smiles. With a shy wave, Yagmur left us and clanked up in the cage elevator to her new quarters.

Selami and I struck out over the lobby, but Karin's angry "halt" stopped us. After I explained our sleeping plans, she charged me for a double room. I didn't like it, but Selami shrugged: "Fair is fair." So I paid her, and we took the corridor. I undid my door lock and flipped on my room's light before Selami stretched out on his prayer mat.

I decked out on my swayback bed and waited, my nerve endings lit up like burning fuses but getting any sleep was impossible. I leaned over and told Selami. He was also too stoked. We needed to get out and unwind.

"Have you gone to the *Kocatepe Camii*? It's our most splendid mosque."

"I made it halfway there, but police business intervened."

"We should go now."

"Hans might be on the prowl."

"Relax, Frank. Hans isn't on the prowl for a good while. Trust me."

That was all I needed to hear. "Lead on."

Karin waiting in ambush stepped out from behind the front desk. She had on that fuzzy, pink shawl and, as always, looked hot.

"I should warn you that Detective Abdullah visited here earlier." She smiled in a catty way. "Naturally I told him the truth when he asked me where you'd gone. I'd no idea. My answer didn't leave him any too happy."

I dealt Selami a wary look. "We don't want the police crawling up our backs."

Selami waved her off. "We're always in his city. He knows that."

Karin shifted the fuzzy, pink shawl on her shoulders. "Suit yourselves. It your funerals, not mine."

The revolving glass door spun us into the hushed evening. I cut for the parked *taksi*, but another tug came at my shirt.

"It's faster to walk it," said Selami.

We struck off headed north. Ten minutes of brisk walking through the dim streets put us at a breathtaking scene. The klieg lights gleamed off the mosque's azure tilework. The main dome was a giant armadillo's shell spiked by a half-dozen minarets. Even now a few ticks before midnight, the worshippers thronged under the high-arched doors. Selami pointed, and we removed our shoes and stashed them in the provided cubbyholes.

"What if our shoes get stolen?"

He shrugged. "So. We'll buy new pairs. Ankara has lots of shoes."

I sock-footed it, following Selami through the carved walnut doors. He steered us to walk in the brighter lights. The mosque's grand interior outmatched its exterior. Lead crystal chandeliers dangled from the high ceilings. Marble elephant-foot pillars supported the inner domes. I saw no pews. Only Turkish carpets covered the shiny granite floor.

A prayerful murmur droned from a knot of bearded men kneeling on their prayer mats. We skirted them. A Caucasian tourist -- a lank man twice my age wearing a straw hat -- took flash photos of the ornate ceiling. Two uniformed officials marched over and referred him to a sign. Apologizing, he put away his camera.

"Amazing, eh, Frank?"

I nodded. "Perfect description."

The panhandler with the bathroom scales had talked to Mercedes in his sightseeing travels. Had he also wandered over to this grand mosque? I persuaded Selami to show Mercedes' photo to the two guards. He quizzed them in Turkish. They gave him grunts and surly looks. He returned my photo. Mercedes hadn't made it this way.

"Do you believe in the power of prayer, Frank?"

"I've said a few in my life. What do we pray for?"

"Your lost man's safe return."

"Omar tells me Mercedes is playing hooky. Wait long enough, and he'll turn up on his own when he's ready."

"Don't listen to Omar. He's a big fool."

"He repeated a story on the Khoja who's crazy like a fox. He thinks Mercedes is like that."

Selami scoffed. "The Khoja stories are fairy tales you tell the kids before bedtime."

"Suppose Omar has it right?"

"Is it Mercedes' habit to drop out of sight?"

"His wife hasn't mentioned a history of it, but she describes him as 'clandestine'."

"It doesn't matter. We'll find him and get our money."

"That's the only reason I'm sticking with it."

We left *Kocatepe Camii* in our own shoes and hurried back. This time the Otel Pamuk looked more inviting and restful. We bedded down again in my room and fell straight asleep.

※

The next morning -- it was Thursday already -- we overslept. The maid's taps on the door must've roused Selami first. I growled at feeling my shoulder being poked after he shooed off the maid.

I showered and shaved while he tanked up at the breakfast buffet. Putting on a fresh shirt let me feel human again, and I caught up to him. Before finishing our second cup of coffee, Yagmur stepped off the cage elevator and padded over to our table. She didn't have on the mechanic's overalls, a relief.

She told us during the night her sympathetic, younger sister had brought over her outfit, a sedate white blouse and modest red skirt. Then Yagmur picked at her eggs, fruit salad, and sausage links. I downed more coffee watching her and trading glances with Selami. Haggard and pale, she'd spent a sleepless night.

She put her cold hand over mine. "I want to help you find Sylvester."

My headshake was automatic. "Bad idea. His wife is paying me, and she doesn't want you involved."

"But she doesn't love Sylvester. I do."

"I won't dispute you on that point, but I can't be responsible for what happens to you."

Yagmur turned to Selami, her eyes pleading. "Make Frank see it my way."

"It's really his show to run as he wishes."

"He's the boss?"

"He's paying me so, yes, that's correct."

"I don't like it."

"Frank is a good man. He'll bring Sylvester home."

I nodded. "That's my job."

I was up in the air over what to do next, but Selami called her a *taksi*. Then using the business card from the

Citadel shop I'd given him, he put in a call to Yagmur's father and gave her the cell phone. She refused it. Selami murmured something in Turkish, translating loosely to mean it was a good time to grovel and mend fences.

She accepted the cell phone, moved off into the lobby, and patched up the rift with her father. She returned teary-eyed to our table. We finished our breakfast in silence. When her *taksi* blared its horn out front, she left us, but not before I gave her some money and promised to call the minute I tracked down Mercedes. PIs were big liars but only to get the job done.

Then Selami spurted off in his *taksi* to grab a shower and return primed to go. His wife might or might not accept his version for our all-nighter. I sat at our table perusing the Turkish Daily News and sipping a juice tasting like cherry cider. Insurgents had struck Coalition forces again, and the death toll incremented by three. I tossed down the Turkish Daily News. Three more Gold Star mothers had their souls cored out.

The four Turkish businessmen trickled down on the cage elevator from their rooms. Two fiddled with their BlackBerries as the others haggled over their bills with Karin at the front desk. I plugged each into my homicide suspect profile, but none of them fit.

The pinstriped suits, charcoal silk ties, and buffed black shoes marked them as entrepreneurs, not killers. The shortest one felt my curious stare and, grinning, dealt me a cavalier wave. I returned it.

Then their entourage, luggage in hand, rumbled out the revolving glass door, and they piled into the airport microbus. It zoomed off, and I never saw them again, though I envied their leaving Ankara, and I hoped soon to follow in their wake.

I grew bored. Karin plucked the cigarette butts from ashtrays' white masonry sand. She'd lost the fuzzy, pink shawl and didn't snarl at my deferential "good morning", an encouraging sign.

"Has Mustafa returned?" I asked her.

"He's a pill. He moped around here until I ordered him a *taksi* to go home. Pembe is dead. All his pitiful grief can't bring her back."

"It amazes me how somebody else's pain doesn't faze you even when you're, in part, responsible for it."

She put a hand on a hip. Her breasts heaved at me. "I didn't pull the gun's trigger killing her. Go peddle your damn guilt trip elsewhere. I'm not buying it."

"Pembe died right over there" -- I pointed a finger -- "at the cage elevator. A killer came in and spilled blood in your lobby. Like it or not, you're on the hook. Your denial doesn't change that fact."

Karin's glare turned poisonous. Her mouth was a chop mark in her face. "This is a stupid argument. Pembe deserted her post, and the killer slipped in here. Her laxness did her the harm. How can you blame us for her death?"

"That's not what happened. The killer lured her upstairs and shot her dead."

"Our police haven't found a shred of evidence upstairs."

"Excuse me, Karin." I breezed by her. "I've got a few phone calls to make."

But any excuse to leave would do. Her rage at Pembe spoke to motive, and she'd also ample opportunity. As I paced off to my room, Nashwinter poked out his door. His blotchy cheeks and bloodshot eyes came from seeing John Barleycorn. He once was my friend, too.

Nashwinter ruffled his burly shoulders as his belligerent swagger approached me. His suit worn every day that I'd known him was beyond any dry cleaning, and his straight-edged razor was still missing.

He saw the <u>Turkish Daily News</u> folded under my elbow and nodded at it. "How goes the war for our side?"

He crowded my space and smelled as bad as a morgue drain. "Our people are making the best of a tough situation, I'd say."

"Do you know what I say? Nuke all the fucking towel heads."

"Nashwinter, get some strong coffee in you, man."

"Drunk, half-drunk, or stone-cold sober, I mean every word. I'm sick of this jihad bullshit. If they hate us, tough titty. We're here, and we're here to stay."

"You trash them, but you're not above taking their money."

"I've got no beef with the Turks. They've earned my respect."

"Spout off your ethnic slurs again, and you'll see what the Turks think. Don't expect any help from me."

"I knew it. Underneath your hardboiled act, you're a yellow-livered son of a bitch."

My busted knuckles ached. Punching out this big lush wasn't worth the pain it'd take me to do it. I stiff-armed him in the chest. Groaning, he stumbled into the wall. He rebounded with a large man's surprising nimbleness. He uncorked a right cross you could see coming a mile away. I feinted, then uncorked a left jab. My fist lanced deep in Nashwinter's soft gut. He staggered a half-step, and I bulled my way around him.

Trying to save face, he stumbled after me. His fist banged on my door locked after I darted into my room. I tuned out his noise. He'd wind up as a corpse in some gasoline alleyway, a Jihadist's knife planted between his shoulder blades. Some men remained stupid. At last he quit clubbing on my door and left for his liquid breakfast served at the bar.

I reviewed the slate of suspects for Mercedes' homicide I'd compiled earlier.

Omar (Otel Pamuk owner)
Karin (Omar's wife)
Joel Nashwinter (U.S. beer salesman)
Mr. Ahmet (Turkish cabbie)(Omar's cousin)

Each suspect could just as well go on a similar list for Pembe's homicide. Mr. Ahmet might be the long shot. Karin and Nashwinter now raced neck-and-neck to win the brass ring. I scribbled a little something to stick in my final report to Mrs. Mercedes when I hit her with my bill.

By now reflexive, I tuned in CNN. Gouts of dense, black smoke and bloodied victims in the rubble chilled the camera lens panning over a mortared hospital in Baghdad. I collapsed on the bed, my eyes riveted on the TV. Our brand of Western democracy just didn't port very well, now did it?

Answering a knock preceded the appearance of Abdullah's imposing frame at my door. He didn't look so happy and stalked by me over to the desk. He flumped down in the chair, sent me a perceptible nod, and studied a scabby wart on his thumb knuckle. I cut off the TV, and took my phone off its hook. He said nothing. I said nothing. A minute played out before I spoke.

"Is any homicide arrest coming?"

"No homicide arrest is coming." His dark eyes in their deep sockets landed on me.

"Is Pembe's autopsy still a go?"

"Yes, I'm pinning all my hopes on it. Anyway how is your situation?"

"A panhandler near the U.S. Embassy saw Mercedes the Sunday morning he vanished."

"Why did he go that way?"

"Maybe he wanted to see Felix for some reason."

"Mercedes' passport has never turned up?"

"It wasn't in his duffel."

Abdullah mashed his dog-tired eyes shut. "You've found nothing on any suspects at the Otel Pamuk?"

Our exchange fresh in my mind, I gave Abdullah the rundown on Nashwinter and didn't hold back on repeating his ethnic slurs.

"If he feels so bitter, why doesn't he get on a plane and leave Turkey?"

"While trashing you, he likes taking your money."

"I see how it is with some of you Americans." Abdullah cast me a sharp appraisal. "You'd never come to live in Turkey, would you, Frank?"

"I'd never master speaking basic Turkish. Apart from that, I'd have no problem staying longer. Of course I couldn't get a job, and I have to eat even if it's just rice and water."

"Oh come now, you'd work off the books. Many do it."

"No way. I'm not out to piss off my cop pals here. By the way, you should know a cabbie named Selami Hanim is now tooling me around Ankara."

Rubbing his eyes, Abdullah nodded. "I know." He smiled at me. "Selami is my first cousin."

"Huh?"

"I put him on you. He picked you up near the Citadel, right? Why do you think my plainclothes cop quit his tail job? Selami will watch you."

My anger spiked. "He never told me this."

"Maybe you never asked him."

I stopped. How much had Selami the Rat filled in his cousin Abdullah the Cop? Where did Selami's true allegiance lie? To the highest bidder, Abdullah or me?

"Get on with your story, Frank."

"We tracked down Mercedes' lady friend Yagmur, but our questioning her hit another stone wall."

"It figures. Do you like a suspect for Pembe's homicide?" Abdullah's severe squint crimped his eye corners. The wrinkles, I saw, weren't just humor lines.

"Any guest at the Otel Pamuk has to go under the microscope. I don't know how many you've checked out since she died."

"Nobody beyond the first interviews. In your PI trade, you must evaluate suspects, so let me pick your brain. What do your instincts tell you about her killer?"

"I'd shake out a solid motive. Who had a burning reason to kill her?"

Abdullah ridged his heavy shoulders. "Who?"

"Omar's wife, Karin, was no friend of Pembe's."

Abdullah smiled. "Oh yes, I've had my eye on Karin. A wife's jealousy will drive her to do in her husband's lover."

"You told me a Luger probably croaked Pembe. Could a small woman like Karin could fire a big gun like a Luger?"

"I also had my doubts," replied Abdullah. "But a Luger's grips are slim. I took our secretary out to our firing range. She's near Karin's weight and height. Our secretary used both hands to aim a Luger and squeezed off a clip. She's a better-than-mediocre shot. If Pembe was boxed in the cage elevator, she was a staked goat. My conclusion is, yes, Karin firing a Luger could murder Pembe."

"If you suspect Karin, put the screws to her."

"We interviewed her in Omar's office. She's a prickly lady." Slapping his hands on both knees, Abdullah bounded to his feet. "We'll haul her off downtown and repeat our questions. Put in a different cage, our canary might sing a different song."

"Leave my name out of it. My manhunt goes on, and the Otel Pamuk is my base of operations. I don't want to get her any angrier at me."

"You should be okay by staying here."

I decided it was time to play my trump card before sitting on it burned me. "Speaking of Karin and Lugers, did you know she keeps one in her purse? I know because I've seen it."

Abdullah's face knotted in dark anger. "You took long enough to tell me this."

"But I didn't recall she had the Luger until just now with our talking about it."

CHAPTER 32

Right after Abdullah left, I backed out of my room and locked up. Omar had relieved Karin at the front desk. If I was a betting man, I'd put money on Abdullah making a beeline to their apartment and ransacking her purse for the Luger. Glancing up, Omar saw me. His scurry over left me to cringe. His disheveled hair and flushed lean face warned me all wasn't quiet on his homefront, as if I cared.

"Frank, I've got something important."

"Later, Omar. I'm busy. Can't stop."

"A gentleman rang through to the front desk asking for you."

"Who was it?"

"Robert Gatlin."

"His message?"

"He said to tell you 'the bird has flown the coop'. Those were his exact words. 'The bird has flown the coop.'"

My heart lurched for a beat. "Oh Christ, not that."

"Is it bad news?"

I just nodded.

Mrs. Mercedes was the bird in the wind. Lufthansa jetted nightly flights out of Washington, D.C. bound for Frankfurt, and she rode on one. Her connecting Turkish Airlines DC-9 in Frankfurt then humped over the Swiss Alps and the Straits of Dardanelles to touch down at Ankara International Esenboga Airport. I left Omar and backtracked to my room. My finger pecked in the numbers, and I greeted Gatlin.

"I got your message. What the fuck is going on?"

"Lois has left. I found her itinerary. She booked a flight to Ankara."

My white-knuckled grip choked the phone receiver. "Why?"

"For the past two days, she's been fuming over your lack of progress. Honestly, I did my best to calm her, but she wasn't having any of it.

"You should've seen her. She was like a big cat pacing the floor. I finally convinced her to sit down and relax a little. No sooner had I gone to fix our highballs than she bounced up to resume that crazy stalking."

"I can see her upset over Sylvester, but why is she coming here?"

"Who knows? She gets intense. I told her she'd jeopardize or hinder your job, but she has her own mind on how to do things."

"She can take Ankara by storm, but throwing your weight around here pisses off the natives. You'll get nowhere by trying it."

"Well, our work is more complicated."

"Our work? I'm the one who's stuck baby-sitting this client."

"I'm always a phone call away, Frank. Or I can hop on the next plane and follow her to Ankara."

That rash proposal left my pulse to stutter. "Let's stay calm ourselves."

"Okay, just park her in the Harrington's best suite. Then ply her with expensive brandy. She drinks like a lord. Coax her down to the casino. Yeah, that's the right stuff. She plays a wicked hand of poker. She's a black jack fiend, too. That should divert her while you continue to comb Ankara for Sylvester. Are you getting any closer to finding him?"

"Yeah, sure. Is your romancing her finished?"

"If it's done with the right lady, Frank, it's called love."

"It's getting deep over here."

Gatlin ignored my barb, had me promise to call him as soon as I knew anything new, and we cut our signal. My next call went to Gerald who was supposed to be on a stakeout in Middleburg. Something had gone haywire.

"Frank, I had the lady in my sights. Then I ducked into a Wawa, and damn if she didn't give me the slip."

I wanted to holler at Gerald.

"Where did she go?"

"Gatlin just gave me the lowdown. She's on a plane coming here. What am I supposed to do now?"

"You need the big dog. I'm on my way, too."

Click.

My phone receiver clattered into its hook. "Great. Now I have two wing nuts on my hands."

After my own pacing my crib for ten minutes, I returned to the lobby and claimed a table in the restaurant annex. Two coffees later other reinforcements arrived. Cutting across the carpet, Selami wore a clean pair of jeans and a T-shirt. I called out and hailed him.

"You look intense." He grabbed a chair.

"My case has taken a turn for the worse."

"Things can't be that bad."

I summarized Gatlin's latest news, but left out Gerald was also en route to Ankara. I'd deal with one snafu at a time. "By now she must be a raving lunatic."

Selami wasn't alarmed. "If her money is green, why do you care if she comes?"

"I also have other headaches." I looked at him. "Abdullah told me he's your cousin."

"That's true, Frank."

"Funny how you didn't tell me. He did."

"It has no bearing on our deal."

"Sure it does. He said you're keeping an eye on me for him."

"I told Abdullah that to make him happy."

"So then, who do you work for, him or me?"

"He's paying me nothing, so I work for you."

"I only hope you mean that."

"Frank, didn't I spring you from the brothel?"

"Yeah, I guess you did at that."

"Besides I've got big news. Remember I put out some feelers on Mr. Mercedes? A cabbie I know dropped by the apartment. He told me a well-dressed, white American the Sunday before last called his *taksi* a block or so from the U.S. Embassy. The fare had to be Mr. Mercedes."

"Sounds like it. Where did your cabbie take him?"

"They didn't stop in the city but took a far, strange trip south on Konya Road."

The shiver tracking up my back felt ice-cold. "To the land of the troglodytes?"

Nodding, Selami smiled. "It takes a half-day to reach Cappadocia. The cabbie, however, returned home alone the next day. Mr. Mercedes had wandered off, and the cabbie had to get back to his duties."

"Then Mercedes had a pressing reason to go and make himself scarce. We can retrace their route. Show around his photo. Ask questions. Maybe pick up an eyewitness. If we work fast, I can find and deliver Mercedes to his wife when she blows into town. I'll get paid, and you'll receive your money. Then I'll wash my hands of her for good."

"Sweet."

"How much do I owe your cabbie for the tip?"

"No charge. Our deal was he'd tell me if I left his name out of it."

"When can we leave?"

"I filled up my tank. Just say the word, and we're off."

Before I could get out another word, however, a visitor loped through the revolving glass door. Auk's glare overlooked Omar's affable wave. I felt the full heat of his eyes land on me. Any cop giving you an extra hard look wasn't a good omen.

A frown broke on Selami's face. "Our trip may get postponed. But then maybe not. Just hang loose, Frank. I'll talk to Detective Auk."

Measuring up each other like two junkyard dogs, both then began yammering in Turkish. Auk, his corded neck livid and his eyes shiny, gestured with emphatic hand chops. His index finger stabbed in my direction. I slouched down in my chair. Selami also expressed his shock and dismay. Unmoved, Auk pushed his wrists together as if to say his hands were tied. He'd no wiggle room to strike any deal with us. Still venting, they tramped to my table.

"Detective Auk has orders to arrest you," said Selami. "Karin at headquarters has told them things. They won't give any specifics. But she's connected you to the Luger they found in her purse."

Auk nodded. "Orders are orders. Please come with me, Mr. Johnson. No manacles are necessary if you do as I ask."

His emotions running hot, Selami wasn't done in. "Frank, stay put, and I'll discuss it with Detective Abdullah. We'll fix this misunderstanding."

"Cry out your eyes. Your cousin won't flip-flop on this. The arrest stands. Mr. Johnson is my prisoner."

"Frank isn't going out that door with you until I've heard it from Detective Abdullah."

Selami went to the front desk. He didn't ask the ashen-faced Omar hovering in his office doorway for permission to use the phone.

Auk shifted to check my path of escape to the revolving glass door. I put an ear to Selami pleading my case. After listening for a bit, he nodded.

"An excellent compromise, Abdullah. Thank you." His excited eyes dancing, he hung up and rejoined us. "Frank, we're still in business. Detective Abdullah agrees with our goals in Cappadocia. We'll keep him up to speed while we're down there."

I felt a spasm of relief course through me.

"This is unbelievable. Your cousin must owe you big time." Derision strained Auk's voice.

"You're welcome to ride along with us, Detective Auk. The more the merrier, see?"

"You just shut up." The dour Auk brushing by Selami had the last say. He charged out the revolving glass door to his squad car and tore off up the hill.

"I'll go pack a bag. Do the same, Frank. Within the hour we'll take off on Konya Road for Cappadocia."

Chapter 33

"Level with me. How did you really talk Abdullah into okaying our trip?" I asked Selami at the helm of his *taksi*. We were clipping along south on Konya Road. It was Thursday afternoon, and our big scene in Cappadocia hadn't been written yet.

"I lied. Did you know we're on the verge of a big break in Pembe's murder case?"

"I see. How do we know her murder is linked to Mercedes' disappearance?"

"But aren't they? Both were at the Otel Pamuk."

"Uh-huh. So either we crack both cases in Cappadocia or . . .?"

" . . . or we gnash our teeth in Izmir's Buca Prison for a very long time."

I put down my window for some air, the free kind.

"Can you do this, Frank? Buca Prison is not for us. Believe me."

"I'll give it my best shot."

Our destination, Cappadocia, sat at the midpoint of rectangular Turkey. Or that's how my eye plotted it on my road map. Before we left Ankara, Selami recorded his odometer reading. (I charge my clients for mileage.) Eating up the two-lane tarmac put Ankara's smog behind us.

Before we'd left, I tipped Omar to hold my room. He didn't like hearing of my road trip. Who'd do the hotel security? I didn't know, but I knew my Cappadocia jaunt had to wrap this up before Mrs. Mercedes spun like a fatal bullet through the revolving glass door. I didn't even want to think of what came after Gerald hit town.

"On their trip down, what did Mercedes tell your cabbie?" I asked Selami, watching the barren, stony knolls on both sides whiz by us. A pack of gray wolves -- "*canavars*" -- trotted along a jagged ridgeline, their snouts canted in the air. The scent of the shepherds' flocks drew their noses keen for the kill. We'd the same thing in the States, only we called them Wall Street bankers.

"He said Mr. Mercedes curled up and slept in the rear seat. Even stranger, he brought no luggage."

"Something hot came up, and he dropped everything and rushed down. Did he carry a cell phone?"

"Everybody carries a cell phone."

I didn't but maybe that was just me. "Getting a call may've flipped him out. I wonder if he does spook work for the Feds."

"Doesn't your embassy know?"

"They'd never tell me. It's too hush-hush." Just then, I smelled something briny beat through my open car window.

"Yes, Frank, we have our own salt lake." Selami's hand directed my gaze. "We call it *Tuz Golu*."

Also intrigued, I saw a zinc gray body of water spreading on our right. The two-laner we followed on the berm hugged the lakeshore. A mist wafted off the water's surface smooth as gravy. The brackish air tingled in my nostrils and unclogged my sinuses. I saw the tire tracks left by the farmers' tractors that pulled up at the bank. The farmers scooped up the briny silt to use as salt licks to fortify their livestock. We boogied on.

"When did your cabbie last see Mercedes?" I asked.

Fingers clawed through Selami's wiry, jet hair. He used his thumb pad and slicked down his mustache. "They got to their hotel after a half-day trip and agreed to meet for dinner in the hotel restaurant. The cabbie ran five minutes late, but Mr. Mercedes never came at all.

"The cabbie found Mr. Mercedes' room and knocked on the door. Getting no answer, the cabbie figured Mr. Mercedes had gone to bed. It wasn't until the next morning, Monday, that the cabbie realized Mr. Mercedes had vanished."

"Was Mercedes' bed slept in?"

"The cabbie got the key, went in, and said the bed looked as if it'd never been touched. He combed the hotel and its grounds but found no sign of Mr. Mercedes."

"Did he tell the hotel manager or local police?"

Selami shrugged. "Mr. Mercedes paid for his privacy."

"Not if he was mugged," I said, incredulous. "Who's your cabbie?"

"No Frank, don't badger me for his name. He did us a favor to come forward. He runs a *taksi*. He isn't a bodyguard. He wants no more trouble."

"I'm not out to jam him up. I'm after the whole story."

"I've told you all. You can trust us." Selami drove another mile before asking, "Do you suspect foul play?"

"No ransom demand rules out kidnapping. That narrows it down to murder in my opinion."

"Got any suspects in mind?"

"At least four, Selami, but all are long shots right now."

⁂

Near the supper hour we rolled into Nevsehir, the largest dot on the narrow roads veining Cappadocia. Selami had rang ahead to set our reservations at a tan stucco hotel, the same place Mercedes had stayed. Its lumpish architecture resembling a cave mimicked the famous subterranean cities. We checked in to our separate caves and ditched our bags. The twilight sun prompted Selami to tow me out of the hotel door.

"Hurry," he said. "Before it's too late."

We sprinted up the street to the base of a columnar

stand of basalt. Elbows flying and knees pumping, we huffed up the zigzag path to scale its height and topped the summit just as Thursday's blood orange sun dipped into the western skyline.

We sat huddled in the windy crows' nest with a clan of other tourists, all enjoying the sunset's visual wonders. Selami fired up a thin, black cigar. A curvy blonde coughed into a crumbled Kleenex. He ignored her dirty looks.

The gumdrop imprints to her nipples protruded under her blouse. Her chattering teeth and blue lips grew more noticeable. Far below us, the loudspeakers on the sandstone minarets to the fifty-two mosques amplified the muezzin's chants calling the faithful to evening prayers.

"Sir, do you mind?" The curvy blonde used a German accent. "Your cigar stinks. I hate its smell."

Smiling, he took out the thin, black cigar. "Yes, I suppose you do. But do you see the blue cottage with the red roof, the one before the first mosque? I was born there. This is my native town. So I ask you, can't a man do as he damn well pleases in his own home?"

"Not if it makes him a rude host." Her hand fanned the cigar fumes away from her sour face.

"Host? How so? I didn't invite you up here as my guest."

"You stink, just like your turd of a cigar."

That was when I nudged Selami. "We better get back to the hotel."

He nodded.

As we took the zigzag paths back down the basalt column, he muttered "god damn Kraut" under his breath. I kept quiet. Selami didn't like the Germans. We got back to our hotel at dark. No floor shows featured belly dancers for their guests' amusement, and Selami approved.

Later in the evening after a dinner of dirty rice and fruit, I repaired to my cave, made a few notes for my final report, and broke out my latest expenses. Then I slept better than I had since landing in Turkey. Funny, I'd expected just the opposite.

Chapter 34

Early Friday morning I had the devil of a time tracking down our hotel manager. Our concierge, however, eyed Mercedes' photo I held up for her. Yes, she'd talked to this gentleman. Oh really? Suspicious, I asked her sharper questions, but I just got phonier answers.

For wasting my time, I didn't tip her a dime. After scouting up a pay phone in the deserted lobby, I got an update from Omar, my pair of eyes back in Ankara. My question was terse.

"No American lady is here," he replied. "No Lois Mercedes has phoned in a reservation."

"She will soon. Remember, don't tip her off where I am. Tell her I grabbed a bus for Istanbul to beat out a hot lead."

He made an impatient noise. "This secrecy costs extra."

"You only offer discretion if the price is right."

"I run a business the same as you do."

"Fine, tack it on my tab."

"When will you return?"

"It shouldn't be more than a day or so."

"Why don't you quit this wild goose chase? I doubt if Mr. Mercedes left Ankara."

"Then I just rode down to soak up Cappadocia's scenery," I said before hanging up.

I skipped calling Gatlin or Abdullah. What was the point? Ravenous tourists had pillaged the breakfast buffet, but Selami had saved me a dish of dirty rice. Between my chews and sips, I spun him up to speed.

"To recap, your cabbie and Mercedes left Ankara bright and early two Sundays ago. They used Konya Road just as we did. That put them in this neck of the woods, say, no later than Sunday noon. What came next?"

"The cabbie said Mr. Mercedes was antsy to see the underground cities on Monday."

"Then he returned to his room, and nobody has set eyes on him since. Yet the cabbie didn't report him missing." I paused, giving Selami a hard look. "Odd."

"Mr. Mercedes paid the cabbie to guard his privacy." Selami set his jaw. "Look, the cabbie isn't the bad guy here. He got Mr. Mercedes to Cappadocia. That was his only job."

I let that ride but felt irked for a different reason. "We'll also go visit the troglodytes' tunnels. I hate doing it. But you know sneaky Mercedes had reason to slip down there. Maybe we'll pick up on just why."

My breakfast finished, we hit the front desk and booked our tour reservations. As always, the expense went on Mrs. Mercedes' tab. The tour coaches departed every two hours, and ours pulled out at nine. Selami used the pay phone. Parked on the hotel's portico bench in front of the irises and hollyhock, I studied the map.

A trident of jagged valleys -- Uhlara, Goreme, and Urgup -- forked through Cappadocia proper. Our tour coach steaming off in less than ten minutes chuffed south of Nevsehir and then cut through the Urgup Valley to dock at the village of Kaymakli. Selami walked up to me.

"My father will meet us in Kaymakli. His name is Joe. Yes, I know, it's a funny name for a Turk, but he likes the way it sounds, so call him Joe. Before we go back to Ankara on Konya Road, we'll visit my baby niece. For now, lend me your photo. Mr. Mercedes probably paid at the front desk."

The desk lady, her hennaed, lank hair the color of a

rusted nail, gave Mercedes' photo a sharp look and frowned. Selami interviewed her in Turkish and came back.

"Mr. Mercedes was here. He also had the nerve to ask if she was available. Married with three kids, she wanted to slap the smile off his face."

"He's a regular Don Juan. She remembers him buying a ticket?"

"She says he bought *two* tickets."

"Interesting. He'd plans for entertaining some company. Maybe they joined the tour at Kaymakli, but their objective was to hit the catacombs."

Catacombs and troglodytes, I thought. The image of me buried alive under a crush of rock froze my blood. Abdullah had told me it was a heathenish way to live and die, and now I believed him.

"Don't look so happy, Frank."

"Yeah well, tight, dark places scare me."

His eyes bright, Selami cocked his head at me. "I'll go with you."

"Do you know the tunnels?"

"We played there. Joe knows them better than I do. But no man lives long enough to explore all the tunnels. The troglodytes dug too many levels and mazes."

※

At nine on the dot, we scooted into our seats on the tour coach. A gang from Germany was our neighbors. Although the landscape was arid and barren, the troglodytes underground cities drew a steady stream of tour coaches like ours groaning over the pitted, twisty gravel lanes.

I gawked out the dirty windows at the Marslike terrain. The valleys the color of iodine looked dry as chalk. I saw busted rocks strewn everywhere. Spindly pinnacles topped with the mushroom caps were "fairy chimneys". The hues to the wind-sculpted rock shapes reminded me of a lemon meringue pie.

"Isn't it as I told you?" Selami grinned at me. "Weird

and beautiful."

I nodded. The overcast skies blotted out the sunlight. Our tour coach laboring up a switchback spewed out a plume of black, greasy exhaust. Did the locals bellyache on the air quality? I would. The Germans muttered and also ogled out the windows. Selami with a surly face watched them.

As our tour coach slogged on, I mulled if I'd wandered too far off the reservation this time. Going underground was radical for me. A chilly rain like that one on my first steps in Ankara pelted us. The tour coach's panel lights flickered off and on.

The diesel engine bogging down had lost power. I watched a stout lady in her fifties route around a box of hard candy to the passengers. When it came my turn, I passed. She took offense despite my disarming shrug.

"Don't you care for any?"

"Sorry, I'm diabetic."

I felt our tour coach gear down as we lumbered into a deserted car lot. Several ladies took along umbrellas. Gazing through the tour coach windows, Selami didn't spot Joe. We piled off and huddled in a ragged circle. At the center, a clean-cut kid wearing a starchy white, buttoned-down shirt and chinos said he was Uzay. He set up the historical stage for the troglodytes.

"When the vigilant sentries posted out on the steppe first spotted the barbarians on the rampage, word was rushed back to the villagers who scurried below the ground like ants on a picnic basket. This huge, round stone was rolled into place and corked the entrance. They felt safe.

"Picture it with me. Life was vastly different in the tunnels. Oil lamps were their only light source. To scrimp on precious oil, the villagers must've sat in the quiet, clammy darkness.

"Sleep was a favorite pastime." Uzay waggled his eyebrows. "Also the other activities dark places invite." That quip earned a run of knowing snickers. He explained our tour. "Kaymakli's underground city consists of seven levels. Archaeologists have mapped the top six, however only levels one through three are open to the public. Today we'll explore each of those three levels. I'll tell you more stories as we go along. Questions?"

Hard Candy Lady ventured one. "You've gotten me a little curious. What's at the bottom of the underground cities? What can you tell us about the seventh level? Can we get there today?"

I saw the blood rush from Uzay's face. He coughed a little as if to clear the frog in his throat.

"Thank you for your important question. A guest on every tour must ask me the same thing. Most passageways to the seventh level have caved in. Archeologists have tried to probe their way down, but it's too dangerous. Several have been injured."

Throwing back her shoulders, Hard Candy Lady jutted her blunt chin. "You haven't answered my question. Is it a big secret?"

"I've heard stories the seventh level is where the troglodytes buried their dead and quarantined their violent lunatics." A chorus of gasps filled the pause Uzay gave for dramatic effect.

"Without further ado, we'll start our tour. I should warn you, ladies and gentlemen. Be ready to bend low. Space gets very tight very fast."

His last remark didn't whet my adventuresome spirit.

"Frank, are you holding up? You look a little green."

"No matter. Mercedes got two tickets. We'll follow in his footsteps and see just why. Have you been through this tunnel?"

But Selami had turned to enter the portal behind the huge, round stone and didn't hear me. Or he acted as if he hadn't. I tilted my face to enjoy the gun-metal gray sky, sucked in a fresh breath of air, and plunged with the others into the underworld's gloom.

Chapter 35

The ingenious troglodytes had chiseled out a huge, round stone to plug their burrow's entryway. Ports notched out in the walls let them stab their lethal spears into the evil hearts of any unwanted trespassers who made it past the huge, round stone. We assembled in the vestibule. Electric lamps blazed down on us.

Uzay smiled and waved. "Follow me on down."

I lingered near the back. Shoulders narrowed and heads lowered, we followed Uzay, filing through the tunnel. My rice diet and shedding a few pounds made it easier for me. Hard Candy Lady nipping on my heels was our rearguard.

The tour members emerged from the tunnel and schooled around Uzay inside a stone chapel. The Christians had worshipped at this altar while the cannibals above drooled for their red meat. Prayers did little good. No angels had flown to the Christians' miraculous rescue. They were on their own.

Bad nerves seeped through our tour group. Hard Candy Lady coughed and then breathed like a creaky bellows. I also shivered. The frescoes on the wall showed Jesus Christ and His Chosen Twelve sitting to chow down at the Last Supper.

Judas Iscariot, the roly-poly, two-faced one, at my first glance resembled Robert Gatlin in Middleburg. Then my wary eyes settled on the altar that had been chiseled from the crusty, blood-red stone. That and the numbing temperature had me picturing us trapped in a meat locker. Who could pray in here? Uzay spoke again.

"Ladies and gentlemen, before we go on, I'll recreate the troglodytes' actual living conditions."

He clapped his hands. The electric lamps mounted in the chapel's ceiling flickered off. Darkness hit us. I blinked, the murk swarming me. I couldn't see, let alone breathe. Maybe we had a glimpse into our own hellish eternity. Then an inhuman howl pierced the chapel.

To my left, Hard Candy Lady caterwauled again. A second lady behind me burst out shrieking. My knees softened into jelly. Just before mass hysteria struck us, Uzay clapped his hands again. The electric lamps seared on again. Our eyes blinked. Terror had slashed up the pale faces I saw except for one. Grinning, Selami squeezed my forearm.

"Spooky stuff, eh?"

"You played in here as a kid?"

"But of course. You get use to it."

"The troglodytes brought down no jackhammers or dynamite. Who did all this stonemasonry?"

"Black magic, Frank."

"Can you get serious?"

"I am serious. Catch up to the others before we get lost."

Maneuvering through a chest-high tunnel, we moved in a conga line. The space grew too cramped for me to turn around and double back. But I could weather this just fine I kept thinking. Then my biggest fear came true: we stopped. My heart cartwheeled as I hyperventilated. A shove plowed me into the next man in the conga line.

He yelled and I muttered an apology.

"Move it!" Again Hard Candy Lady tried to bulldoze me.

"We're stuck," I yelled back at her. "Just chill out."

She made a rodent noise. "I'm losing my mind."

"No you're not. Take a deep breath. Hold it."

She said nothing as our conga line crawled along again.

The tunnel gave way to a shell-shaped space high enough for us to stand up in. Stretching my arms overhead, I moved away from Hard Candy Lady. Selami's eyes were glowing embers. He got off on this extreme spelunking. He edged over to me.

"Frank, I believe I've shed light on your mystery. The answer lies below our feet."

"How so?"

"Mr. Mercedes never made it out of the tunnels. He's dead, buried seven levels down."

"No, that can't be. Uzay said you can't get there from here."

Selami was a hard-ass for accuracy. "Uzay said 'most passageways' are blocked."

"Good. You can go find the secret tunnel. The only place I'm going is topside." My thumb pointed to show where.

Selami's eyes smoked. He felt the juice to finish our manhunt. I knew he was right. We needed to get paid. He'd also concocted a plan.

"When the others enter the next tunnel, we'll go last and splinter off."

"What then?"

"I'll get us there. Stick close."

I grabbed his sleeve as he turned. "Away from the electric lamps, how do we see our way around?"

"Sneak back to the tour coach. It carries flashlights."

We hotfooted it back through the labyrinth of tunnels, chambers, and portals. After busting out of the vestibule before the huge, round stone, we found the rain had lifted. The slashes of sunbeams gave the eggplant dark sky a starburst appearance.

We raced across the car lot to the tour coach. Everybody had gone below, leaving us alone. After stabbing my fingers into the crack, I pried open the collapsible door. The leaner Selami turned sideways to mash through the crevice.

"Stealing buses, I see. I'll bring you biscuits in Buca Prison."

Our heads jerked around to see a fireplug of a man dressed in a blue shirt unbuttoned to reveal a wifebeater T-shirt over his chino pants. No socks covered his knobby feet shod in a pair of tire rubber sandals. Arms crossed on his chest, he reveled in having caught us. Lookalike father and son broke into grins.

"Joe, shakes hands with PI Frank Johnson."

He nodded at me. "I've watched some wild movies on you guys."

I gave a noncommittal grunt as we pumped hands. His palm rough as pumice used a viselike grip. Selami with my occasional inputs sketched out our quest. Listening, Joe, a half-head shorter than Selami, stared down at the ground. His emphatic nod came at Selami's memory that a passageway led to the seventh floor.

"I know of the one hole in the stone wall that links to a little-used stairway," said Joe. "But it's not for beginners to tackle."

Selami reassured Joe. "We'll do fine. Have you visited the seventh level? My friends never explored that far below."

"Once long ago and it's darker than doomsday. We'll need to take along big flashlights. The tour coach carries emergency flares but as for flashlights, I don't think so."

"It's our best shot." Selami refitted in the crevice to the tour coach's door.

A padlocked tool box stored under the rear seat came out. The other two men glanced at me, but lock picking skills weren't bulleted on my résumé. Selami rousted a tire iron from under the spare tire compartment and rented apart his second cheap padlock. He dug out a tin flashlight from under the pliers and box-end wrenches. His flicking the switch produced a pitiful spark.

"It's no better than a candle." The more experienced Joe started for the huge, round stone. "I recall emergency kits are kept in the tunnels. They should include flashlights."

The coast still clear, we padded over the car lot and

skirted the huge, round stone to re-enter the vestibule. We could pick up the human chatter bubbling from the tunnel. A tour group was that near us. Hearing an engine noise, Selami, our sentry behind the huge, round stone, gave us a second bad report.

"A new tour coach just pulled up. We're sandwiched by the tourists from both sides." Selami cut his eyes to me. "What now, Frank?"

I used the old last-ditch rule. "When in doubt, do nothing."

Chapter 36

Acting as if we belonged there, we milled in the vestibule and then mingled with our tour group surging up from the tunnel. I nodded at Hard Candy Lady leading their exodus. Breathing in gasps, she tramped around the huge, round stone to rehab in the fresh air and bright sun. Uzay not far behind herded the others by us.

Joe pretended to inspect the shallow pit carved in the floor and used for stomping wine grapes. He needn't have bothered. Everybody stampeded right by us. After the wild-eyed stragglers cleared the vestibule, we barreled down the same tunnel. Joe explained on the way.

"Our generations have mapped these cities. How else do we have our fun?"

Selami grunted. "This isn't fun to Frank."

"Why?"

"He freaks when he gets in tight, dark places."

"Frank will do okay," I told them. "Just don't slow down. Thinking too much gets Frank into trouble."

We cornered the tunnel's last turn. Selami leaned backward for a quick check. "I can hear the new tour group coming behind us." He looked at Joe. "The man Frank searches for lies on the seventh level."

The smile fell off Joe's face. "Are you sure? Getting down there is dangerous."

"We'll go. This is about murder."

Joe's dark eyes pierced us. "Murder? Who killed this man?"

I had a suggestion. "First we'll find the man before we look into his murder."

It was plain Joe was reluctant to take us, but we hurried on to beat the tour group. The electric lamps placed every ten paces or so in the new connecting tunnel's ceiling lit up the nebulous path for us.

"I'll give the killer mad props for original corpse disposal," I said trying to make light of our situation.

Neither Turkish man responded. I'd no clue what curses they muttered under their breaths, but I also picked up my pace. We clawed and scrabbled our way down the next series of low tunnels. We pulled up at the last familiar spot where Selami and I had U-turned to the tour coach.

Joe spoke from a cowboy crouch. "The emergency kit isn't here. I swear it was along this wall."

Selami darted a glance behind us. The curiosity seekers in the new tour group were already clambering down the same tunnels we'd just taken. I heard their rambunctious tread echo off the stone walls. Selami joined in Joe's urgent poking along the walls, looking for the niche containing the emergency kit.

"We can't stay here," said Selami. "Either we push on, or we sneak back to the car lot and tour coach."

Joe agreed. "Frank, it's your call."

But I was also crabbing on all fours. My frenzied hands groping the rough stone walls found the mouth to a cubbyhole. My fingers darted inside it, and I grabbed the edge to a wood box. Unlike the toolbox on the tour coach, I felt no padlock. I drew out the heavy wood box, lifted its lid, and pawed through its contents. Shovels, coils of rope, and five three-cell flashlights shook out.

With all five flashlights switched on, we carved a brilliant swath through the tunnel's murk. Joe left first. Soon he branched off at a dipping curve, and we entered an alcove. His flashlight beam directed our eyes.

"There it is, Frank."

Doubtful, I saw the skunk hole the troglodytes had

chipped through the stone wall. The stairway we hoped to use waited on the other side for us.

"Selami, you're first. Make it snappy."

Smaller and more agile, they squirted through the skunk hole easier than I could. I peered through it at them.

"Is this the right way?"

Joe nodded.

"Frank, hurry," said Selami. "We're on the homestretch."

By squishing in my gut, I wriggled through the skunk hole. No cage elevators, escalators, or ladders waited to shuttle us below. As Joe had recalled, the troglodytes had notched out the steep, angular steps into the stone.

The stairs spiraled down into a natural chasm. Our descent made my ears pop. My sinuses were on fire. Twice my shoes skidded on the treads. I shuddered and not just from the chill since I'd no railing to clutch. One false step and that was all she wrote.

Our flashlights wigwagged light beams in our front. We rumbled on for another several hundred feet, but getting winded, I hollered out, "Yo, take five, guys!" We flumped down on the stairs, Selami and Joe sitting a few steps below me. My head turned up the way we'd plunged, but I heard no hot pursuit or spotted the glimmers to any flashlights.

"Joe, I'm with Frank. After this, I won't return to any part of Cappadocia where the sun doesn't shine."

Joe swallowed hard. "I've also had more than my fill. But we're not done. Hurry before our muscles cramp on us."

We dragged up and mushed on, keeping our wits and scuffing our feet on the hard steps until they petered out at last. We'd hit the rock bottom of Cappadocia. It was as inky dark as Joe had described it.

My conical beam roved to and fro, scraping a bright oval across the red dust. My shaft of light caromed off a human skull bleached white. "Whoa there." Its rictus marked the right spot. Selami and Joe stared after my whistle of amazement.

Our flashlight beams delved into the sepulcher's further recesses. My heart pinged too fast in my chest. Skeletal remains -- the long and short bones -- lay strewn about the red dust, the stark remnants of the cannibals' barbecues. If the bones could talk, they'd warn us to turn back.

Then I noticed shoeprints, both sets left by small-framed men, stamped in the red dust tracking over to an irregular, wine-colored slab. My flashlight beam nudged their rapt eyes over to it. Selami using a scratchy voice stated the obvious.

"It's got to be a crypt. Frank, you get the honors."

After a chesty cough, Joe had few words. "Do it."

I left them at the bottom step, my shoes tramping over the few inches of red dust. Particles eddied at my ankles and swirled up into my flashlight's beam. I used care not to disturb the original sets of shoeprints.

Behind the wine-colored slab I observed a pair of drag marks gouged in the red dust. Something bulky had been towed over, dunked in the crypt, and sealed under the wine-colored slab. I planted my flashlight by its butt end on the floor and yelled over for extra light, and they hit me with the other cascading beams. I squatted down.

Sucking in a breath of the foul air, my fingers grabbed the wine-colored slab. It was abrasive and heavy. I gave the slab a shove, and it skated over the gritty red dust.

"Phew!"

I recoiled. A rotten flesh stench from the crypt I'd uncapped flew up into my nose. The stab to my flashlight beam revealed why. The flaccid, mottled face I squinted down at was the spitting image of every photo I'd ever seen of him.

Hello, Sylvester Mercedes. Except for his beige suit and tie needing a whisk broom, he was coffin-ready. The white gardenia boutonniere Omar had recalled on my first day was pinned to a lapel. The white gardenia, I thought, looked better preserved than Mercedes did.

Selami's forearms barred his face. "What a stink. Well, Frank . . . ?"

I removed the two cigars from Mercedes' breast pocket. They were maduro like the tobacco aroma I'd smelled in his hotel room and on his clothes. From the same pocket I fished out his passport verifying his identity. What a coup. I did a fist pump.

"What did you dig out, Frank?" asked Selami.

"Mercedes lies here. A slug to the heart killed him."

Joe's jet eyes lifted to the ceiling. "Allah be thanked."

Selami jerked his head at us. "Let's get the hell out of here."

Chapter 37

Their salvage job went like clockwork. The local authorities sent their most nimble detectives down the rock stairway with us to Mercedes' mausoleum. A lady photographer with a powerful flash snapped off a series of crime scene shots. A detective took a plaster mold of the shoeprints. Nobody wanted to stick around for long. We packed up the dead load, knocked off the red dust, and hustled topside to join the living and breathing under the sun again.

A band of tourists from the latest tour coaches milled behind the yellow police line tape tethered between the boxy squad cars. What was the big allure to tramp through the dark, narrow tunnels where the troglodytes centuries ago had eked out a so-called life? I was at a loss to comprehend it.

The crime scene honcho, a fussy, carrot-haired lieutenant named Baykal, questioned us. What had sent us into the hole? I never lie to the cops. There's no percentage in it. So, I spilled my guts.

Frowning, Lieutenant Baykal asked for my passport. His Ankara colleagues had it, I told him, but I offered my PI license. Not a big fan, he grunted, pushing it away. He phoned a flabbergasted, then freaked Abdullah. They talked in brash tones.

"You will return to Ankara," Lieutenant Baykal instructed me after they'd hung up. "I'm to guarantee it."

"I've got no driver's permit. Selami better haul me in his *taksi*."

"Yes, yes." Lieutenant Baykal spat on the ground. "I want you both out of Cappadocia. Go, go. Now."

The uniforms rolled Mercedes, flat and stiff under a dingy sheet, on a gurney over to load in the meat wagon. A lady cop detached the yellow police line tape. At last, the antsy tourists got to file into the vestibule behind the huge, round stone. Little did they know they'd come out never quite the same again.

"It'll be okay," said Joe, shaking my hand.

"Thanks for everything, Joe."

"It was the least I could do for you." Joe smiled. "May Allah go with you, Frank."

Lieutenant Baykal escorted Selami and I back to our fake cave hotel. He oversaw us packing our duffel and watched us steam off in Selami's *taksi*. We pitstopped at a Shell station to gas up. Petrol in the no-name stations outside the towns often sold you smuggled, cheap-grade fuel. We left.

Some umpteen miles north of Nevsehir on Konya Road at high noon, I saw our four squad car escort, their roof bar lights flaring red-blue glints, peel off. They U-turned and streaked south for their home back in Cappadocia.

"They don't like us doing their jobs for them." A little further, Selami brought up something weighing on both our minds. "I'd just as soon not talk about why Mercedes went into the tunnels."

I nodded. I wanted to forget it all, too, but I couldn't, not if we were going to stay out of Buca Prison and get paid. We humped along doing seventy. I conjured up my suspects list and ran a detection program in my head. This time it all seemed to fit into place. I thought I knew who'd slain Mercedes and Pembe and why.

"Sorry we didn't visit your little niece."

Selami stroked his jet mustache and wagged his head. "Don't sweat it, Frank. My little niece can keep, but solving these murders sure can't. We can talk about them if you like."

"I believe I know who the killer is and their motive. I wouldn't be surprised if Detective Abdullah has already nailed it together."

"I hope so or, we'll wear a number at Buca Prison. When do I get paid?"

"As soon as I get my money, you'll get yours."

"Sounds good."

Without fanfare we swooped into downtown Ankara and parked on the right street. The city air was smoky. We bulled through the revolving glass door where Abdullah and Auk met us in the Otel Pamuk's lobby.

I knew by their short-tempered grunts that they'd been sitting there stewing for some time. That didn't aid in my chances. Abdullah propelled me by the elbow to the restaurant annex. Now late afternoon, no diners sat at the tables. We occupied one in a corner.

Auk sat at one end, and Abdullah staked the other. I was on his right. Selami spun a chair around and straddled it backward. He dealt me a wink. Catching it, Abdullah snorted. Then Selami winked at Abdullah.

"Don't push it, cousin. You're in plenty of hot water, too."

"Abdullah, just be cool. You don't have all the facts yet."

"That's why we're here. To get at the truth wherever it may lead us."

Selami scoffed. "Frank has done it all. You should thank him."

"I think I'll wait and see, thanks."

"Suit yourself."

I saw the burly uniforms deployed at the revolving glass door carried automatic assault rifles. SWAT, I guessed. Security was that damn heavy. No hotel guest came or went without Abdullah's say-so. Sweat soaked through my shirt fabric on my back and under my armpits.

This shootout was for all the marbles to clear me and pave my way home. I flushed away a blood-chilling specter of imagining me corn-holed, chained, and starved in a prison cell. Abdullah kicked off the proceedings.

"Mr. Johnson, kudos on your successful Cappadocia treasure hunt. But you haven't tidied up here. A killer is still at large, and I hold your passport."

I tap danced. "What if I clear Mercedes and Pembe's homicides? Will that win me back my passport?"

His wrinkled forehead smoothing, a more relaxed but skeptical, Abdullah leaned back in his chair. "It might. But your last chance ebbs away. Talk fast. We'll see where the chips fall."

"Fair enough. First, we'll need to convene a quorum." I ran a silent head count at the table. "Has Mrs. Mercedes arrived?"

Auk nodded. "She stormed up to her room."

"Only she can make this work. Plus Omar and Nashwinter should be present."

"Detective Auk, invite Mrs. Mercedes, Omar, and Mr. Nashwinter to come and join us. If they complain at all, handcuff and force them." Abdullah's hooded eyes fell on me. "Who else?"

"Mustafa and Berk, the casinos guards, had better come. Omar's wife Karin is a big player, too."

"Or maybe not. The Luger we took from her purse didn't match Pembe's death slug. So I released her."

My nod stiff, I acknowledged Abdullah. Karin wasn't Pembe's killer. That one hurt. One house of cards fell through on me. I'd go with my second scenario.

Still short a cook, Omar charged out the batwing doors. Auk stuffed him at my left. We didn't speak. Abdullah conversed with Omar in Turkish. He seemed to protest. Then he saw the wisdom in playing nice with the cops. He left to use his desk phone and bring Karin from home.

Abdullah ordered an Efes from the server. Auk and four burly uniforms bustled out the revolving glass door into the street and stomped up to the two hotel casinos to usher back Mustafa and Berk. Joel Nashwinter, the beer peddler, in his rumpled suit rattled out of the corridor, doddered over, and scooted up a chair to sit by Selami.

All but Abdullah sat on thorns. He saw fit to tell us how from his front row seat he'd watched John Steinbeck's <u>Of Mice and Men </u>at the state opera hall. This was his second time. At the climax, he said, a posse carrying real flickering torches chased Lenny and George through the aisles of spectators. For all his smiles, Abdullah took his manhunts to heart.

Auk and his burly uniforms with Berk and Mustafa sat down before Karin bustled out of the *taksi*. We lined the table, a tight-lipped bunch. Our bright eyes converged on Abdullah. Shaking with displeasure, he asked Auk if he'd sent Mrs. Mercedes an engraved invitation.

The indefatigable Auk clanged up in the cage elevator. No sooner had Abdullah polished off his next Efes than Auk and a lady who I took as Lois Mercedes burst through the stairway exit and ambled over to us.

"My welcoming committee," she said in that autocratic, nasally cadence I'd grown to cringe at hearing over the phone connection. "Which of you is my abysmal shamus?"

I gave a slight head shake. "That'd be me, ma'am."

"I see."

But then I also saw. Lois Mercedes stood in profile, the sketchy light not stinting any striking aspect. I could almost forgive Gatlin for his gullible lust. She was a looker. Her hair, cropped and curled on end, glinted coppery red. Her face, slim and elegant, was a classic one highlighted by her cobalt blue eyes and high cheekbones.

My eyes drifted lower. Her J Lo curves shined through her pair of throw on jeans and a sweatshirt as much as if she'd come in a clingy Versace gown with a sweetheart neckline. She packed her top drawer, too.

"My *taksi* dropped me a short while ago. I freshened up and intended to take a nap to get over my jet lag. Then this pernicious lackey" -- she gave the deadpan Auk a dismissive glance -- "insisted I trot down to the lobby. So, here I am. Talk. I'm all ears."

Abdullah gestured with his hand. "Be seated, Mrs. Mercedes. I'll emcee this show, not you. Now, our topic is murder. Two murders, actually. Pembe's was here at the Otel Pamuk, and Sylvester Mercedes' was down in Cappadocia."

"No!" Everybody looked at Mrs. Mercedes. "That can't be. Sylvester is dead? I can't believe it." Swooning into a chair, she gasped, her fingers rising to her eyes to cup the instant tears. She repressed a sob as her shoulders quivered. "Sylvester died in Turkey."

"Sorry for your loss, ma'am. You hired me to track him down. I did. He rotted at the bottom of a hellhole."

"His killer, I hope, has been apprehended."

I stared at her. "Not yet but soon, I think. Lucky me served here at your pleasure. Chasing my tail was a major part of the masquerade. But you bring a solid alibi, don't you?"

Leaping up, Mrs. Mercedes' eyes speared me. "I've flown for over seven thousand miles worth of an alibi. Is that enough for you?"

"Mrs. Mercedes, that will do." At the end of the table Abdullah waved a hand at her. "Sit down, please. We'll hash this out in a civil way. Your patience and restraint are appreciated."

Aiming her eye's death rays to zap me, she had a seat. She'd changed. Her beauty had morphed into a scary, haggish creature I might run from in a nightmare.

"Mr. Johnson, you've got the floor. Go on, please," said Abdullah.

"Mercedes' disappearance has kept me behind the eight ball. I've racked my brain on it. Then returning from Cappadocia I thought: it's the motive, stupid. The motive is hate. Who hated Mercedes enough to want him dead?"

"Sylvester and I were in love," said Mrs. Mercedes, her domineering arrogance a large part of her defense. "Say otherwise, and I'll sue you for slander."

I just looked at her. She had brass.

"You'll do nothing except sit there and shut up," said Abdullah. "Or I'll ask Detective Auk to gag you."

"Your passion for Mercedes ran deep," I said. "Except I believe it ran the opposite way you claim. You'd grown to loathe the man. Hell, you took your own lovers. But what to do with him? First you had to recruit an assassin. Happy days came when that part fell in your lap. A willing agent was here at the Otel Pamuk where Mercedes stayed."

"Be specific, Mr. Johnson."

Selami horned in. "Abdullah, patience. Let's give Frank a chance."

Abdullah nodded. "I'm nothing but a patient man. Go on, Mr. Johnson."

My scan about our table first targeted Karin. She stirred her long legs. I cut to Nashwinter, and he yawned into his palm. Next on my short list was Mr. Ahmet, the cabbie. For the time being, I shelved him. That brought me to the killer. Or so I hoped. I pressed on.

Chapter 38

"My leading theory says Mrs. Mercedes and Omar united by accident. Maybe she phoned the Otel Pamuk, and Omar fielded her call. Anyway they talked and discovered their mutual hatred of Mercedes. They hatched a sweet, little conspiracy. From there, the murder plot solidified."

"Lies," said Omar.

But Abdullah nodded as if he ranged miles ahead of me. His hooded gaze singled out Omar. "Care to make a confession? Spare us more trouble, and you more guilt?"

"This is sheer fantasy. You've got no evidence."

Omar's vehement denial had an innocent man's ring of honesty. My heart worked harder. I'd given my PI ability too much credit. This was a busted flush. I stared at him. All at the table also watched him. Then his upper lip twitched like how an angler's hook sets before reeling in the prize trout. That was my reminder to go on before he slipped the hook.

"Proof does exist. Omar talked to Mrs. Mercedes on her cell phone. Her records will show when, but it was within days before Mercedes fell off the face of the earth. She probably kicked in some blood money. An electronic money trail is there for it."

"I did no such thing," she said.

Abdullah glared at her. For once, she piped down.

Karin used a resigned tone. "Why?"

"Lust and rage," I replied. "Wealthy playboy Mercedes had an affair with Pembe. Also a womanizer, Omar grew jealous. Maybe as her boss, he tried to coerce her into sleeping with him. Maybe she wasn't as free with her favors as he figured she'd be."

"You filthy swine!" Mustafa lurched up from his chair. "You touched my wife. I'll kill you with my bare hands."

The stolid Auk's hands clutched Mustafa's shoulders to restrain him in his chair. Three burly uniforms sprang up and assisted Auk.

Omar shook his head. "It wasn't like that."

Swallowing my doubt, I plowed ahead, talking faster. My gut cramped in knots, but I kept the old calm MP mask on my face.

"I shook out Pembe's lacy, red bra in Mercedes' room. They made love in there. Only the last time she must've felt rushed and left her bra behind. Omar skulked into Mercedes' room after I went up. He must've seen the bra where I put it on the nightstand. He recognized who owned it, knocked me out, and grabbed it."

"Omar killed Mercedes to have Pembe all to himself," said Abdullah, tracking my line of logic. "But then why did he bump her off?"

I breathed a bit easier. "The night Pembe was murdered, she wore the lacy, red bra the ever hopeful Omar had returned to her. Maybe they'd struck a *quid pro quo*. He'd keep quiet about where he'd found it and her affair with Mercedes in exchange for sex. But then she reneged. Ticked off, Omar used a ruse to lure her upstairs.

"He killed her and rigged the murder scene to appear like a robbery gone bad in the lobby. He ditched the Luger. The Otel Pamuk has lots of nooks and crannies. My money says his precious Luger will turn up sooner or later. After all, he planned to fish it out after the heat wore off. He'd never bear to part with one."

Defiant or desperate, Omar writhed under the burly uniforms anchoring him to the chair as their prisoner. "A lacy, red bra? So what? Any young lady has a drawer of them."

My head shook. "I was married once. A husband might give this intimate, expensive gift to his young wife. Pembe wore it the day she died, but not for your gratification."

Mustafa snarled his words. "What Mr. Johnson says is true. I gave it to her. She wore it that morning. We had a romantic evening in mind. You're the pig who killed her. You'll pay."

I felt sorry for Mustafa. His late wife's tragic infidelity hadn't yet registered on him. Maybe it never would, but he deserved better than this.

"I can confirm she came to our morgue wearing it," said Abdullah.

Karin's speech was hollow. "I'm able to confirm I own no such piece of lingerie."

Berk contributed a tidbit. "You know, I recall now Mercedes once told me he was scared of his wife. He swore up and down she was out to kill him."

"I heard the same story from him," said Nashwinter.

All the heads swiveled to regard Mrs. Mercedes.

"The bunch of you can go to hell," she said, acid in the words she hurled at us. "Johnson, you can't prove your accusations. Why would I hire you to identify me as Sylvester's killer? What does that say about me?"

"It says you're sitting pretty, and you'll fly out of Ankara unscathed. The evidence isn't there to make a homicide charge stick. Omar did all your dirty work. He'll take the fall for it alone.

"Detective Abdullah may detain you to squeeze a little harder. But no firm evidence will surface. All you'll have to do is bury Mercedes' remains, and your hands will stay clean."

"Wait," said Omar. "What's all this? Not a shred of proof shows I killed Mercedes in Cappadocia."

Abdullah's eyebrows canted at me. My taking more creative leaps tried to connect the free dots still left.

Chapter 39

I went on. "There is proof. Detective Abdullah told me Mercedes died from a 9 mil. I'd say your still hidden Luger will match the death slug the M.E. digs out of his heart. Probably the same slug you put in Pembe came from the same Luger. I'd say Mr. Ahmet, your cousin and willing accomplice, ran you to Cappadocia in his *taksi*.

"He goes there. I saw a Cappadocia map in his rear seat when he brought me from the airport. I know you two are tight. I'd say you thumped me over the head for my wallet, and it's probably in your office desk. A pack rat like you keeps everything."

Abdullah wore a broad smile. "I like this. Go ahead."

"I can make an educated guess how the Cappadocia murder went. Omar duped the skirt chaser Mercedes into thinking a hot babe waited for him. Maybe he met 'her' online, and they agreed to meet there.

"He sure dressed to the nines to wow somebody. He slipped out of here on Sunday morning to flag a cab, and once in Cappadocia bought a pair of tickets to the underground cities to entertain his mystery lady. Witnesses can attest to both facts. Men driven by their lust do dumb things."

I stole a hasty glance at Karin sitting there delectable as she'd been on the day bed watching CNN. Her cancer couldn't diminish her beauty. After swallowing, I finished up spinning my Turkish murder yarn.

"Mercedes probably slipped away from his hotel in

Cappadocia to hook up with his mystery lady on the sly. Only he bumbled into a fatal ambush. Then there was a corpse to hide. Omar, you bribed your way into the underground city during the off-hours."

"No. You're wrong," said Omar, less than convincing.

My tale continued. "Selami and Joe say the locals know the tunnels. Also a local, Mr. Ahmet probably guided you to the crypt on the seventh level to stash Mercedes.

"Who'd find him there? Two small-framed men left two sets of shoeprints in the red dust. Forensics will match the shoeprints to Mr. Ahmet and you. You also left scuff marks from your dragging the corpse."

"I won't give up my other Lugers for testing."

"I already did it," said Karin, her face a study in agony and betrayal. "Detective Abdullah asked me after my Luger was cleared. I said, fine, take all of your damn junk. I'm sick of looking at it, and I'm sick of looking at you, Omar."

"In fact, our ballistics have already proven Pembe's death slug matches the Luger with Omar's handprint on it," said Abdullah. "The ballistics on Mercedes are pending."

No wonder Abdullah had let me run my mouth, I thought. He'd already cobbled it all together. I just parroted everything he already knew.

Smiling, Abdullah pointed. "I've got you, Omar. Detective Auk will remove you peaceably. The hotel guests don't have to know. My dragnet will snag Mr. Ahmet."

Mouth agape, the perspiring Omar couldn't process it fast enough. He mopped a napkin at his bald pate. "You're arresting me?"

"But of course." Abdullah nodded. "Book him, Detective Auk. Two counts of murder for Pembe and Sylvester Mercedes. Omar, advise Karin to find you a criminal lawyer. You'll need one."

"Omar, call one from your jail cell," said Karin. "Our marriage is over. I hate you. You'll never see Açelya or Zeynep again for as long as I have any say in it."

Omar groaned.

Abdullah turned to me. "Mr. Johnson, on your way to Esenboga Airport drop by my office. I'll return your passport after I know a plane will fly you from my city. Never come here again."

I nodded. Abdullah was a square shooter. His booting me out of Ankara wasn't personal. I took my lumps without a beef. He had more cop business.

"Mrs. Mercedes, I believe you're guilty as sin. But it's too thorny for us to prove it in our courts. You've got twelve hours to clear out. If not, I'll throw you in a hole far darker than any dug in Cappadocia."

Paling but still haughty, she arose to her feet.

We disbanded, all free to go except Omar braced between a pair of burly uniforms. I took a step over to have a kind word with Mustafa. His face stitched with raw grief warned me off. Shifting, I let him trudge by me. Dead man walking, I thought.

I guessed Selami had cut out a side door. I didn't see him, the bum. Then the pit of my guts fell away as I watched Mrs. Mercedes saunter over the red carpet. Waiting on the cage elevator, she skewered me with her arsenic green eyes. But I didn't drop my eyes in our staredown. She was evil and smart. She knew it. Now I knew it, too. All in all, she'd beaten me. I didn't like it.

I squared my hotel tab with Karin at the front desk.

"Do you want a receipt?" Her voice was flat.

"No thanks. I don't need it now."

Chapter 40

Mrs. Mercedes the murderess had skated and taken a nice chunk from Mercedes' estate in the bargain. Maybe hate as well as greed had corrupted her. But like I'd said, her hands pulling the right marionette strings in Ankara had no bloodstains. She was clean.

I pictured Mercedes suffering in his cold, dark hole as his weakening heart flatlined, and he groaned to give up the ghost. I shuddered. Nobody deserves to die a lonely, fearful death. It isn't decent.

My call to the front desk got Karin. Her same flat voice gave me Mrs. Mercedes departure time. Smelling trouble, Nashwinter had booked a seat on the same plane. I avoided that outbound flight. But a Turkish Airlines flight to Frankfurt took off in ninety minutes. If I hustled, I could just make it, and I called in my reservation at the airport.

As I'd promised, I rang up Yagmur at her father's house and gave her the third act on Mercedes in Cappadocia. It wasn't a jolly chat -- she was bawling her eyes out by the end -- and it sank me into a blacker Irish rage. Her dream for a better life had gone bust.

Next I hit Abdullah. I had an aisle seat on a Turkish Airlines DC-9 out of his city. But only my passport put me on said DC-9. He heaved out a laugh, invited me to his office, and then I'd leave Ankara for keeps.

"Look for me in a few," I said before hanging up.

My packed duffel went on the bed. A few shirts were still at the laundry, but I'd leave them for the poor people.

The paperback sailed into the wastebasket. I'd had enough gut-wrenching excitement without reading any potboilers. I gave my potential suspects list a wry glance.

Omar (Otel Pamuk owner)
Karin (Omar's wife)
Joel Nashwinter (U.S. beer salesman)
Mr. Ahmet (Turkish cabbie) (Omar's cousin)

When I wrote the list, I hadn't even been close on who -- the victim's wife -- was behind Mercedes' homicide.

A tap came at my door. I pulled it inward, expecting Karin or my favorite maid. My upswept eyes crossed lasers with the arsenic greens. Mrs. Mercedes wanted to get in the last word.

"Are you going to invite me in?"

"Fuck no."

"Honestly, Robert said you were brusque, but this stretches the point. Regardless, we should settle our arrears."

"No sale. No charge. You can tear up our contract."

"You can afford to spurn a paying client?"

"Hardly but in your case it's easy to make an exception. Believe me, I'd love to nail you for Mercedes' homicide, but I'm not smart enough to get the goods on you."

"Believe what you like, but I'd nothing to do with Sylvester's death. I wanted to find him. That's why I paid you to come here."

I thought she was full of it. "Well, I found him. You don't look too choked up over it."

"I won't shed too many tears. Our marriage had tanked long ago."

"Now you can fly home liberated and probably a lot richer."

"We really should try to get along, Frank."

"Fat chance. We've parted ways. Go rot in hell, Mrs. Mercedes."

"I won't be Mrs. Mercedes much longer. It'll soon be Mrs. Robert Gatlin."

That bombshell floored me. I gasped to regain my breath. "If that's true, he and I are done." I choked on the last word.

Seeing my reaction amused her. Her barbed smile left me hanging as she slinked down the corridor. My door whammed shut. The phone receiver jumped into my hand, and I thumbed in the right numbers.

Gatlin wasn't at his cabana. I dialed his posh Middleburg office. His greeting boomed out in the cocky tone I knew so well. I laid it out blunt as I'd heard it from the lady herself.

"Well Frank, you can see she's a ravishing beauty."

"Bullshit. She's a ruthless, calculating killer. Don't act all shocked. You had to suspect it. Playing the stooge for getting her off scot-free makes my day."

"What? Lois killed Sylvester? Impossible. Preposterous. Anyway, we fell in love by accident. Who can predict when cupid's arrow will hit? I proposed, and she accepted."

"Then that's it. We're finished."

He backpedaled, almost contrite. "Now Frank, don't go off half-cocked. Simmer down. Just tell me what you know. How did things finally tie together?"

"Ask your fiancée. She had a front row seat. If you ever get back some brains, call me."

Our signal died, initiated this time from my side. I had to wonder why I'd flown to Ankara, why she'd hired me to scout up Mercedes. I played my part of the window dressing to make it look good for her as the grieving widow. She figured I wasn't a smart enough PI to find him in Cappadocia, but I'd had an able assist from Selami and Joe.

The notes for my final report and expense report went shredded up into the wastebasket. I erased all my memory. I'd never bopped down to Cappadocia. Yeah, that felt better. I'd never uncapped that crypt of bones. I'd never taken on Lois Mercedes as a client.

My Turkish Airlines ticket came from the inner lining of my smaller bag. I'd get to enjoy my Indian summer and visit Dreema in Richmond. Maybe I'd bring a diamond ring. I decided to deposit the rest of Mrs. Mercedes' advance at the front desk with Karin for Selami to pick up. He'd earned every penny. The phone shrilled, and I grabbed it.

"Frank, Gerald here. I just dug up my passport."

"Forget it. I'm on a flight home within the hour."

"Man, you sound low as a cockroach."

"I'm still broke. I didn't get paid."

Gerald blew it off. "Hell, I've got bail skips coming out the wazoo. Come and get my back."

"Okay, that's some work."

"Good. Dreema called me."

"Why?"

"Said she's worried about you."

"This is all finished here."

"Uh-huh. Where's your hub?"

"Frankfurt. Tomorrow a.m."

"You hang tight in Frankfurt. Our paths will cross there."

"See you then." I hung up, feeling less bent. We leaned on our friends to carry us through the shit storms blowing up in our lives.

It was time to kick. I hefted up my duffel and strolled down to the lobby. Emotions clawed at my insides. Gatlin and I had had a grand run, seven years in all. Maybe it wasn't done. I'd left a crack in the door, and I kept a slim hope alive he'd see the light on Mrs. Mercedes. I entered the lobby.

Karin leaned over writing at the front desk. Scars and all, she was now a single mom raising two girls and running a hotel alone. But she packed a Luger to warn off any man getting up in her face. Much to her credit she'd stuck by Omar to the end.

My lips parted. I started to speak, to apologize for the bloody damage left here. But I didn't. Couldn't. I felt as if I cruised seven miles high, winging it over the Atlantic, booking west for Dulles Airport, and home.

Even if I owed the IRS, it'd be sweet homecoming. My eyes fell from her. I also didn't leave her Selami's cash. I could always tap Western Union.

The revolving glass door spun me out where I caught a final whiff of Ankara's gritty air. My heart said I'd be back someday. At the sunny cabstand, I waved a hand, gesturing for a *taksi*.

It screeched up to a stop. My shadow fell short in its rear door flapping out. I gazed up, saying, "Esenboga Airport. Step on it."

With a grin, Selami turned around. "Going home, Frank?"

I threw in my duffel and nodded at him.

THE END

About The Author

Ed Lynskey's fiction has appeared in Mississippi Review, HandHeld-Crime, and Plots With Guns. A short collection, Out of Town a Few Days, appeared in 2004 and a novel titled The Blue Cheer is scheduled for 2006.

Ed's flash fiction titled, "Referee Gone Wild," appears in the October 2005 issue of Alfred Hitchcock Mystery Magazine.

Also From Mundania

The Dirt-Brown Derby

PI Frank Johnson is hired by Mary Taliaferro, a wealthy aristocrat owning a horse estate near Middleburg, Virginia.

Mary's teen-age daughter Emily has died in a riding tragedy. The local law enforcement says it's an accident. Mary thinks it's murder.

Frank is broke and the money Mary offers is too good to pass up, but his case quickly becomes more complicated when the stable manager is murdered one day after he starts his investigation.

Frank soon discovers that there is much more going on here, and he is determined to get to the truth, even if it kills him!

Pelham Fell Here

MP and part-time gunsmith Frank Johnson finds his cousin Cody Chapman killed by a twelve-gauge shotgun. Enraged, Frank wants some answers, and fast. Was Cody involved in an arms smuggling scheme?

The mystery grows when a pair of murderous deputy sheriffs ambush Frank. Killing them in self-defense, Frank must take it on the lam while he continues his investigation.

Eventually he discovers a group of Neo-Nazis, holed up at a remote castle, who may be behind his cousin's murder. Luckily, a couple of bounty hunter pals throw in with Frank to even up the odds.

LaVergne, TN USA
02 October 2009
159724LV00001B/4/P